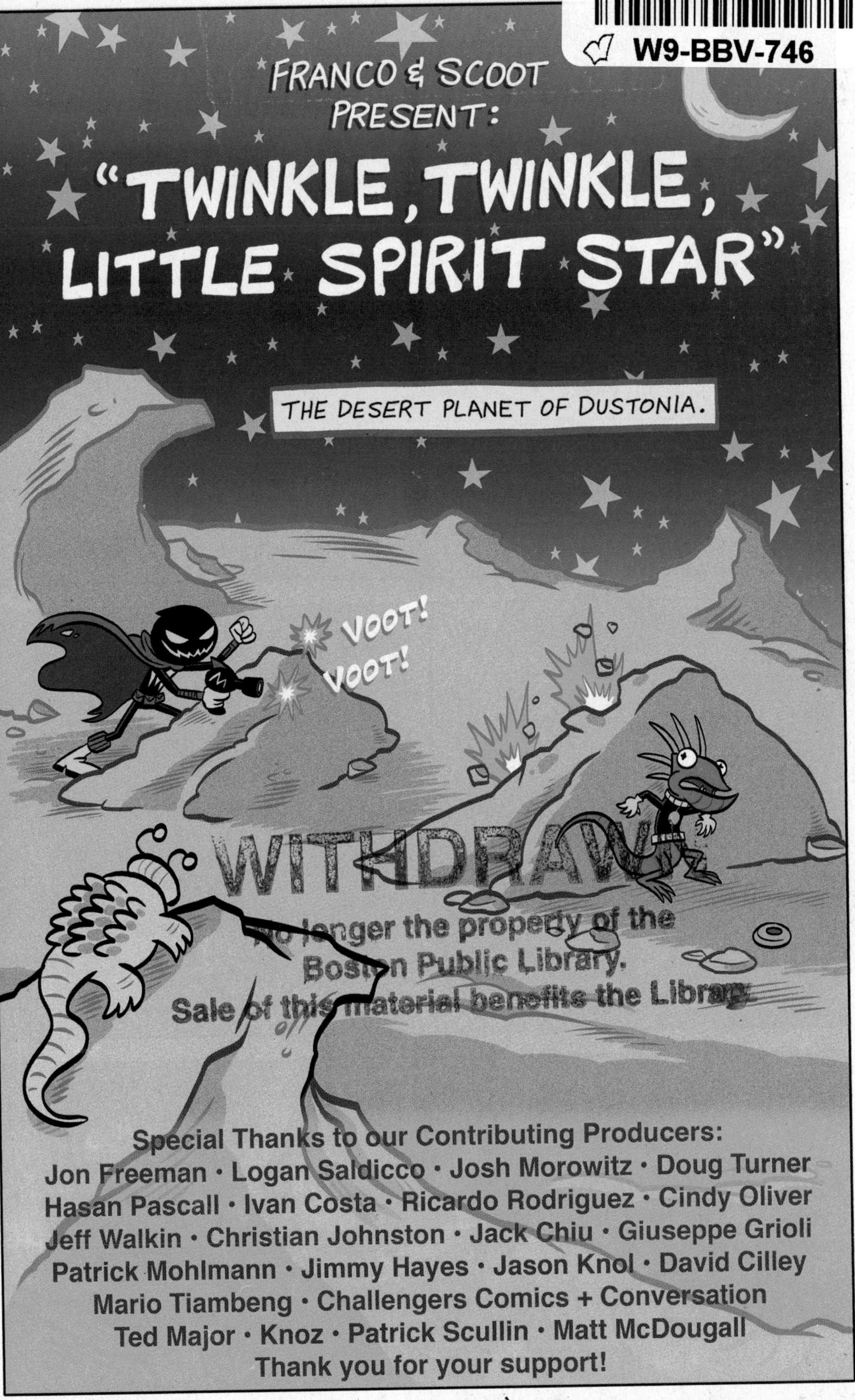

FRANCO & SCOOT
PRESENT:
"TWINKLE, TWINKLE, LITTLE SPIRIT STAR"
THE DESERT PLANET OF DUSTONIA.
VOOT!
VOOT!

Special Thanks to our Contributing Producers:
Jon Freeman · Logan Saldicco · Josh Morowitz · Doug Turner
Hasan Pascall · Ivan Costa · Ricardo Rodriguez · Cindy Oliver
Jeff Walkin · Christian Johnston · Jack Chiu · Giuseppe Grioli
Patrick Mohlmann · Jimmy Hayes · Jason Knol · David Cilley
Mario Tiambeng · Challengers Comics + Conversation
Ted Major · Knoz · Patrick Scullin · Matt McDougall
Thank you for your support!

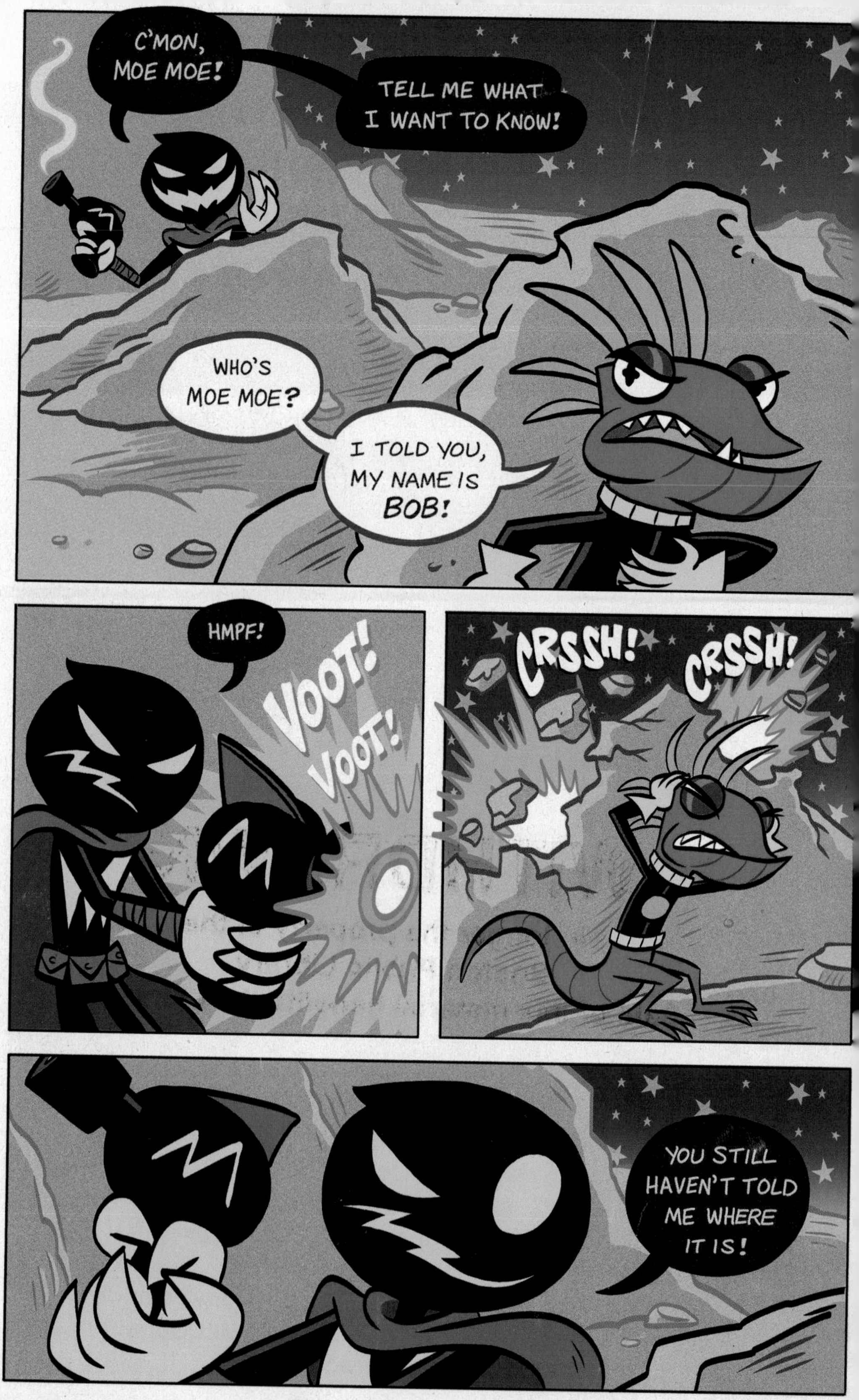
C'MON, MOE MOE!
TELL ME WHAT I WANT TO KNOW!
WHO'S MOE MOE?
I TOLD YOU, MY NAME IS BOB!
HMPF!
VOOT! VOOT!
CRSSH! CRSSH!
YOU STILL HAVEN'T TOLD ME WHERE IT IS!

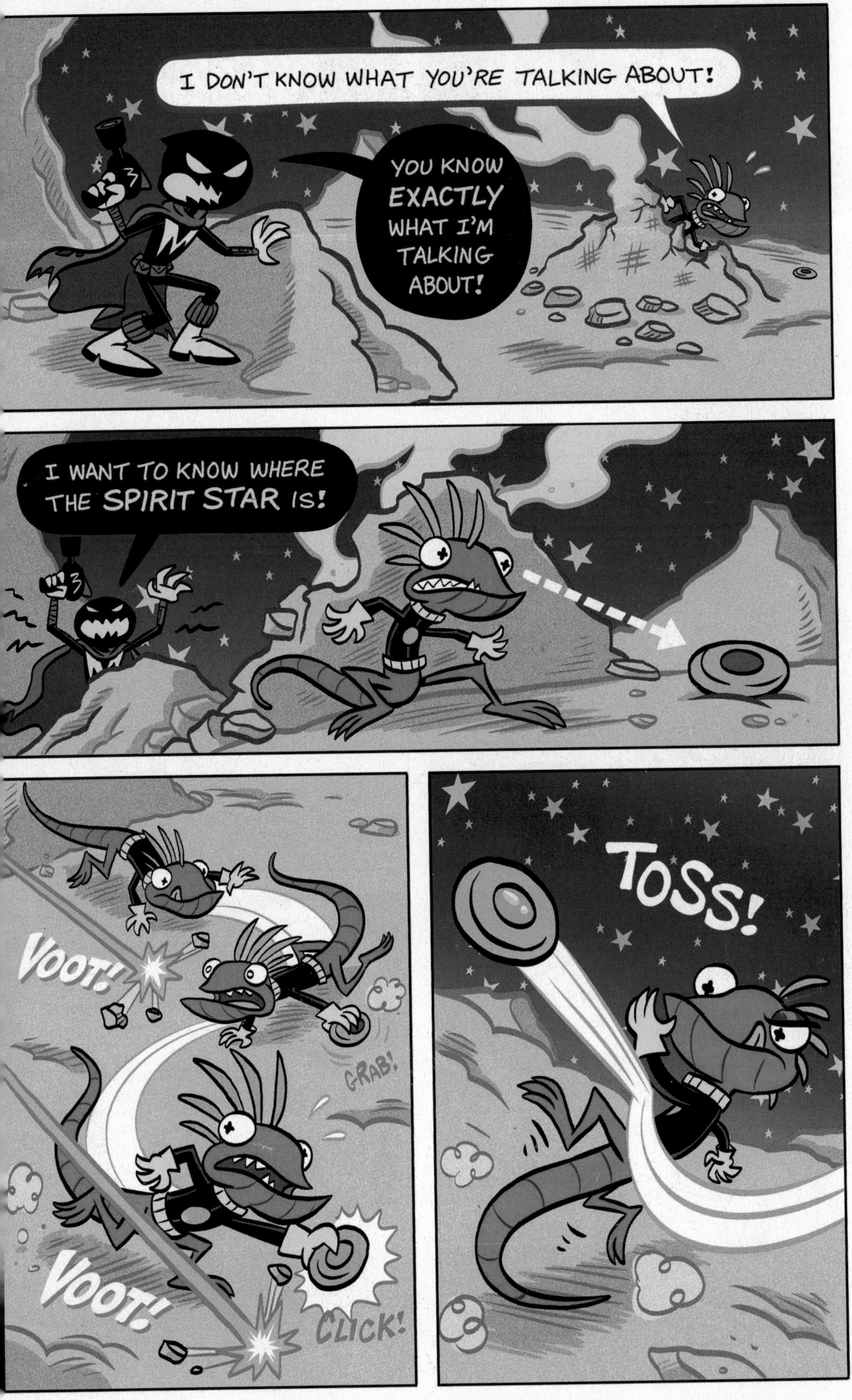
I DON'T KNOW WHAT YOU'RE TALKING ABOUT!
YOU KNOW EXACTLY WHAT I'M TALKING ABOUT!
I WANT TO KNOW WHERE THE SPIRIT STAR IS!
VOOT!
GRAB!
VOOT!
CLICK!
TOSS!

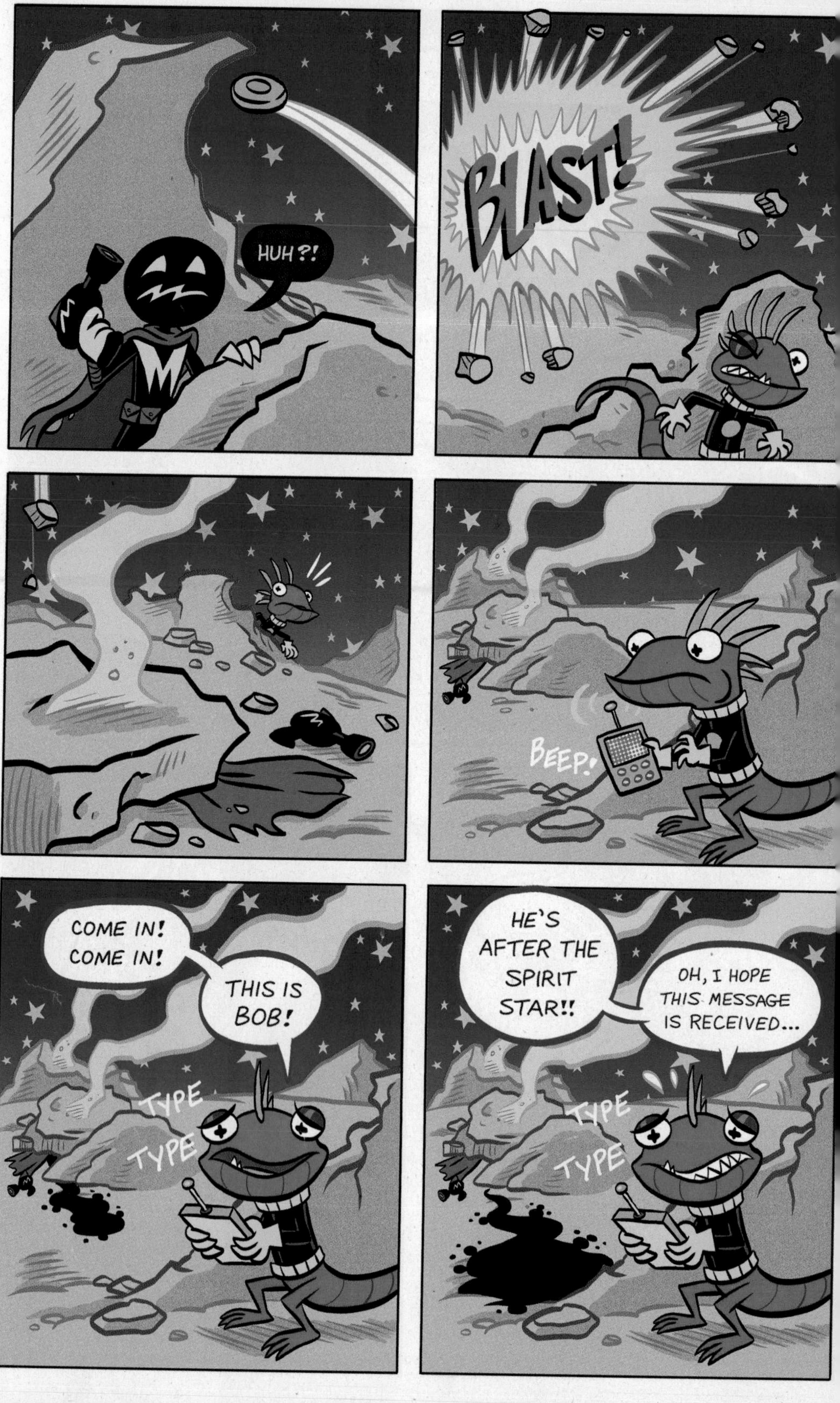
HUH?!
BLAST!
BEEP!
COME IN! COME IN!
THIS IS BOB!
TYPE TYPE
HE'S AFTER THE SPIRIT STAR!!
OH, I HOPE THIS MESSAGE IS RECEIVED...
TYPE TYPE

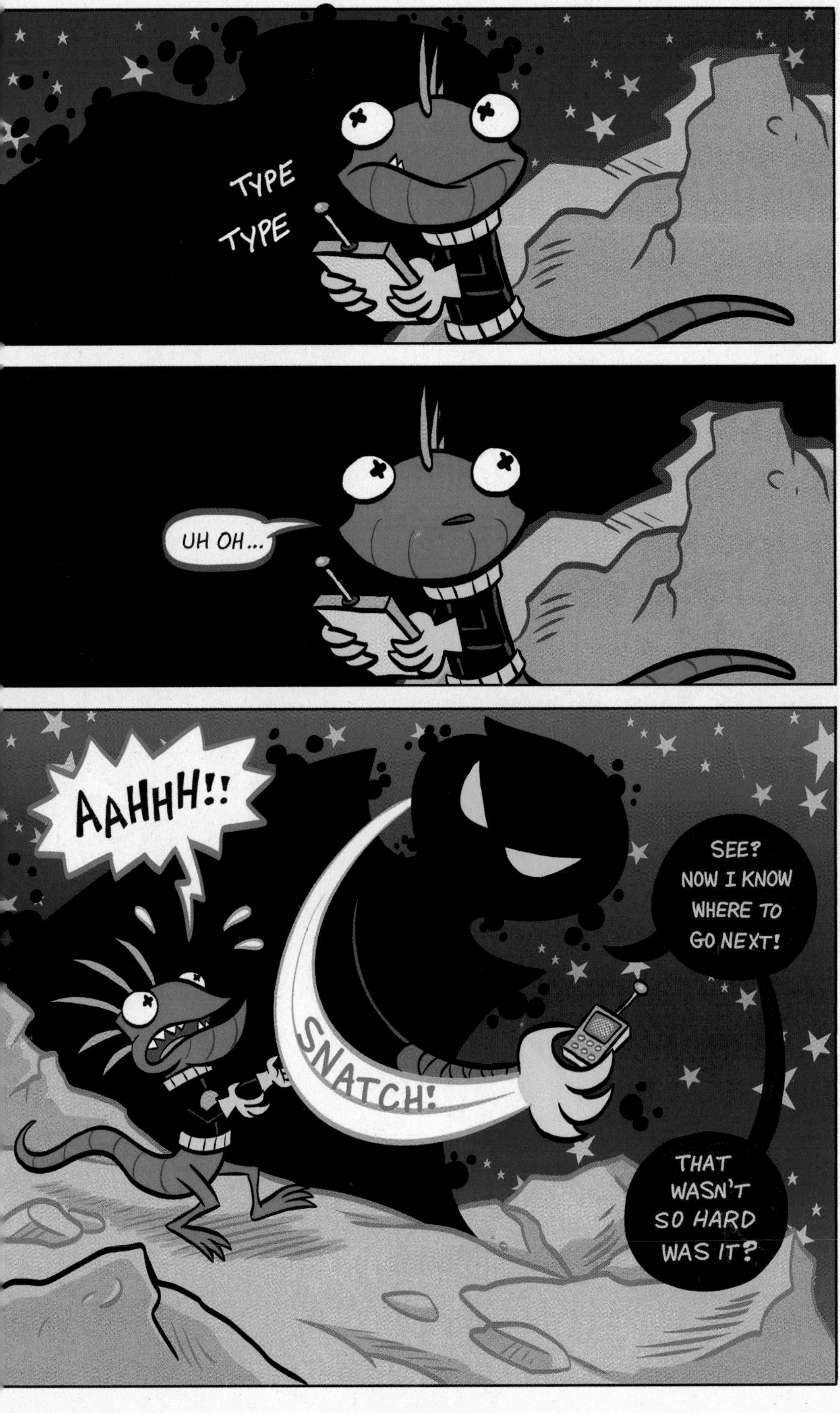
TYPE
TYPE
UH OH...
AAHHH!!
SNATCH!
SEE? NOW I KNOW WHERE TO GO NEXT!
THAT WASN'T SO HARD WAS IT?

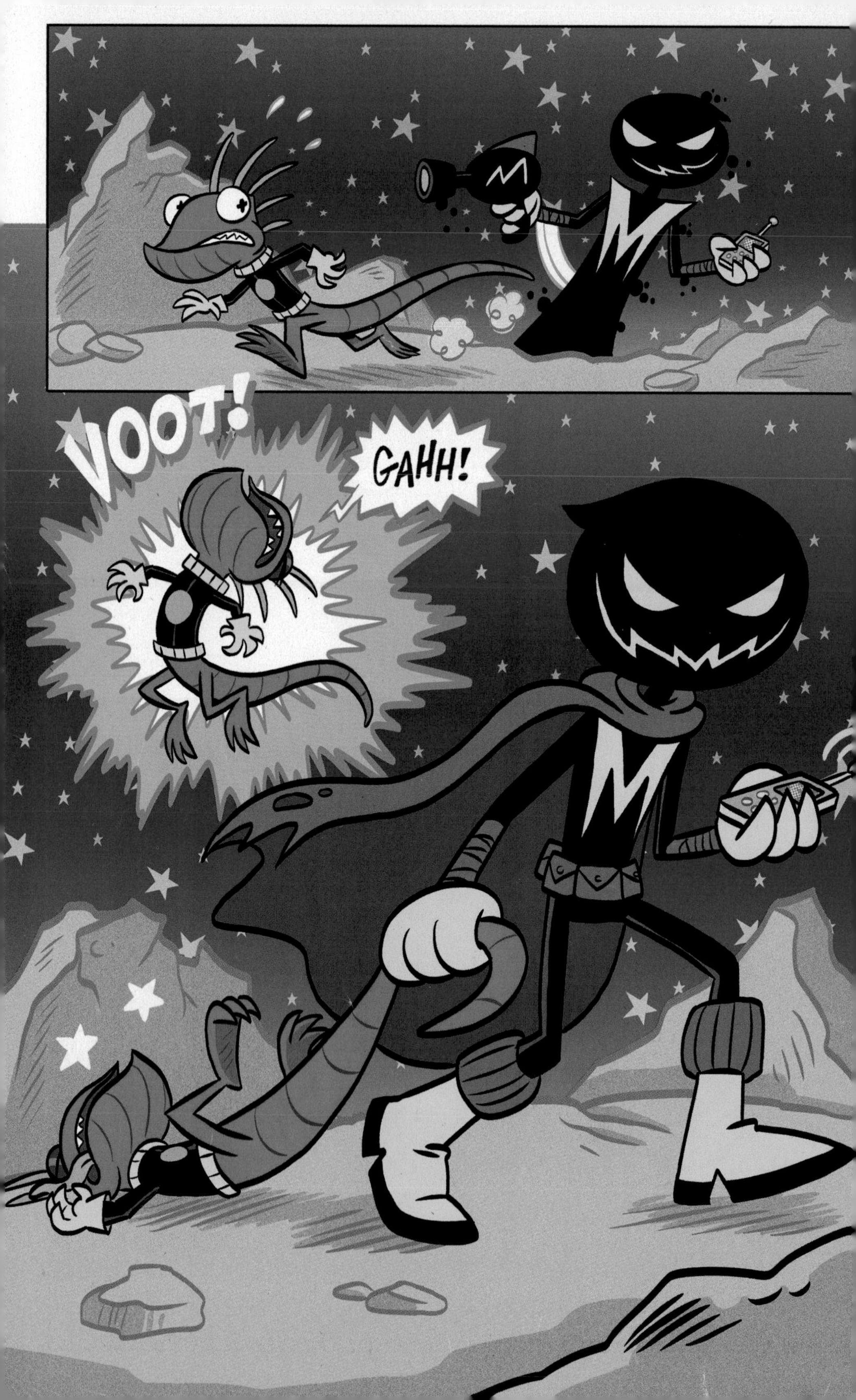
VOOT!
GAHH!

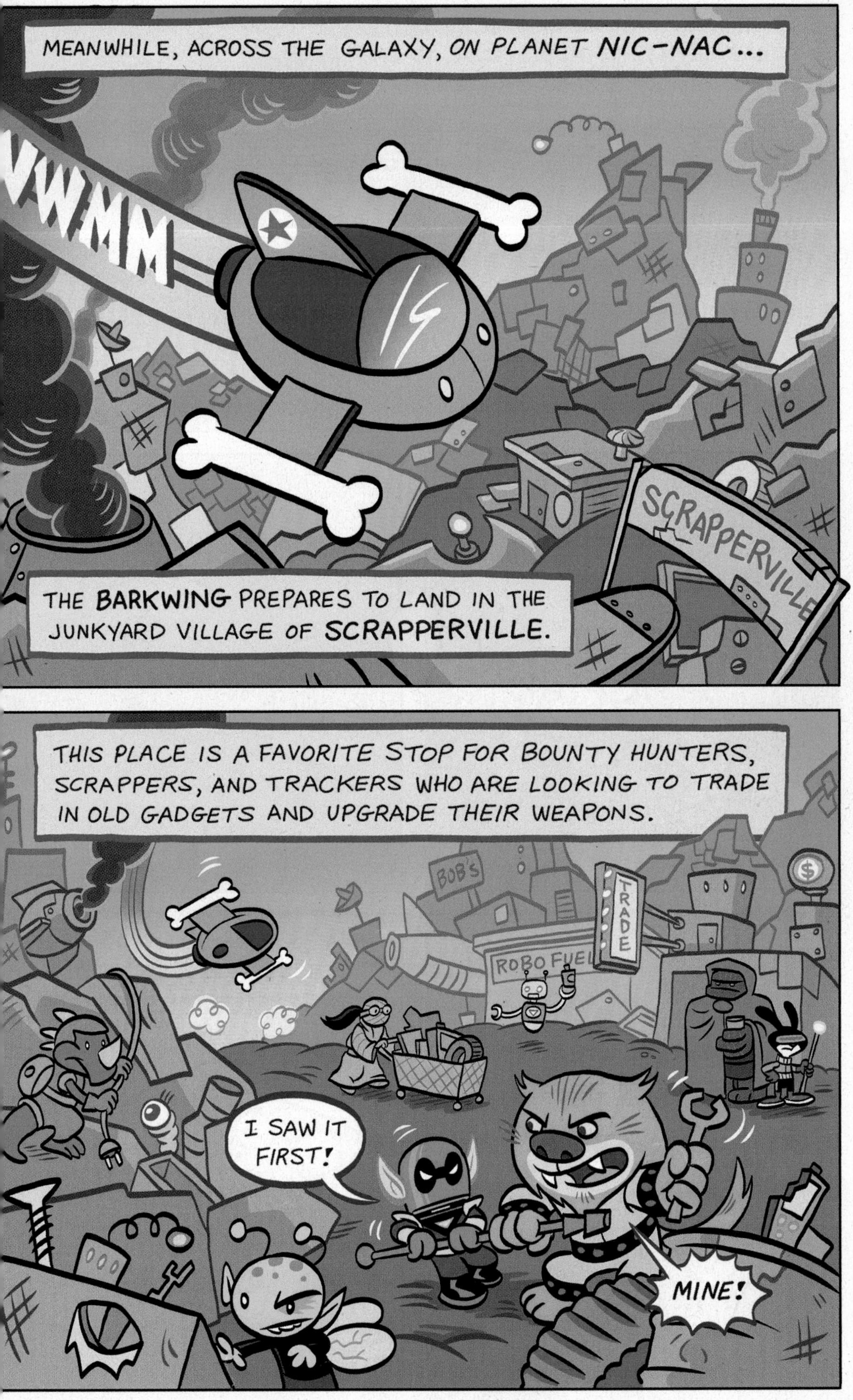
MEANWHILE, ACROSS THE GALAXY, ON PLANET NIC-NAC...
SCRAPPERVILLE
THE BARKWING PREPARES TO LAND IN THE JUNKYARD VILLAGE OF SCRAPPERVILLE.
THIS PLACE IS A FAVORITE STOP FOR BOUNTY HUNTERS, SCRAPPERS, AND TRACKERS WHO ARE LOOKING TO TRADE IN OLD GADGETS AND UPGRADE THEIR WEAPONS.
BOB'S
TRADE
ROBO FUEL
I SAW IT FIRST!
MINE!

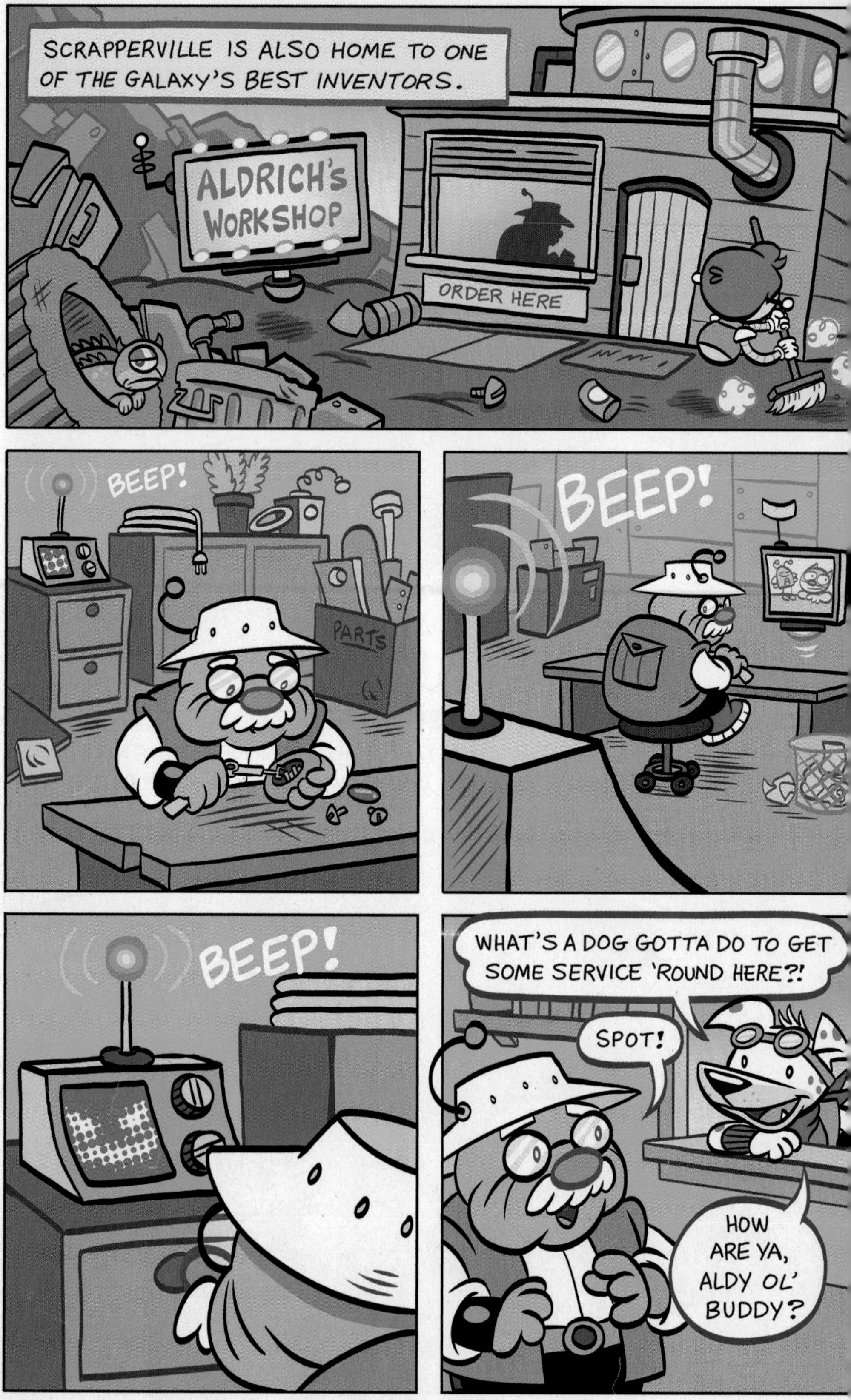
SCRAPPERVILLE IS ALSO HOME TO ONE OF THE GALAXY'S BEST INVENTORS.
ALDRICH's WORKSHOP
ORDER HERE
BEEP!
PARTS
BEEP!
BEEP!
WHAT'S A DOG GOTTA DO TO GET SOME SERVICE 'ROUND HERE?!
SPOT!
HOW ARE YA, ALDY OL' BUDDY?

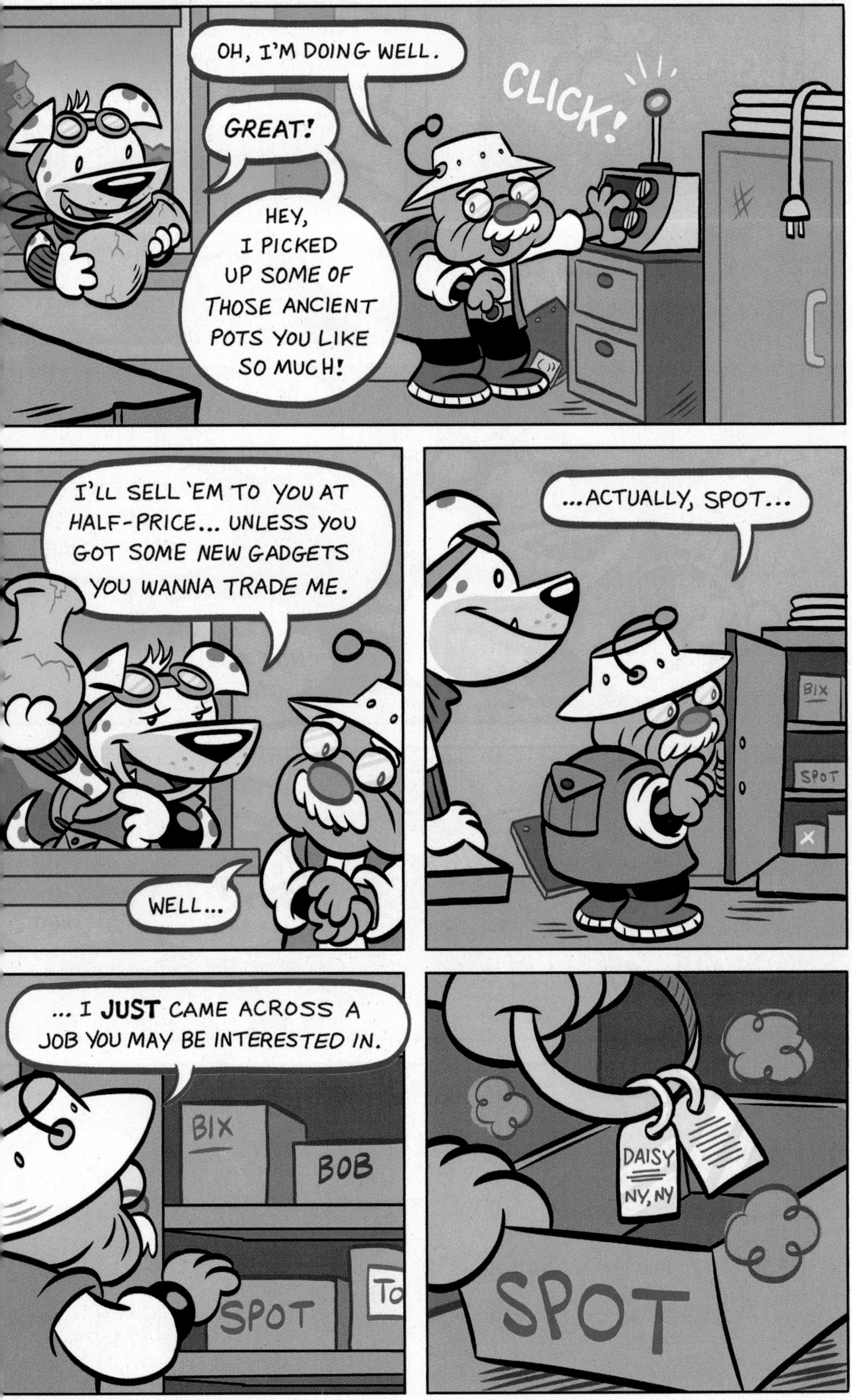
OH, I'M DOING WELL.
GREAT!
HEY, I PICKED UP SOME OF THOSE ANCIENT POTS YOU LIKE SO MUCH!
CLICK!
I'LL SELL 'EM TO YOU AT HALF-PRICE... UNLESS YOU GOT SOME NEW GADGETS YOU WANNA TRADE ME.
WELL...
...ACTUALLY, SPOT...
BIX
SPOT
... I **JUST** CAME ACROSS A JOB YOU MAY BE INTERESTED IN.
BIX
BOB
SPOT
DAISY
NY, NY
SPOT

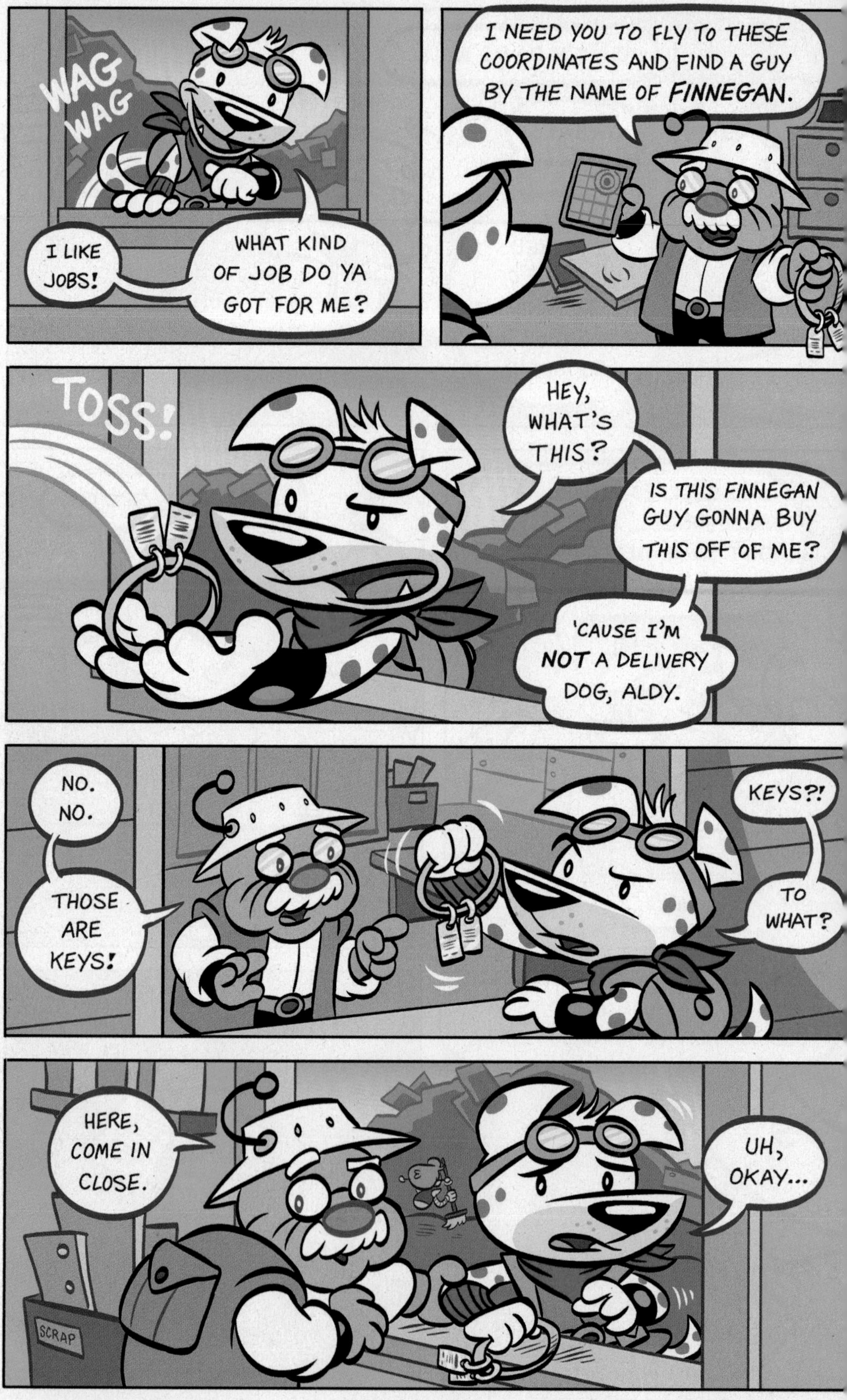
WAG WAG
I LIKE JOBS!
WHAT KIND OF JOB DO YA GOT FOR ME?
I NEED YOU TO FLY TO THESE COORDINATES AND FIND A GUY BY THE NAME OF FINNEGAN.
TOSS!
HEY, WHAT'S THIS?
IS THIS FINNEGAN GUY GONNA BUY THIS OFF OF ME?
'CAUSE I'M NOT A DELIVERY DOG, ALDY.
NO. NO.
THOSE ARE KEYS!
KEYS?!
TO WHAT?
HERE, COME IN CLOSE.
UH, OKAY...
SCRAP

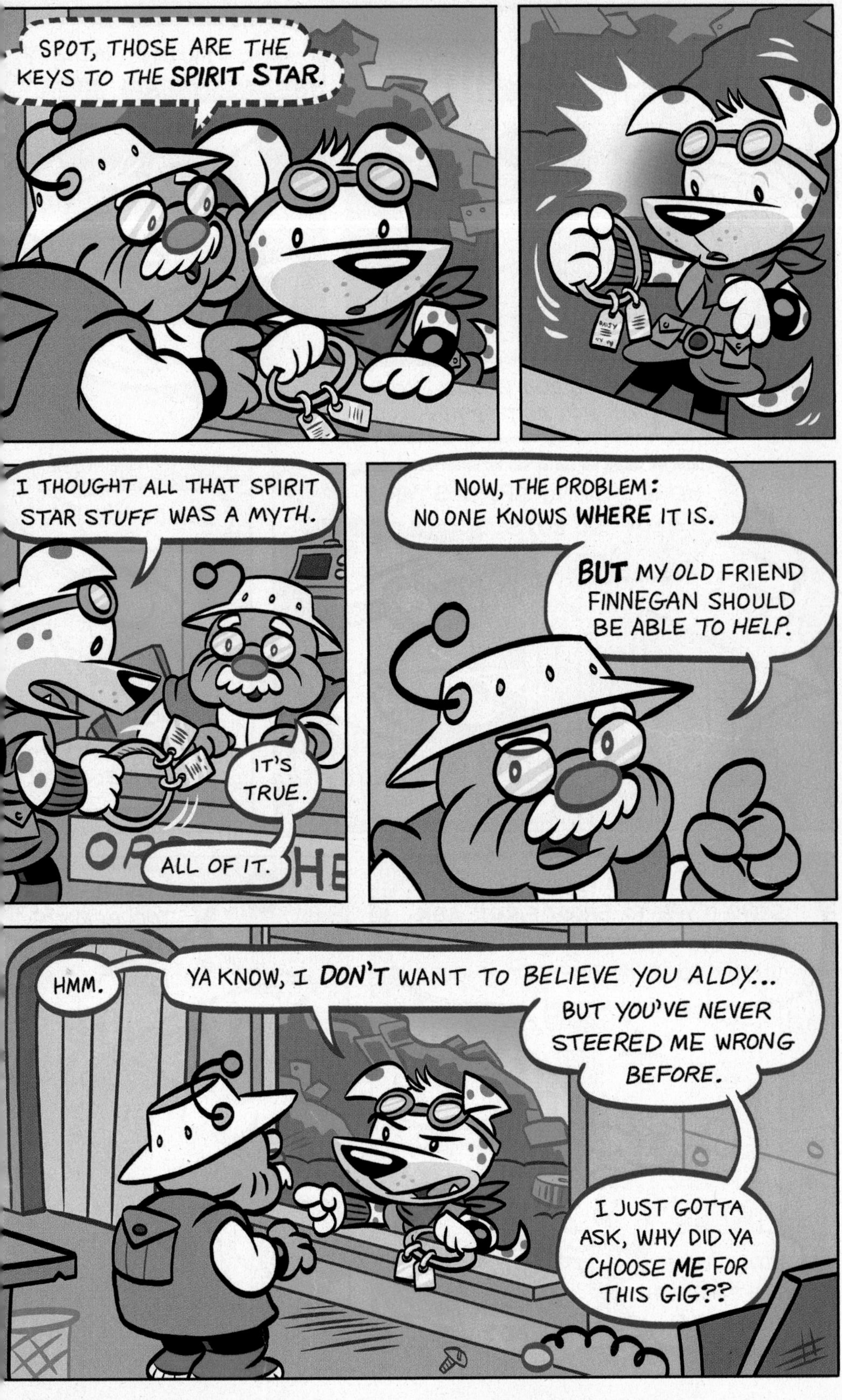
SPOT, THOSE ARE THE KEYS TO THE SPIRIT STAR.
I THOUGHT ALL THAT SPIRIT STAR STUFF WAS A MYTH.
IT'S TRUE.
ALL OF IT.
NOW, THE PROBLEM: NO ONE KNOWS WHERE IT IS.
BUT MY OLD FRIEND FINNEGAN SHOULD BE ABLE TO HELP.
HMM.
YA KNOW, I DON'T WANT TO BELIEVE YOU ALDY...
BUT YOU'VE NEVER STEERED ME WRONG BEFORE.
I JUST GOTTA ASK, WHY DID YA CHOOSE ME FOR THIS GIG??

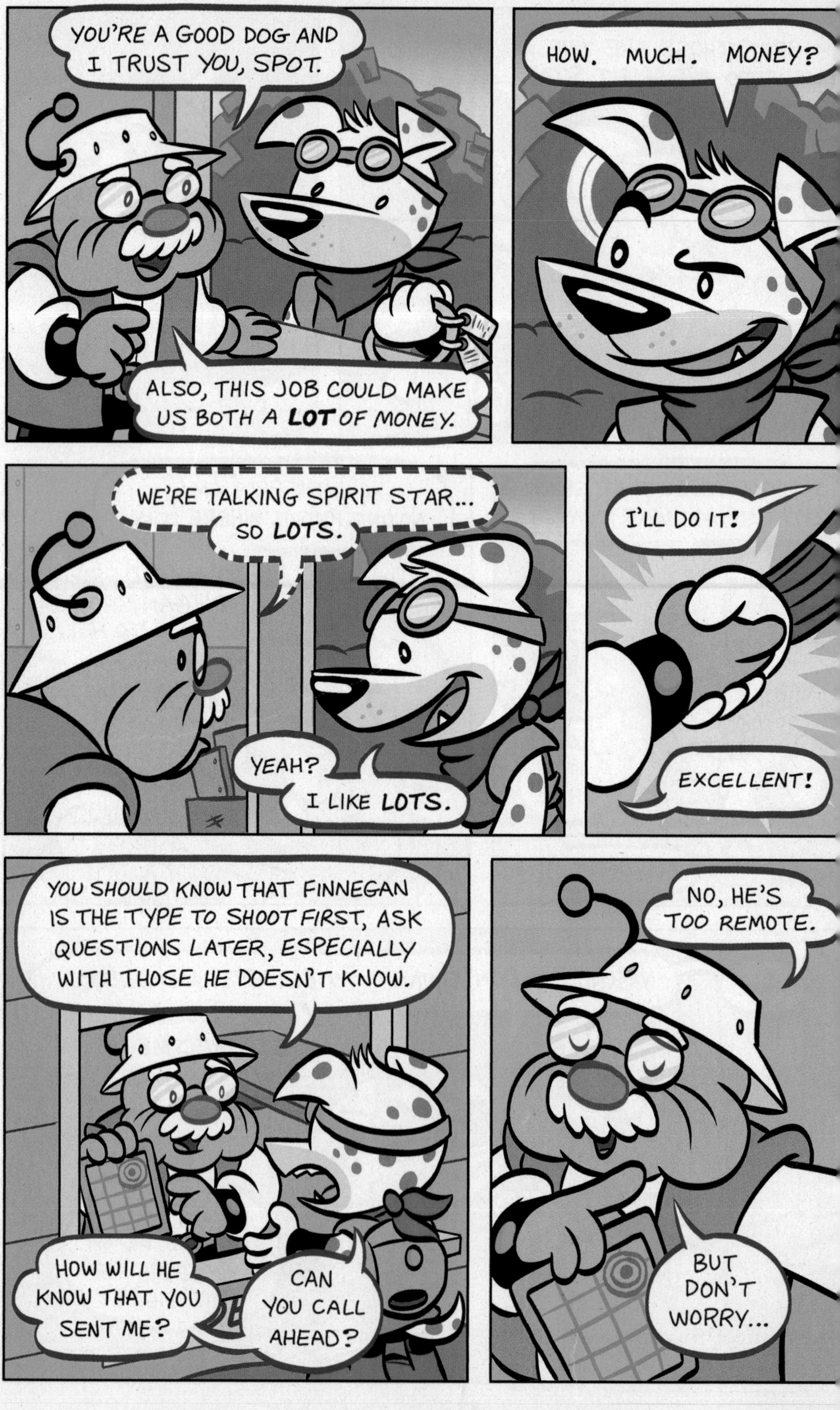
YOU'RE A GOOD DOG AND I TRUST YOU, SPOT.
ALSO, THIS JOB COULD MAKE US BOTH A LOT OF MONEY.
HOW. MUCH. MONEY?
WE'RE TALKING SPIRIT STAR... SO LOTS.
YEAH? I LIKE LOTS.
I'LL DO IT!
EXCELLENT!
YOU SHOULD KNOW THAT FINNEGAN IS THE TYPE TO SHOOT FIRST, ASK QUESTIONS LATER, ESPECIALLY WITH THOSE HE DOESN'T KNOW.
HOW WILL HE KNOW THAT YOU SENT ME?
CAN YOU CALL AHEAD?
NO, HE'S TOO REMOTE.
BUT DON'T WORRY...

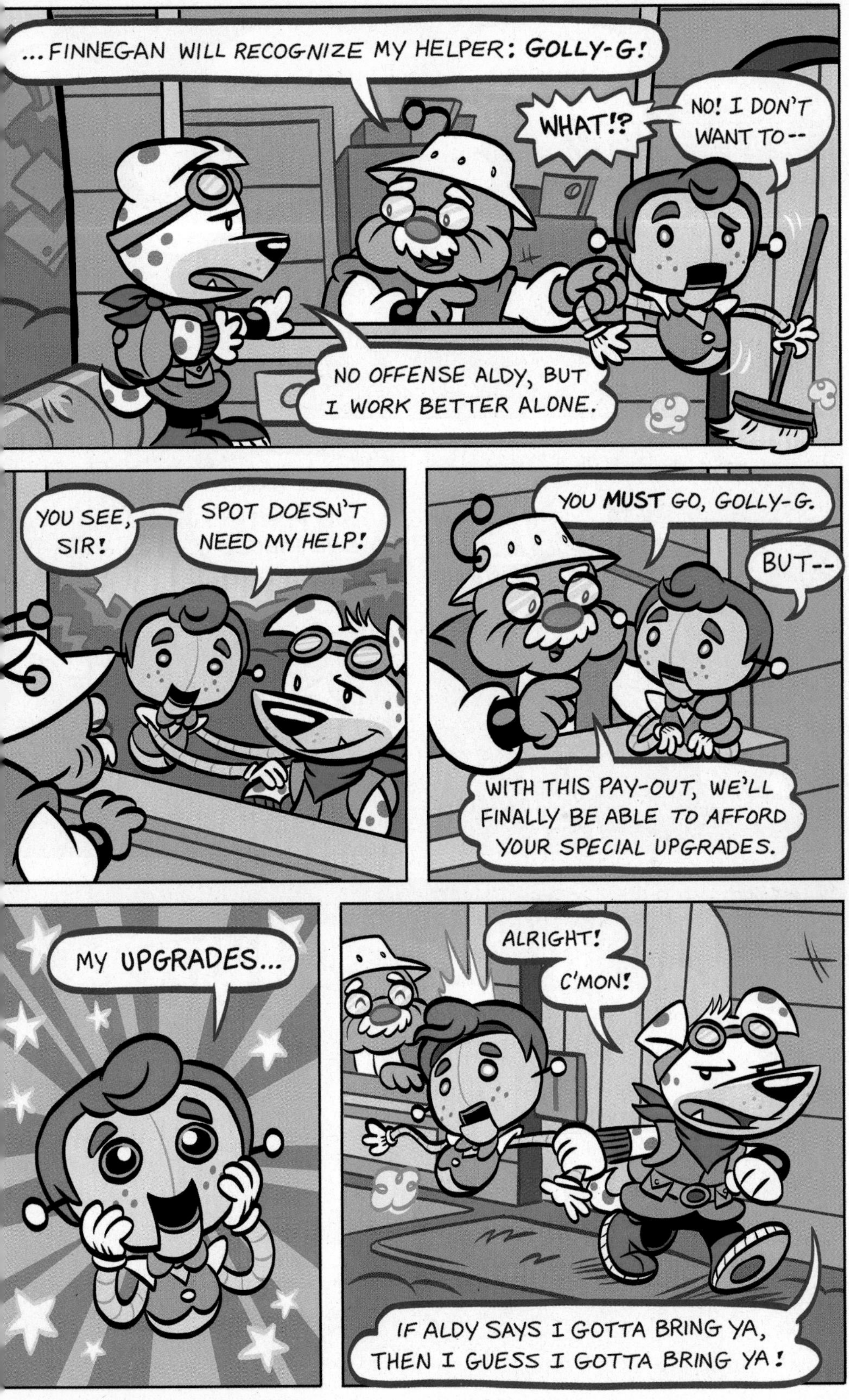
...FINNEGAN WILL RECOGNIZE MY HELPER: **GOLLY-G!**
WHAT!?
NO! I DON'T WANT TO--
NO OFFENSE ALDY, BUT I WORK BETTER ALONE.
YOU SEE, SIR!
SPOT DOESN'T NEED MY HELP!
YOU **MUST** GO, GOLLY-G.
BUT--
WITH THIS PAY-OUT, WE'LL FINALLY BE ABLE TO AFFORD YOUR SPECIAL UPGRADES.
MY **UPGRADES...**
ALRIGHT!
C'MON!
IF ALDY SAYS I GOTTA BRING YA, THEN I GUESS I GOTTA BRING YA!

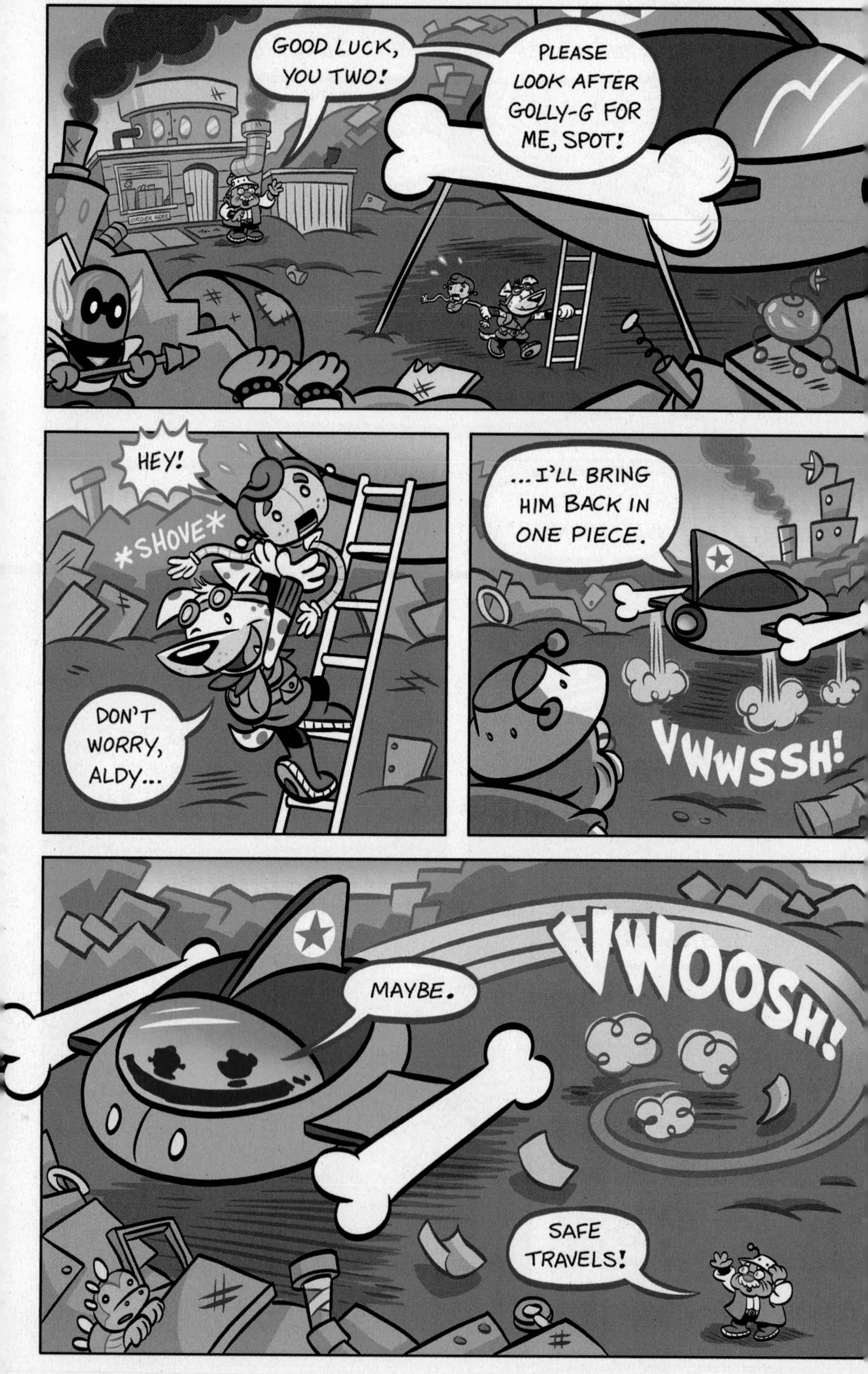
GOOD LUCK, YOU TWO!
PLEASE LOOK AFTER GOLLY-G FOR ME, SPOT!
ORDER HERE
HEY!
SHOVE
DON'T WORRY, ALDY...
...I'LL BRING HIM BACK IN ONE PIECE.
VWWSSH!
MAYBE.
VWOOSH!
SAFE TRAVELS!

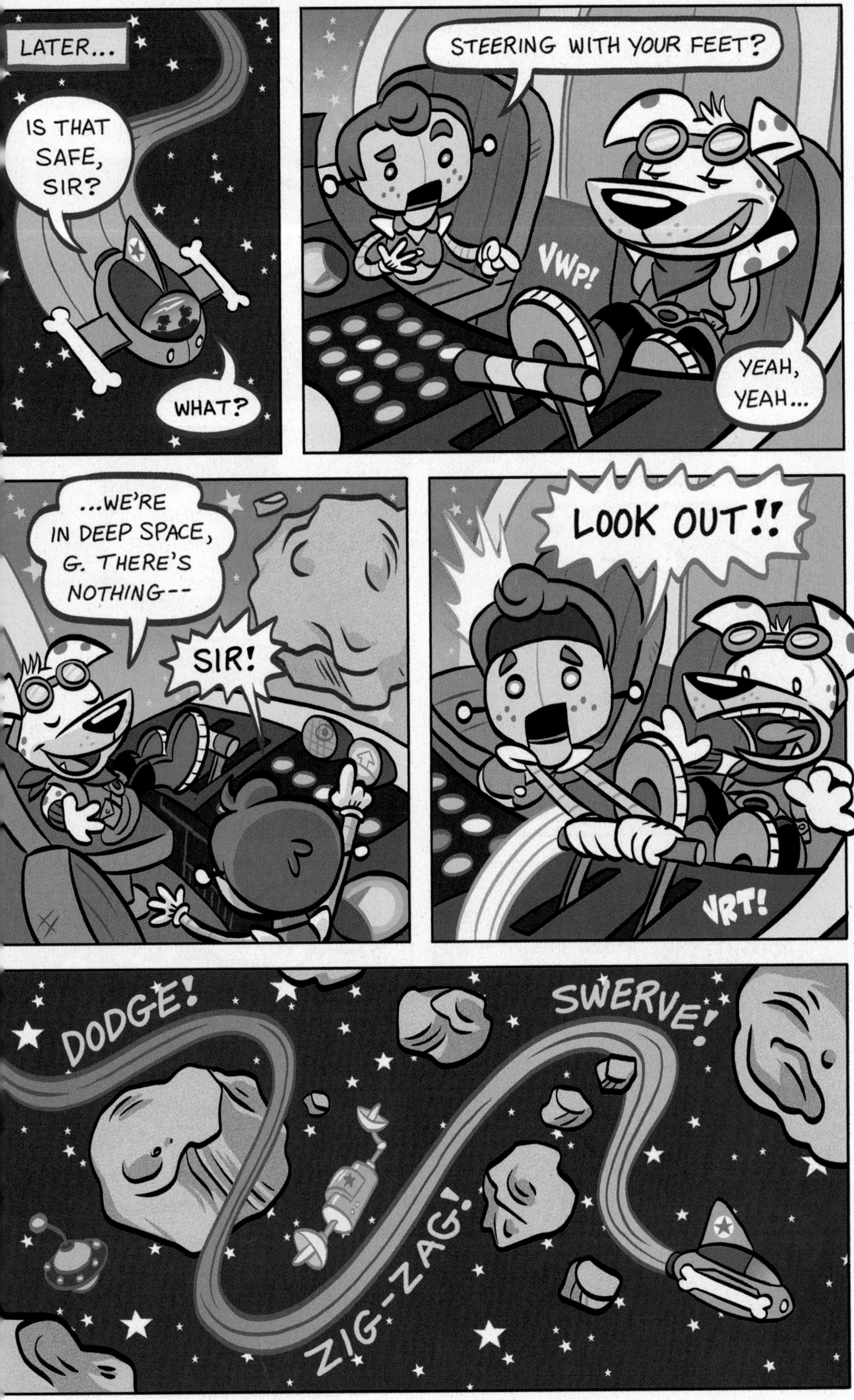
LATER...
IS THAT SAFE, SIR?
WHAT?
STEERING WITH YOUR FEET?
VWP!
YEAH, YEAH...
...WE'RE IN DEEP SPACE, G. THERE'S NOTHING--
SIR!
LOOK OUT!!
VRT!
DODGE!
SWERVE!
ZIG-ZAG!

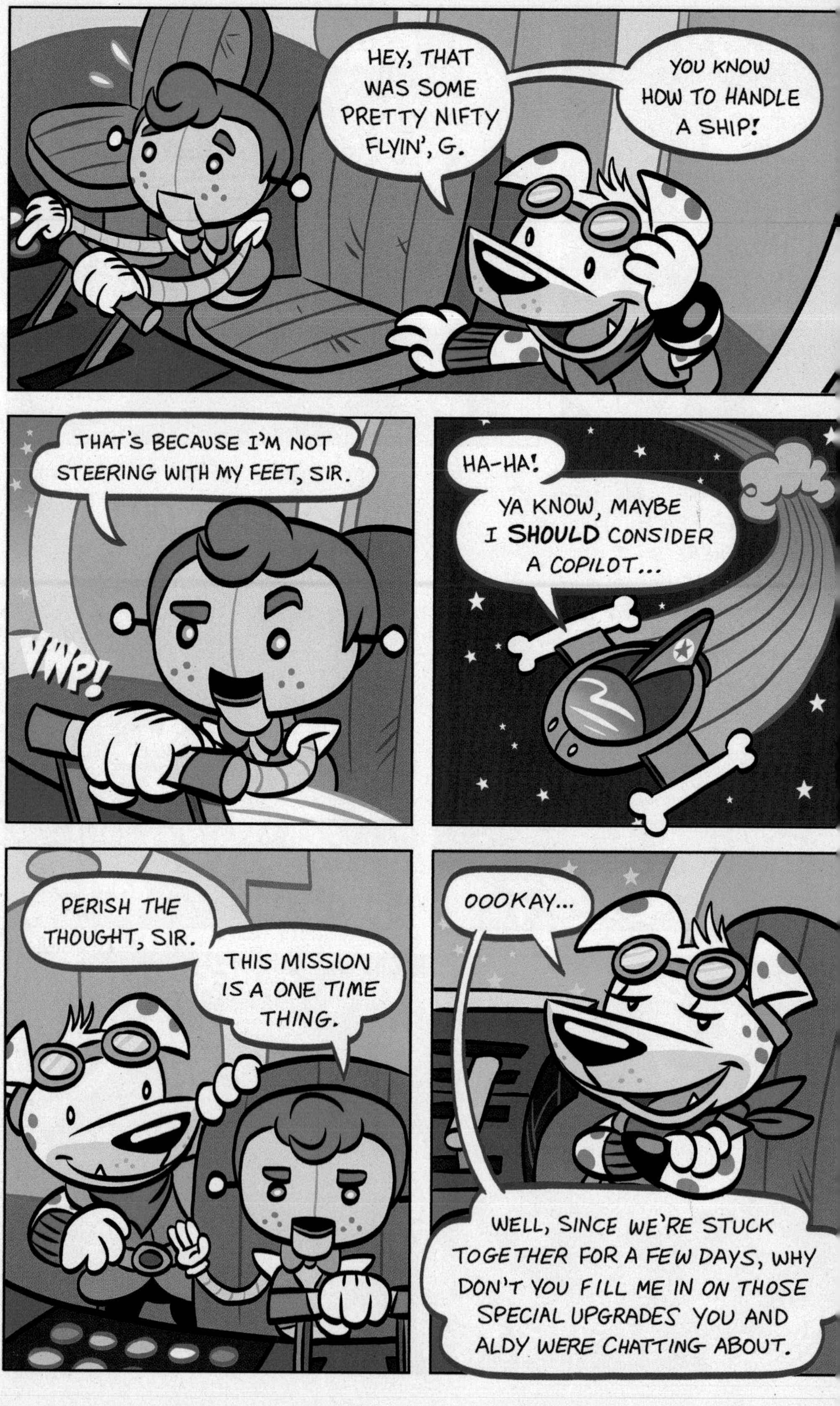
HEY, THAT WAS SOME PRETTY NIFTY FLYIN', G.
YOU KNOW HOW TO HANDLE A SHIP!
THAT'S BECAUSE I'M NOT STEERING WITH MY FEET, SIR.
VWP!
HA-HA!
YA KNOW, MAYBE I **SHOULD** CONSIDER A COPILOT...
PERISH THE THOUGHT, SIR.
THIS MISSION IS A ONE TIME THING.
OOOKAY...
WELL, SINCE WE'RE STUCK TOGETHER FOR A FEW DAYS, WHY DON'T YOU FILL ME IN ON THOSE SPECIAL UPGRADES YOU AND ALDY WERE CHATTING ABOUT.

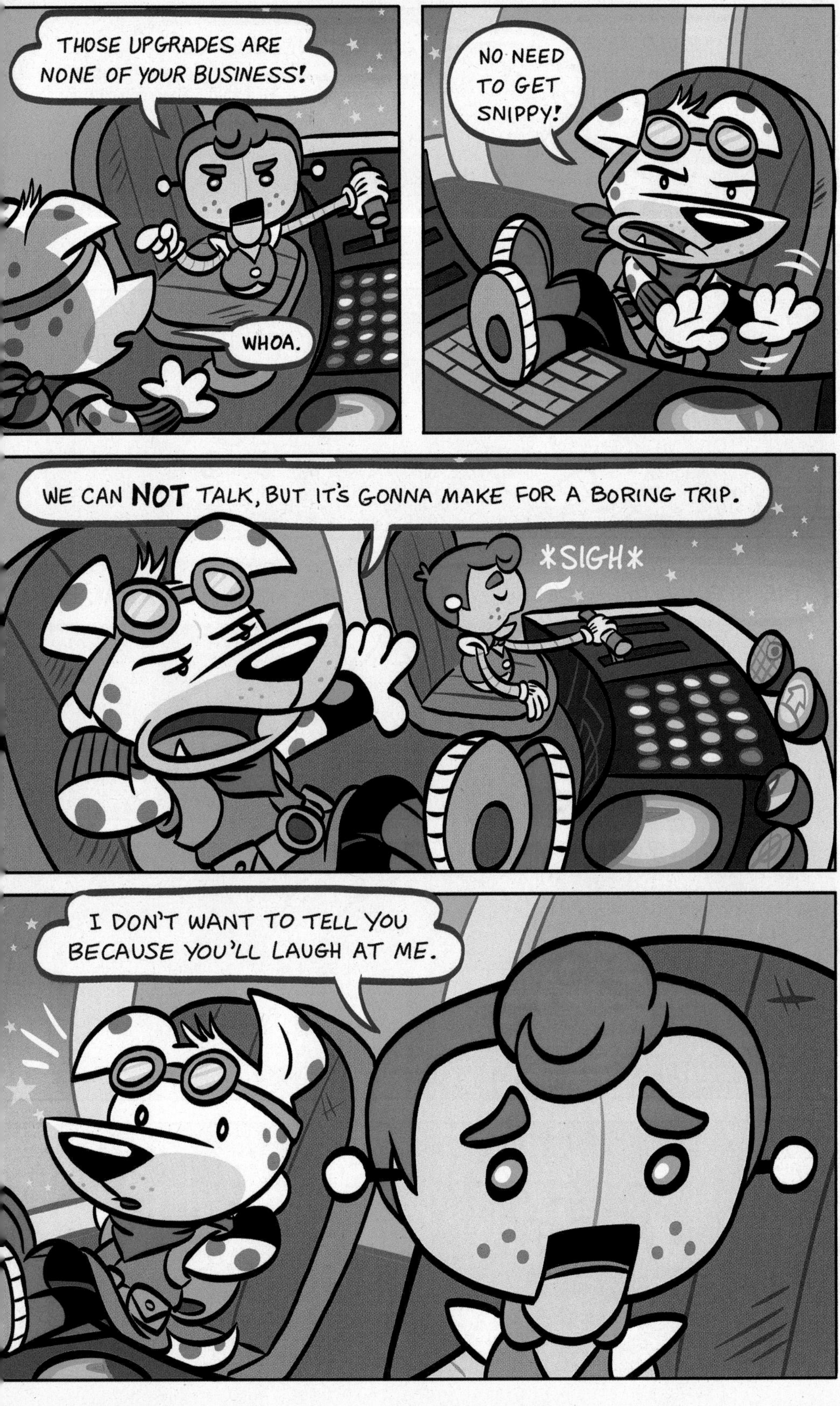
THOSE UPGRADES ARE NONE OF YOUR BUSINESS!
WHOA.
NO NEED TO GET SNIPPY!
WE CAN NOT TALK, BUT IT'S GONNA MAKE FOR A BORING TRIP.
SIGH
I DON'T WANT TO TELL YOU BECAUSE YOU'LL LAUGH AT ME.

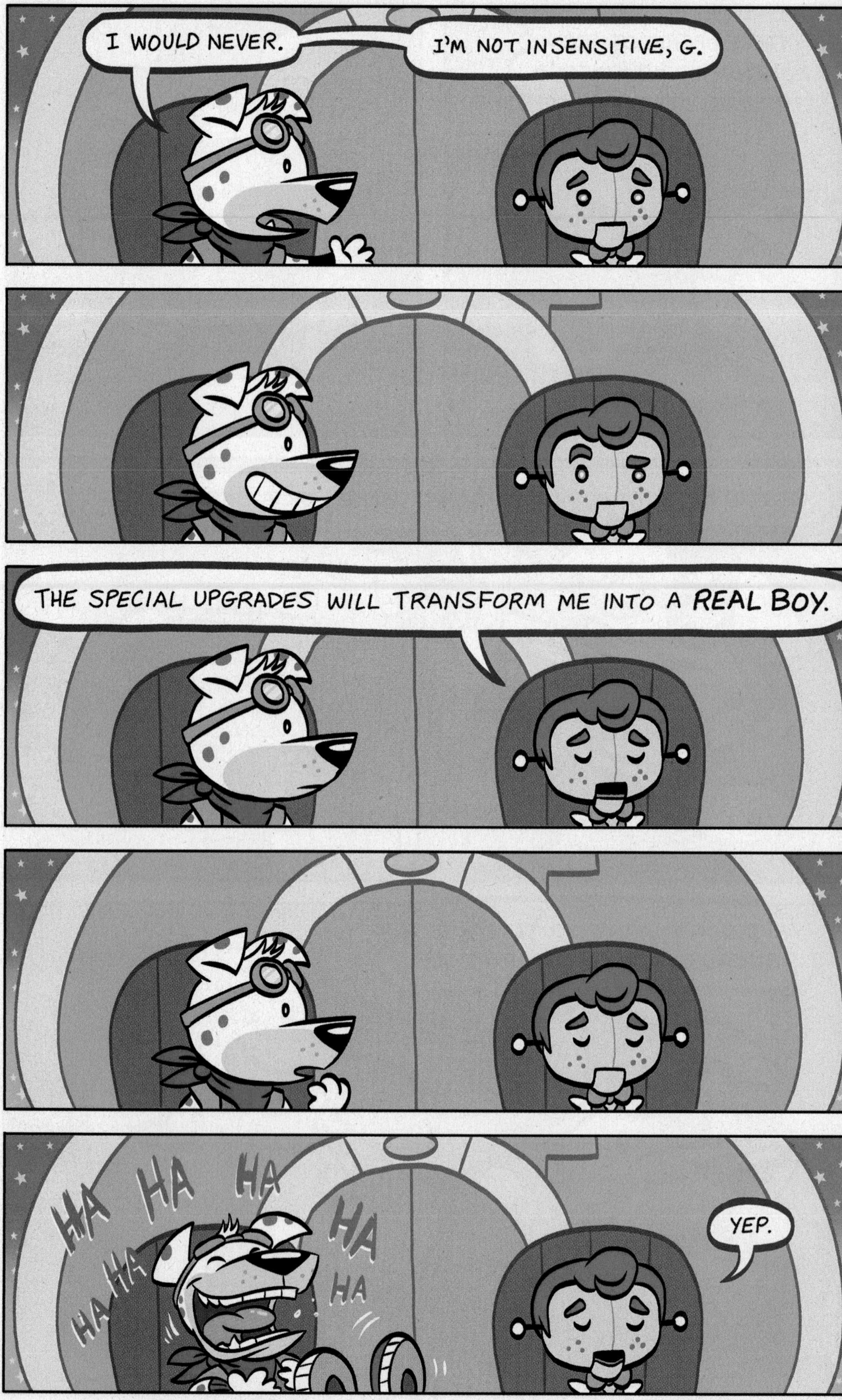
I WOULD NEVER.
I'M NOT INSENSITIVE, G.
THE SPECIAL UPGRADES WILL TRANSFORM ME INTO A REAL BOY.
HA HA HA
HA
HA HA
HA
HA
YEP.

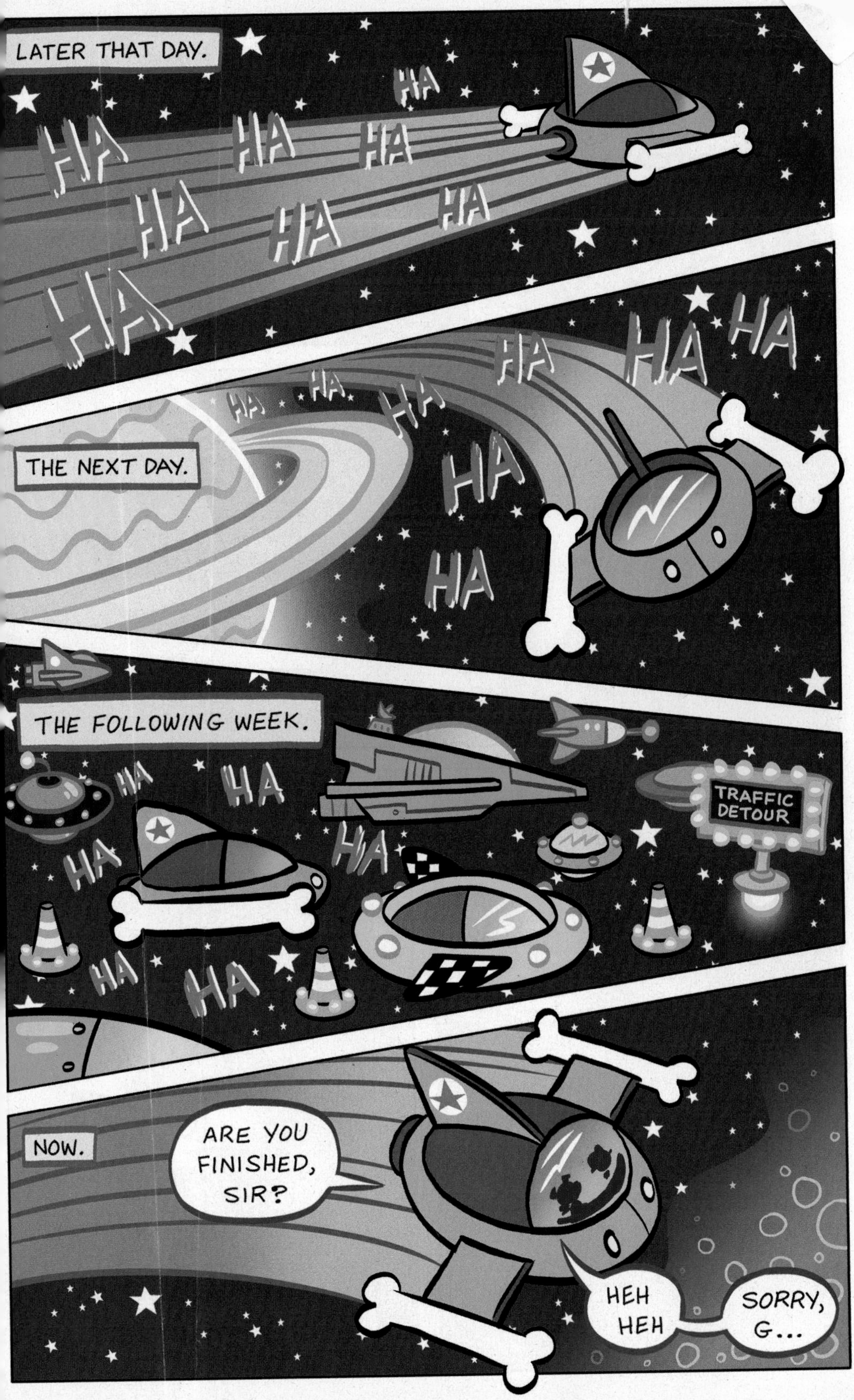
LATER THAT DAY.
HA HA HA HA HA HA HA HA
THE NEXT DAY.
HA HA HA HA HA HA HA HA HA
THE FOLLOWING WEEK.
HA HA HA HA HA HA
TRAFFIC DETOUR
NOW.
ARE YOU FINISHED, SIR?
HEH HEH
SORRY, G...

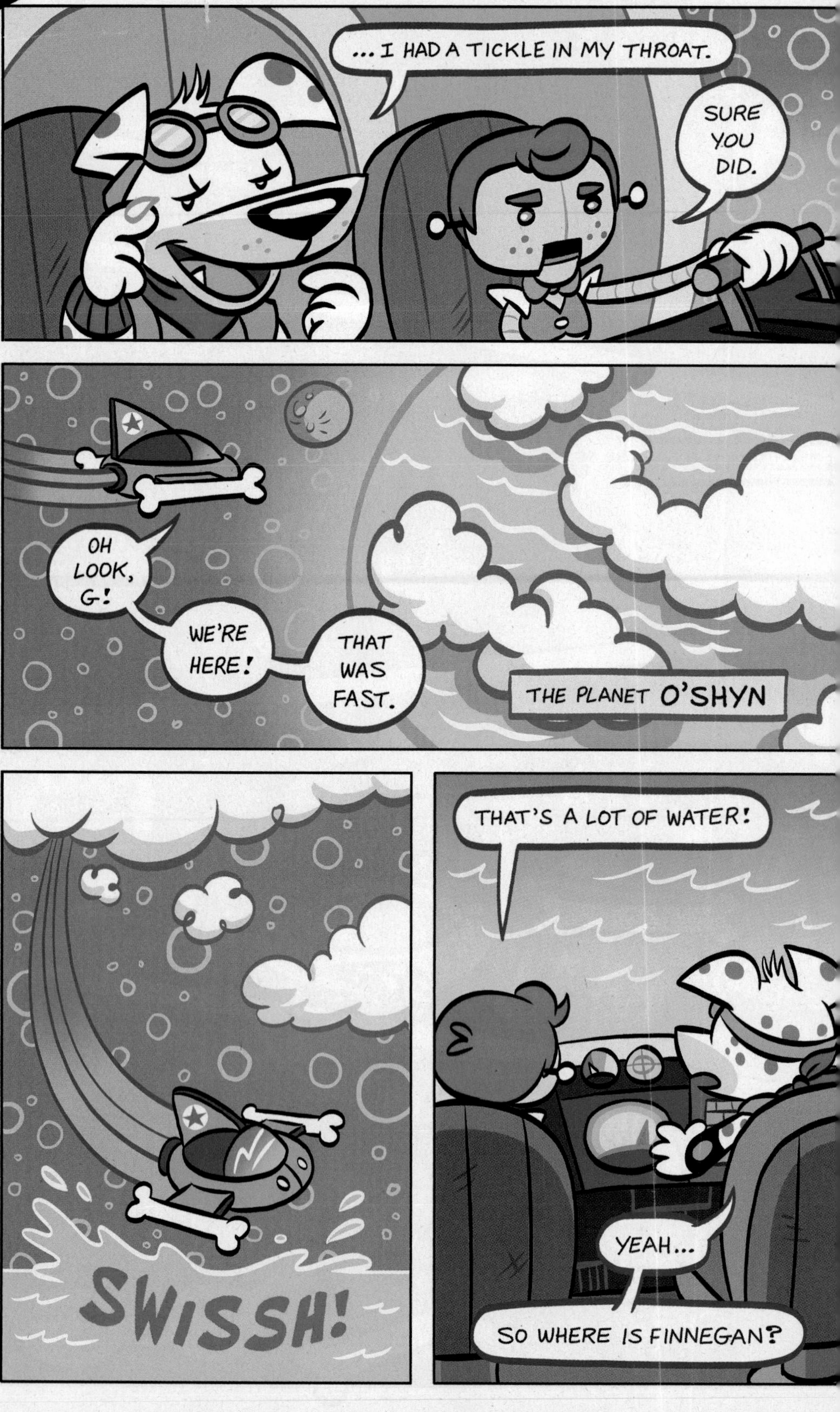

...I HAD A TICKLE IN MY THROAT.
SURE YOU DID.
OH LOOK, G!
WE'RE HERE!
THAT WAS FAST.
THE PLANET O'SHYN
SWISSH!
THAT'S A LOT OF WATER!
YEAH...
SO WHERE IS FINNEGAN?

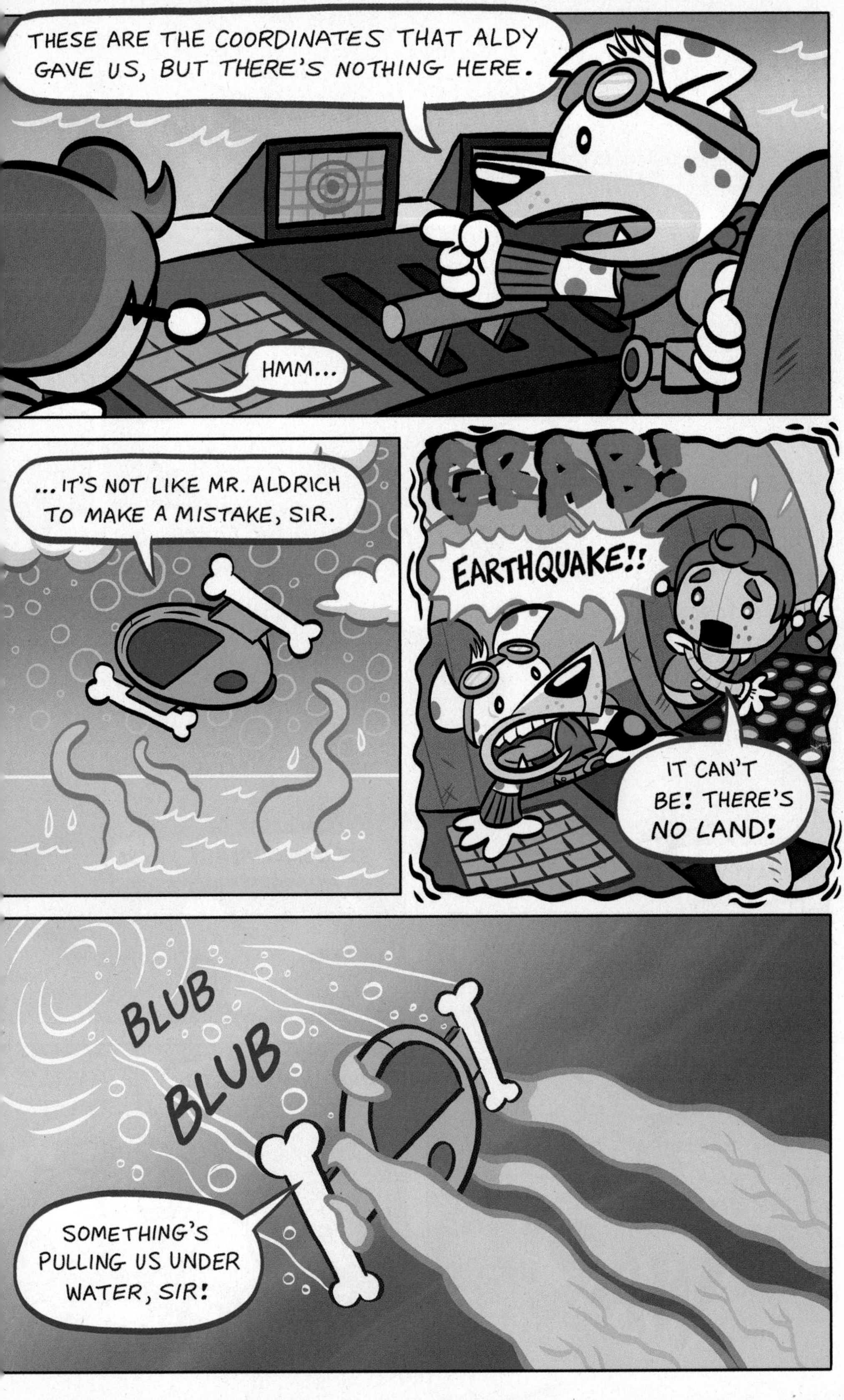
THESE ARE THE COORDINATES THAT ALDY GAVE US, BUT THERE'S NOTHING HERE.
HMM...
...IT'S NOT LIKE MR. ALDRICH TO MAKE A MISTAKE, SIR.
GRAB!
EARTHQUAKE!!
IT CAN'T BE! THERE'S NO LAND!
BLUB
BLUB
SOMETHING'S PULLING US UNDER WATER, SIR!

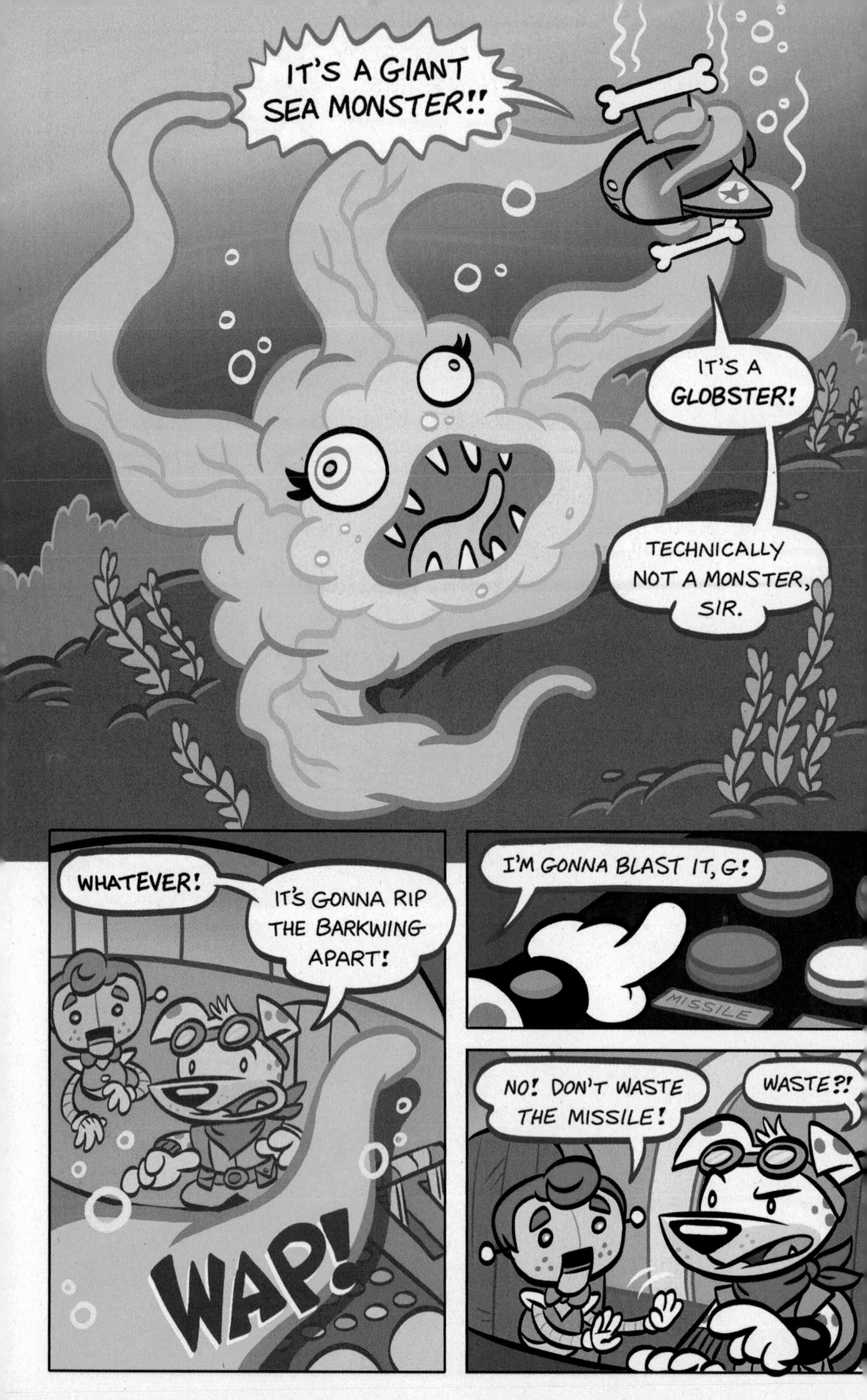
IT'S A GIANT SEA MONSTER!!
IT'S A GLOBSTER!
TECHNICALLY NOT A MONSTER, SIR.
WHATEVER!
IT'S GONNA RIP THE BARKWING APART!
WAP!
I'M GONNA BLAST IT, G!
MISSILE
NO! DON'T WASTE THE MISSILE!
WASTE?!

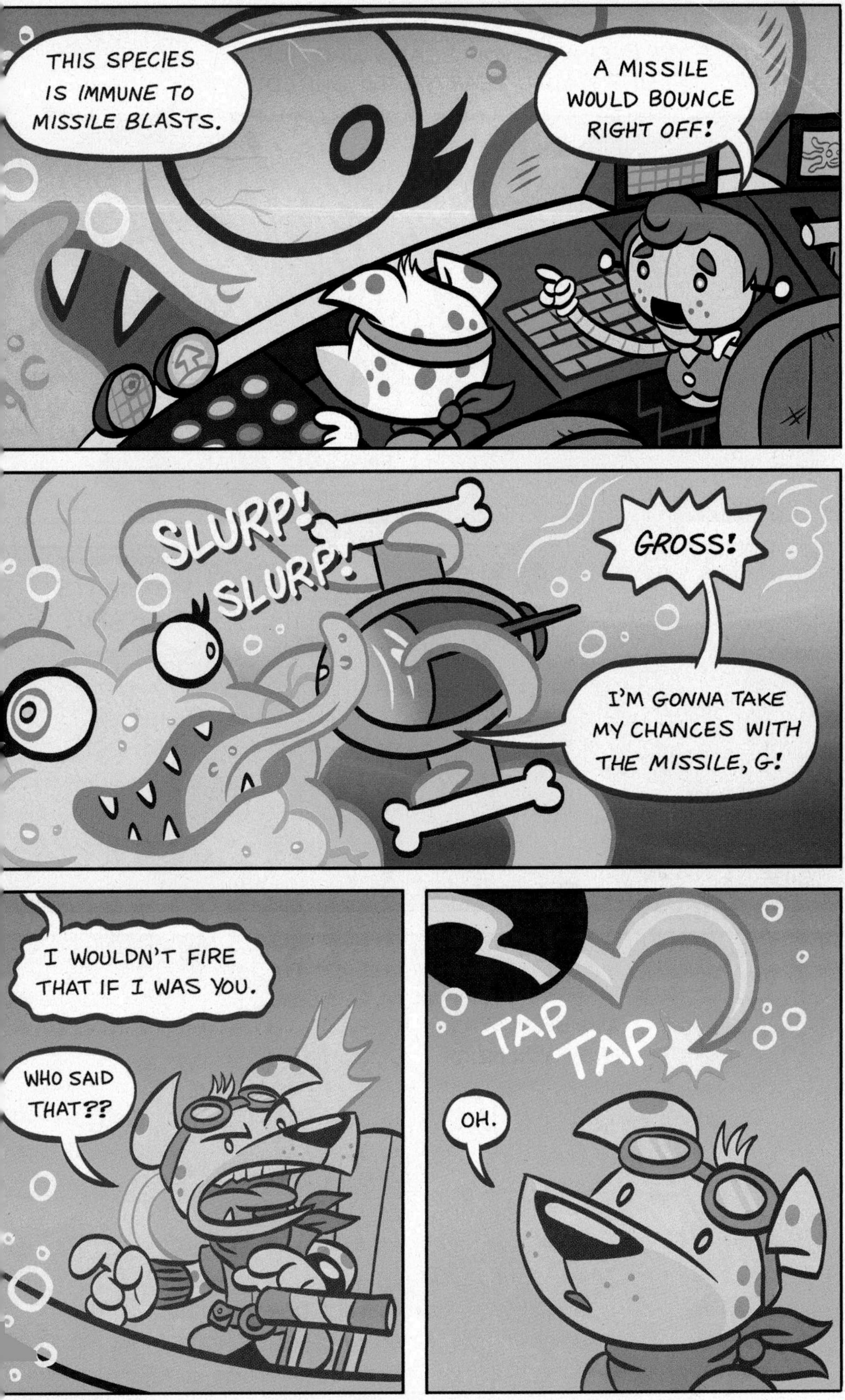
THIS SPECIES IS IMMUNE TO MISSILE BLASTS.
A MISSILE WOULD BOUNCE RIGHT OFF!
SLURP! SLURP!
GROSS!
I'M GONNA TAKE MY CHANCES WITH THE MISSILE, G!
I WOULDN'T FIRE THAT IF I WAS YOU.
WHO SAID THAT??
TAP TAP
OH.

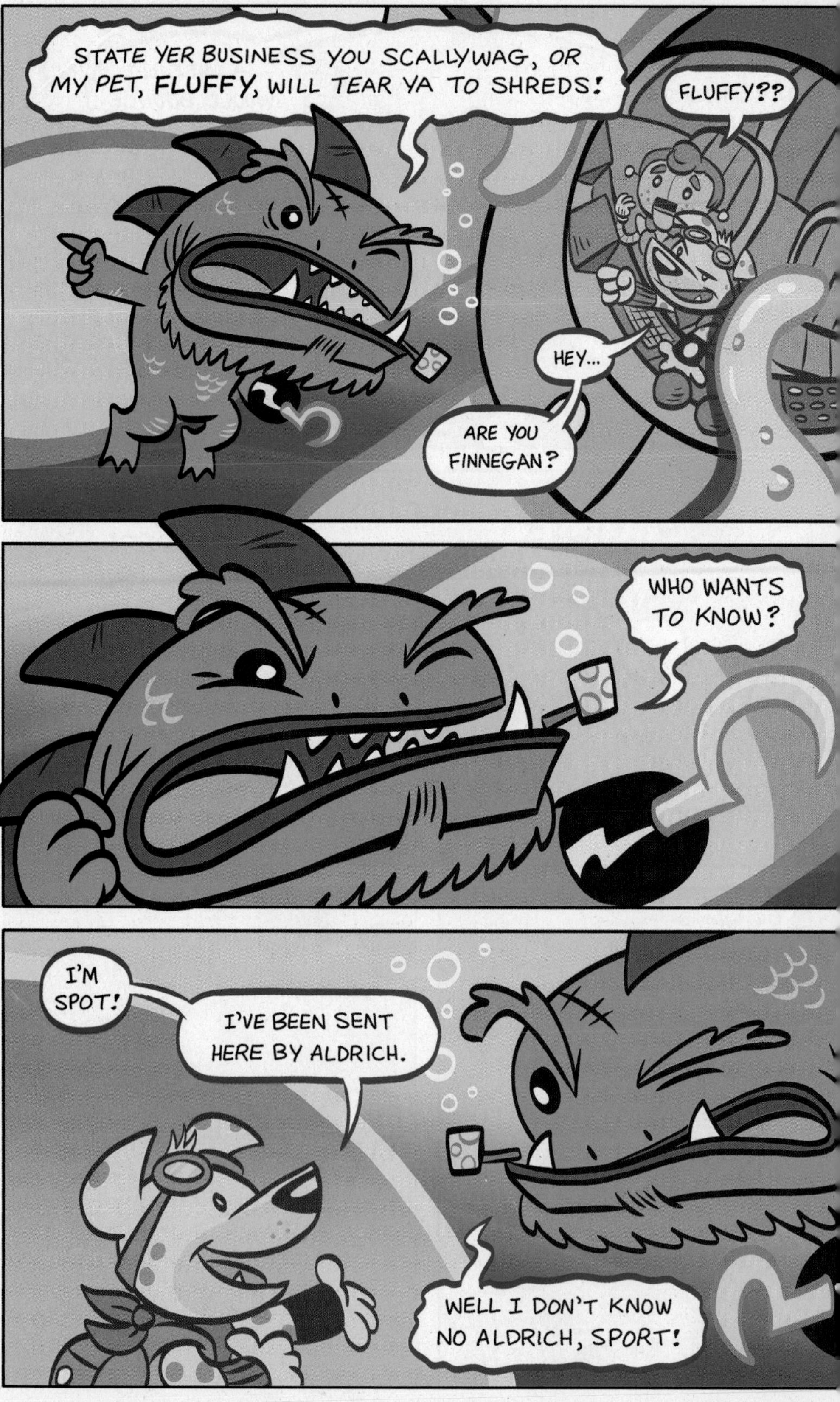
STATE YER BUSINESS YOU SCALLYWAG, OR MY PET, FLUFFY, WILL TEAR YA TO SHREDS!
FLUFFY??
HEY...
ARE YOU FINNEGAN?
WHO WANTS TO KNOW?
I'M SPOT!
I'VE BEEN SENT HERE BY ALDRICH.
WELL I DON'T KNOW NO ALDRICH, SPORT!

AH, HE SAID YOU MIGHT BE SCEPTICAL, SO...

...HE SENT *GOLLY-G* HERE TO PROVE IT!

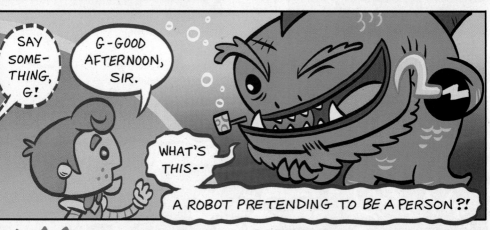

SAY SOME-THING, G!

G-GOOD AFTERNOON, SIR.

WHAT'S THIS--

A ROBOT PRETENDING TO BE A PERSON?!

EXCUSE ME??

PRETENDING??

YOU DON'T RECOGNIZE ALDRICH'S HELPER, HERE?

AW NO...

CALM DOWN, G!

I ALREADY TOLD YA, SPORK--

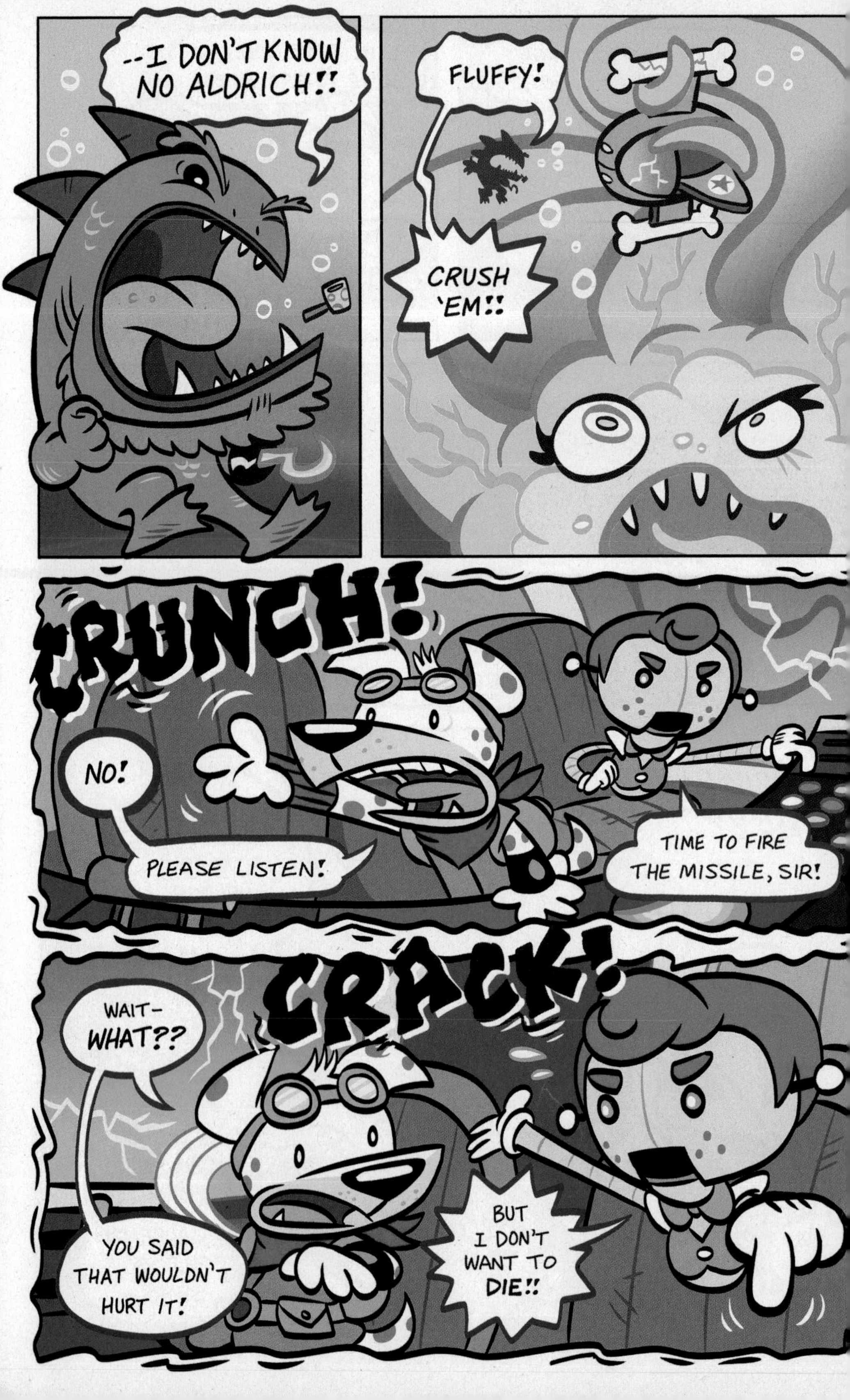
--I DON'T KNOW NO ALDRICH!!
FLUFFY!
CRUSH 'EM!!
CRUNCH!
NO!
PLEASE LISTEN!
TIME TO FIRE THE MISSILE, SIR!
CRACK!
WAIT- WHAT??
YOU SAID THAT WOULDN'T HURT IT!
BUT I DON'T WANT TO DIE!!

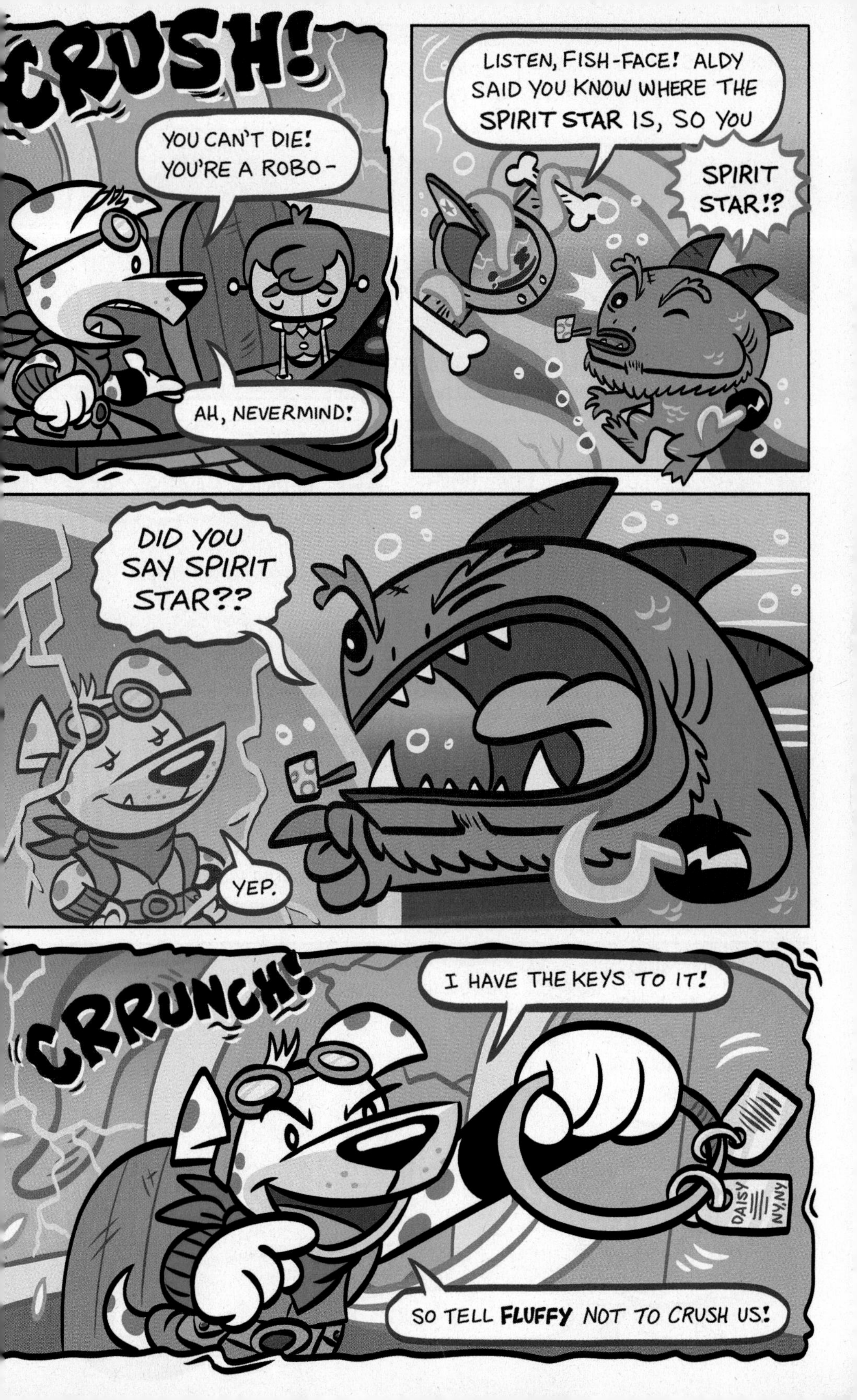
CRUSH!
YOU CAN'T DIE! YOU'RE A ROBO-
AH, NEVERMIND!
LISTEN, FISH-FACE! ALDY SAID YOU KNOW WHERE THE SPIRIT STAR IS, SO YOU
SPIRIT STAR!?
DID YOU SAY SPIRIT STAR??
YEP.
CRRUNCH!
I HAVE THE KEYS TO IT!
DAISY
NY, NY
SO TELL FLUFFY NOT TO CRUSH US!

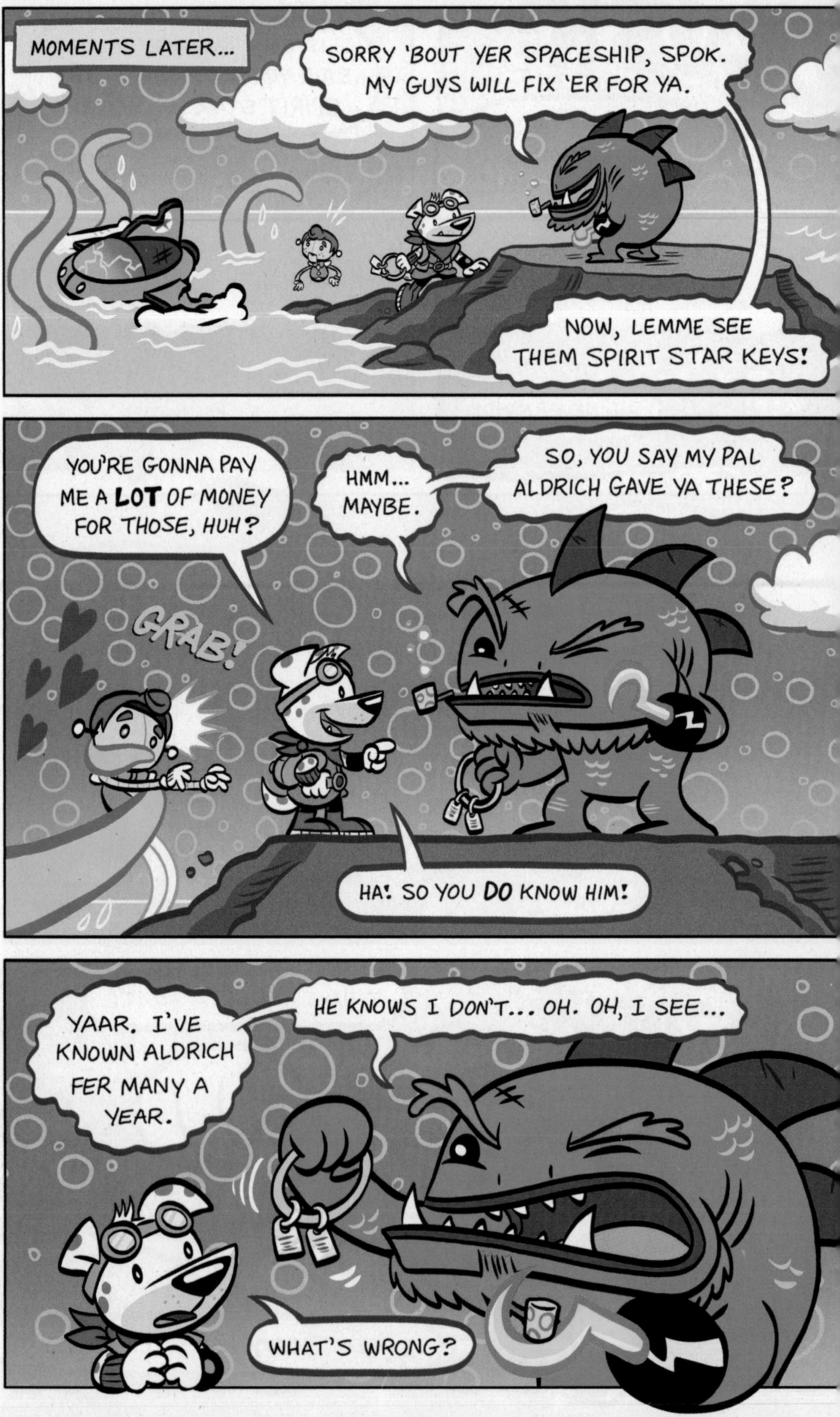
MOMENTS LATER...
SORRY 'BOUT YER SPACESHIP, SPOK. MY GUYS WILL FIX 'ER FOR YA.
NOW, LEMME SEE THEM SPIRIT STAR KEYS!
SO, YOU SAY MY PAL ALDRICH GAVE YA THESE?
HMM... MAYBE.
YOU'RE GONNA PAY ME A LOT OF MONEY FOR THOSE, HUH?
GRAB!
HA! SO YOU DO KNOW HIM!
YAAR. I'VE KNOWN ALDRICH FER MANY A YEAR.
HE KNOWS I DON'T... OH. OH, I SEE...
WHAT'S WRONG?

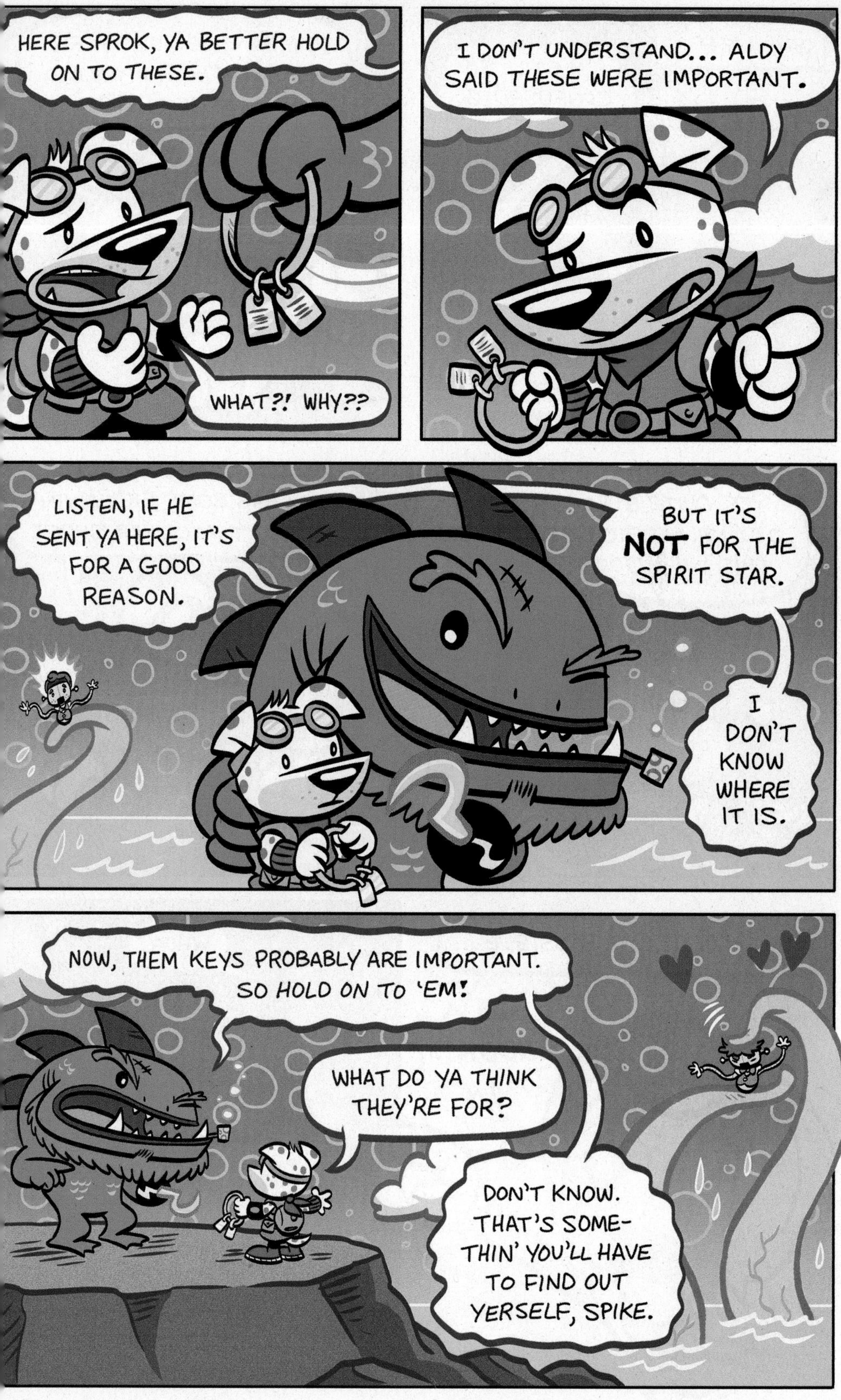
HERE SPROK, YA BETTER HOLD ON TO THESE.
WHAT?! WHY??
I DON'T UNDERSTAND... ALDY SAID THESE WERE IMPORTANT.
LISTEN, IF HE SENT YA HERE, IT'S FOR A GOOD REASON.
BUT IT'S **NOT** FOR THE SPIRIT STAR.
I DON'T KNOW WHERE IT IS.
NOW, THEM KEYS PROBABLY ARE IMPORTANT. SO HOLD ON TO 'EM!
WHAT DO YA THINK THEY'RE FOR?
DON'T KNOW. THAT'S SOME-THIN' YOU'LL HAVE TO FIND OUT YERSELF, SPIKE.

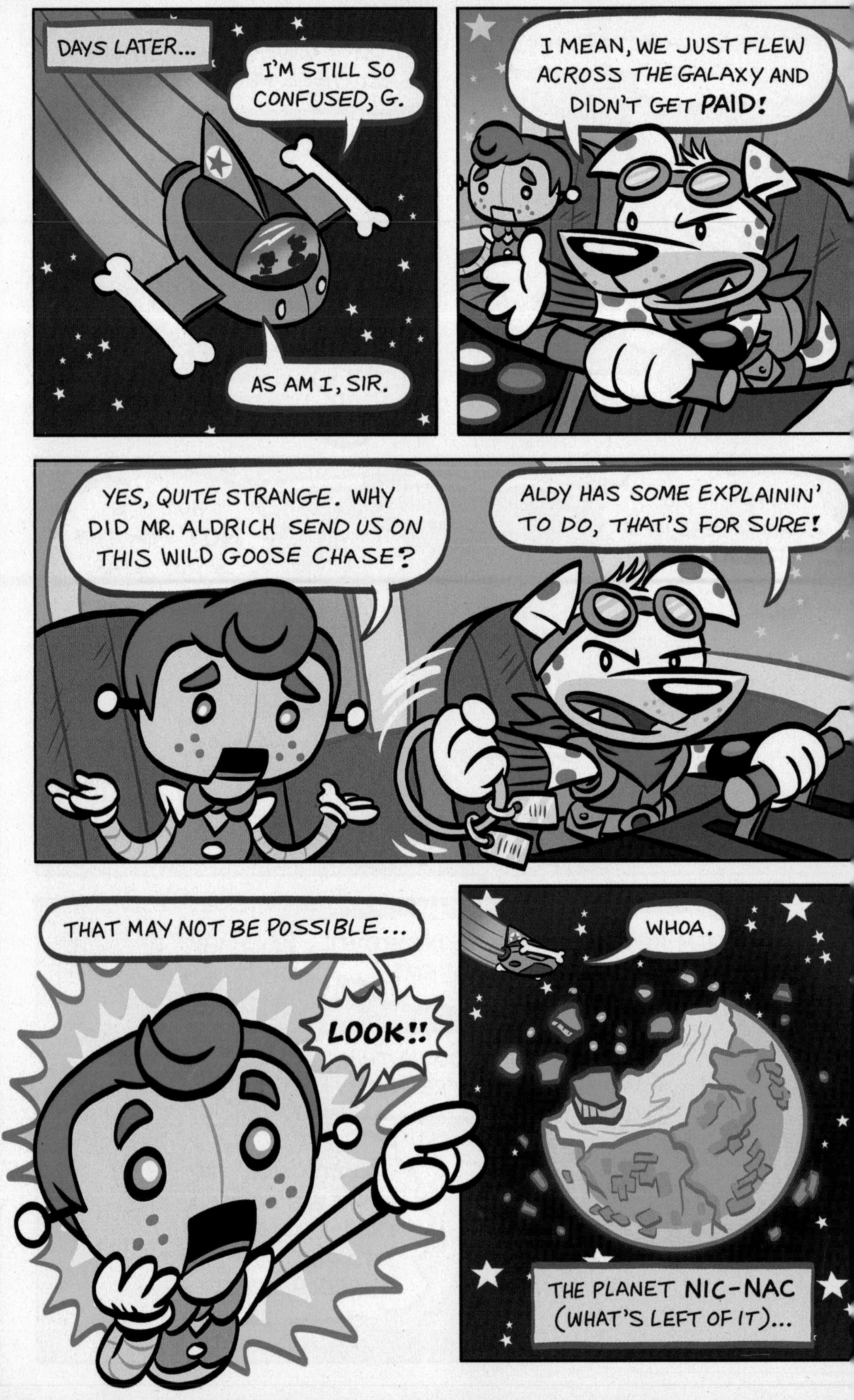
DAYS LATER...
I'M STILL SO CONFUSED, G.
AS AM I, SIR.
I MEAN, WE JUST FLEW ACROSS THE GALAXY AND DIDN'T GET PAID!
YES, QUITE STRANGE. WHY DID MR. ALDRICH SEND US ON THIS WILD GOOSE CHASE?
ALDY HAS SOME EXPLAININ' TO DO, THAT'S FOR SURE!
THAT MAY NOT BE POSSIBLE...
LOOK!!
WHOA.
THE PLANET NIC-NAC (WHAT'S LEFT OF IT)...

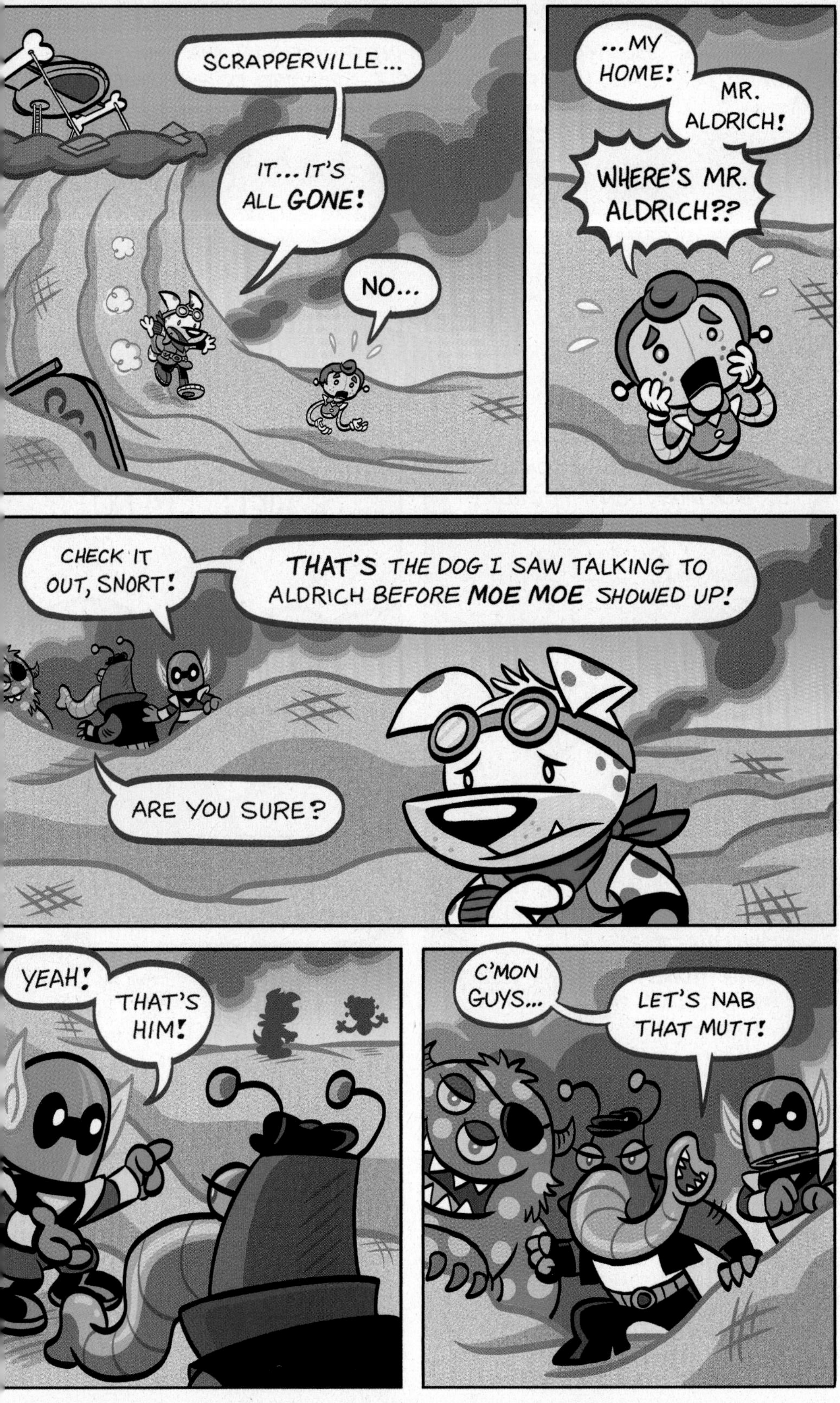
SCRAPPERVILLE...
IT... IT'S ALL GONE!
NO...
...MY HOME!
MR. ALDRICH!
WHERE'S MR. ALDRICH??
CHECK IT OUT, SNORT!
THAT'S THE DOG I SAW TALKING TO ALDRICH BEFORE MOE MOE SHOWED UP!
ARE YOU SURE?
YEAH!
THAT'S HIM!
C'MON GUYS...
LET'S NAB THAT MUTT!

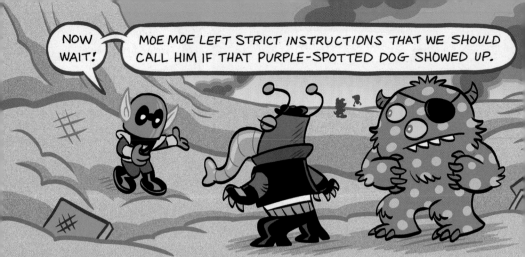

NOW WAIT!

MOE MOE LEFT STRICT INSTRUCTIONS THAT WE SHOULD CALL HIM IF THAT PURPLE-SPOTTED DOG SHOWED UP.

SOUNDS LIKE **BIX** IS SCARED OF MOE MOE, DON'T IT GRUX?

GRAH!

WELL I'M NOT!!

IF MOE MOE WANTS HIM, THAT MEANS SOMEONE, SOMEWHERE, IS WILLING TO PAY **BIG MONEY** FOR HIM!

SO, WHY NOT SPLIT THE BOUNTY BETWEEN THE THREE OF US?

GAWR.

IT'S **OUR TIME** TO CASH IN!

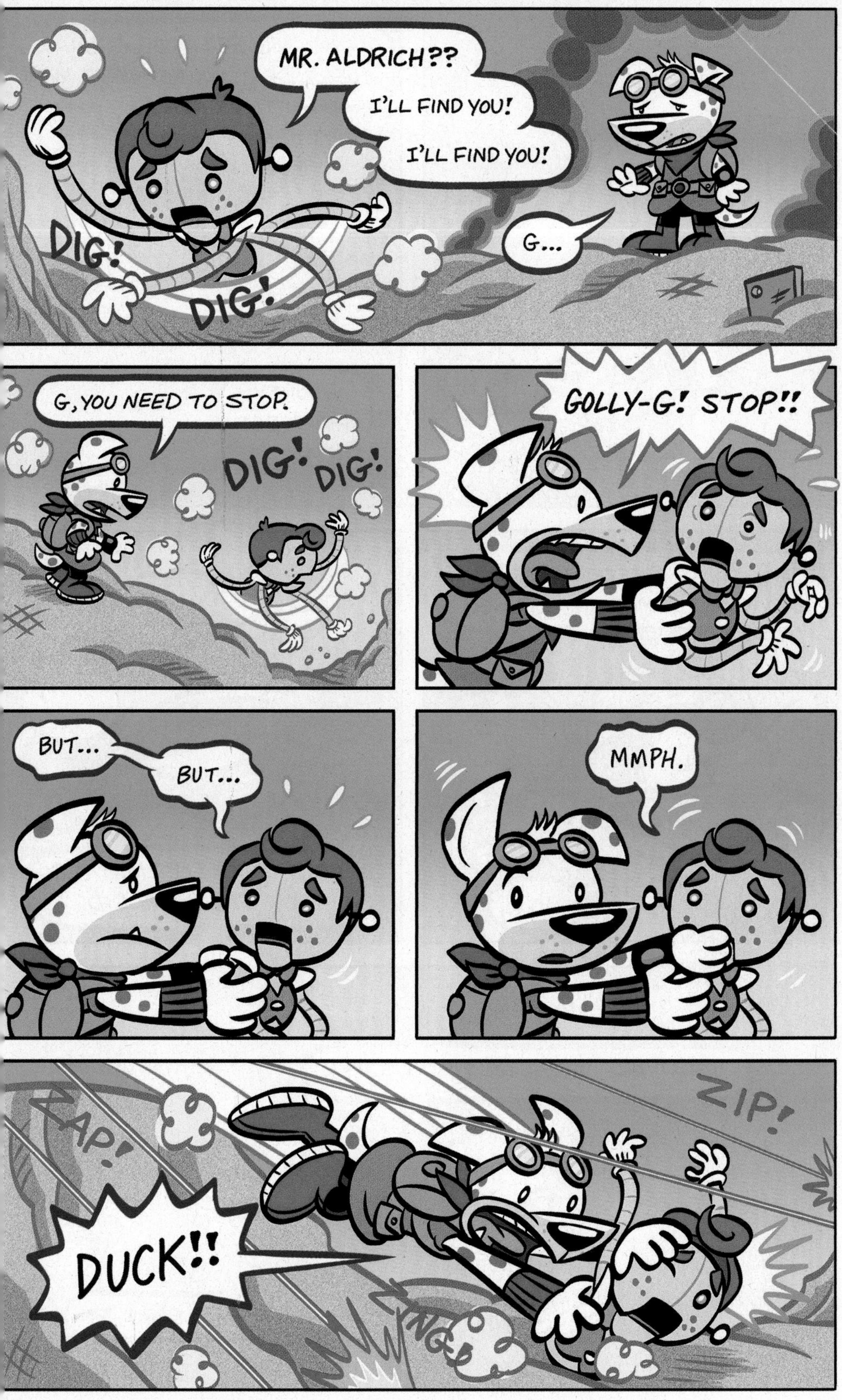
MR. ALDRICH??
I'LL FIND YOU!
I'LL FIND YOU!
DIG!
DIG!
G...
G, YOU NEED TO STOP.
DIG!
DIG!
GOLLY-G! STOP!!
BUT...
BUT...
MMPH.
ZAP!
ZIP!
DUCK!!
ZING!

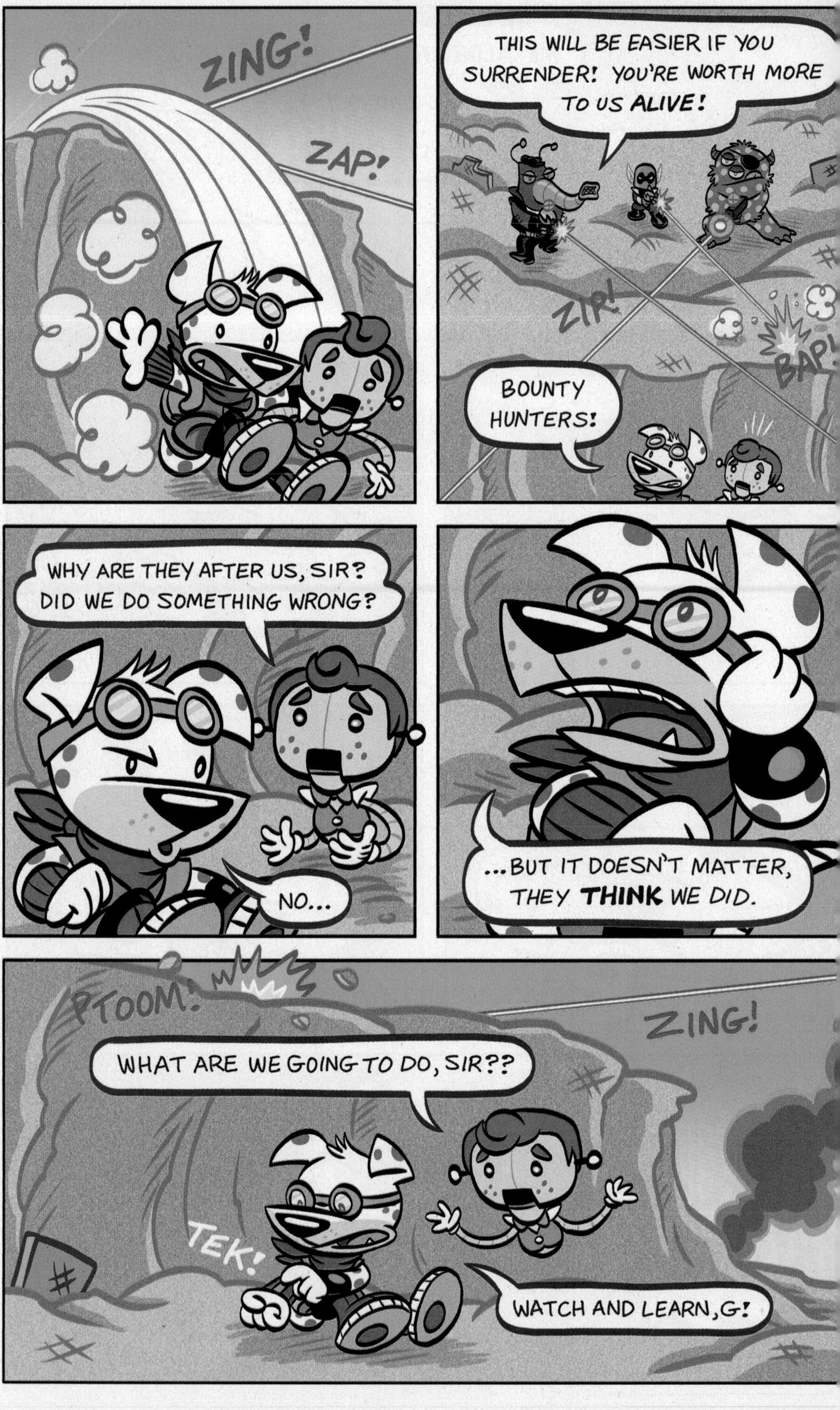
ZING!
ZAP!
THIS WILL BE EASIER IF YOU SURRENDER! YOU'RE WORTH MORE TO US ALIVE!
ZIP!
BAP!
BOUNTY HUNTERS!
WHY ARE THEY AFTER US, SIR? DID WE DO SOMETHING WRONG?
NO...
...BUT IT DOESN'T MATTER, THEY THINK WE DID.
PTOOM!
ZING!
WHAT ARE WE GOING TO DO, SIR??
TEK!
WATCH AND LEARN, G!

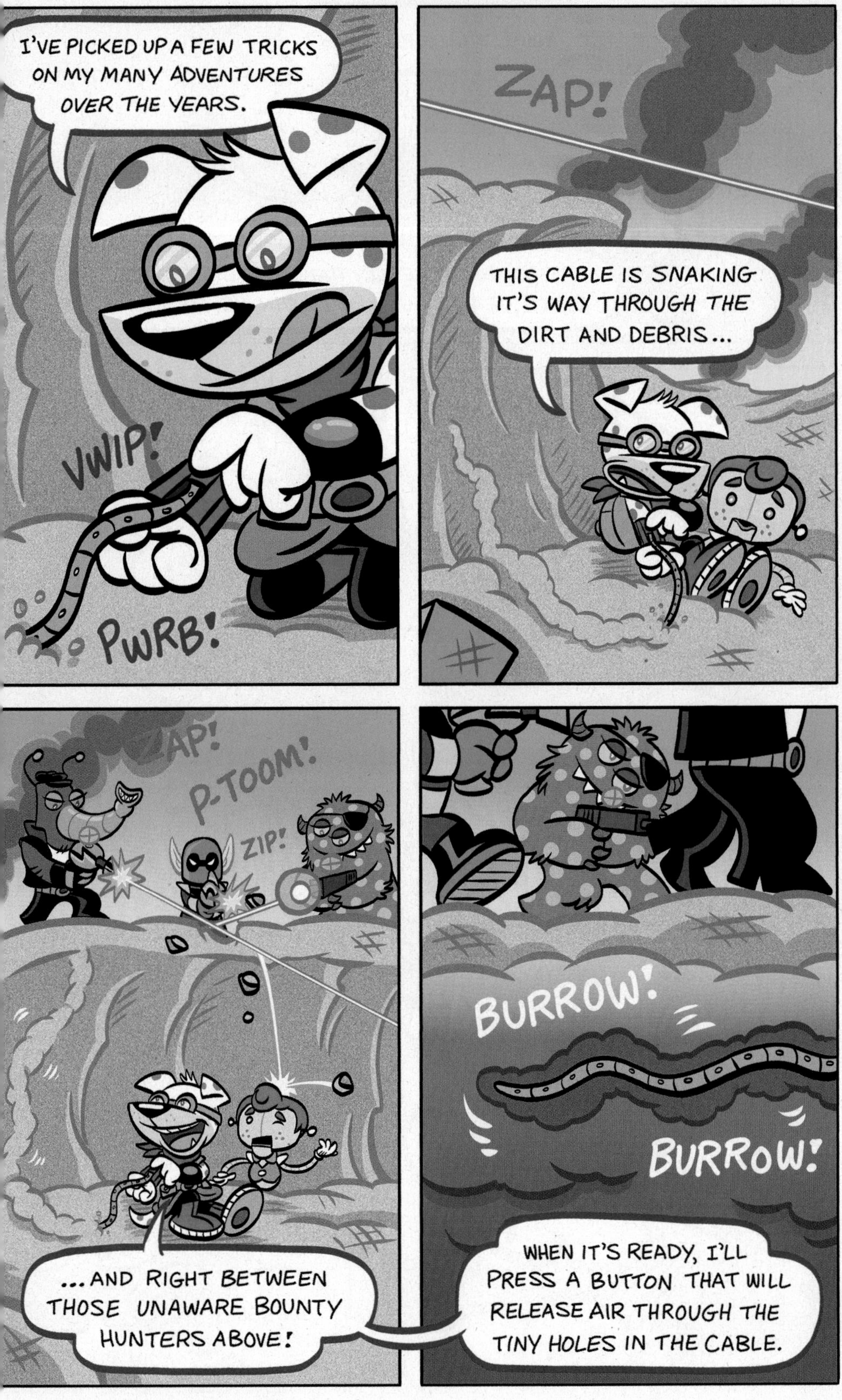
I'VE PICKED UP A FEW TRICKS ON MY MANY ADVENTURES OVER THE YEARS.
VWIP!
PWRB!
ZAP!
THIS CABLE IS SNAKING IT'S WAY THROUGH THE DIRT AND DEBRIS...
ZAP!
P-TOOM!
ZIP!
...AND RIGHT BETWEEN THOSE UNAWARE BOUNTY HUNTERS ABOVE!
BURROW!
BURROW!
WHEN IT'S READY, I'LL PRESS A BUTTON THAT WILL RELEASE AIR THROUGH THE TINY HOLES IN THE CABLE.

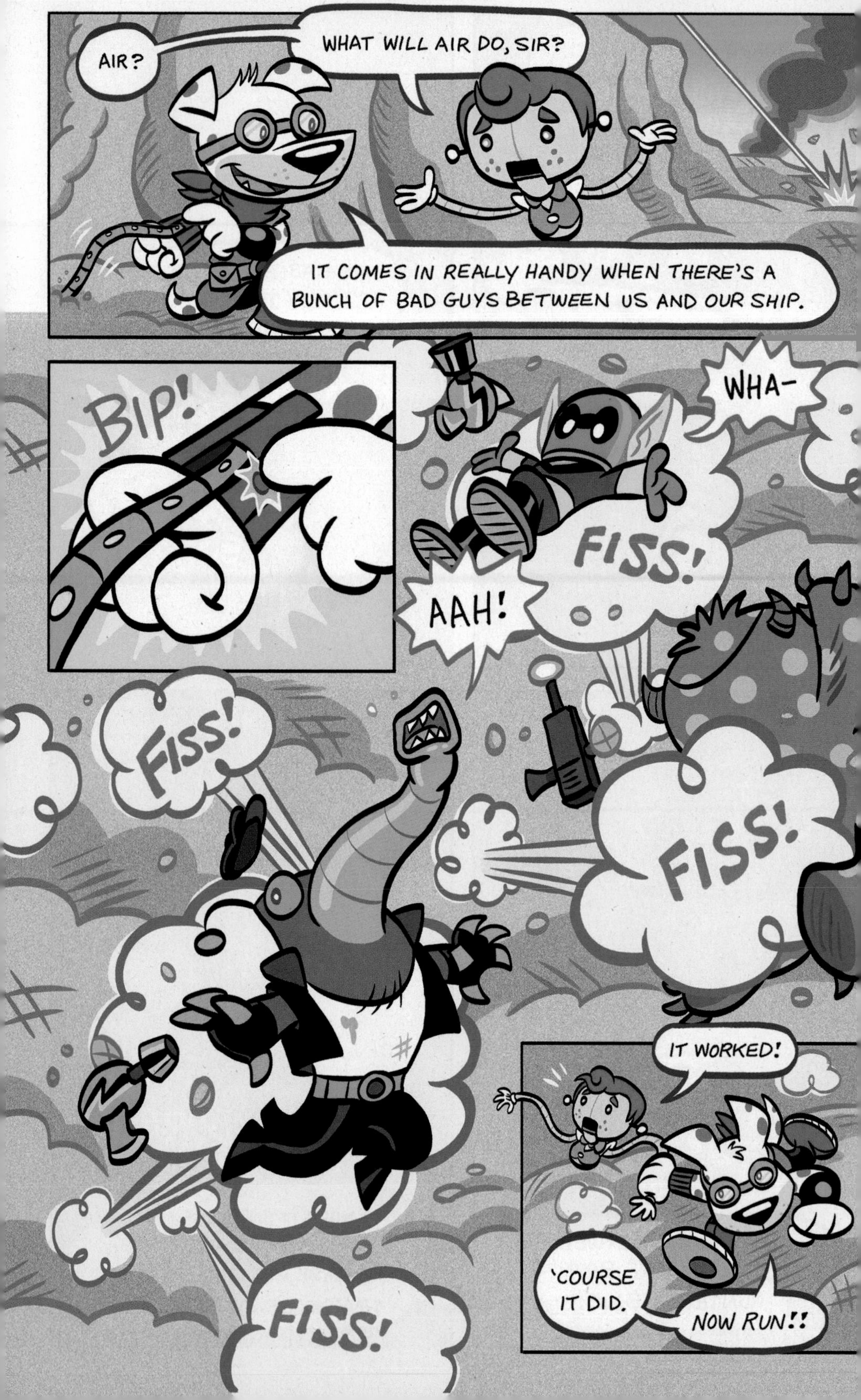
AIR?
WHAT WILL AIR DO, SIR?
IT COMES IN REALLY HANDY WHEN THERE'S A BUNCH OF BAD GUYS BETWEEN US AND OUR SHIP.
BIP!
WHA-
FISS!
AAH!
FISS!
FISS!
FISS!
IT WORKED!
'COURSE IT DID.
NOW RUN!!

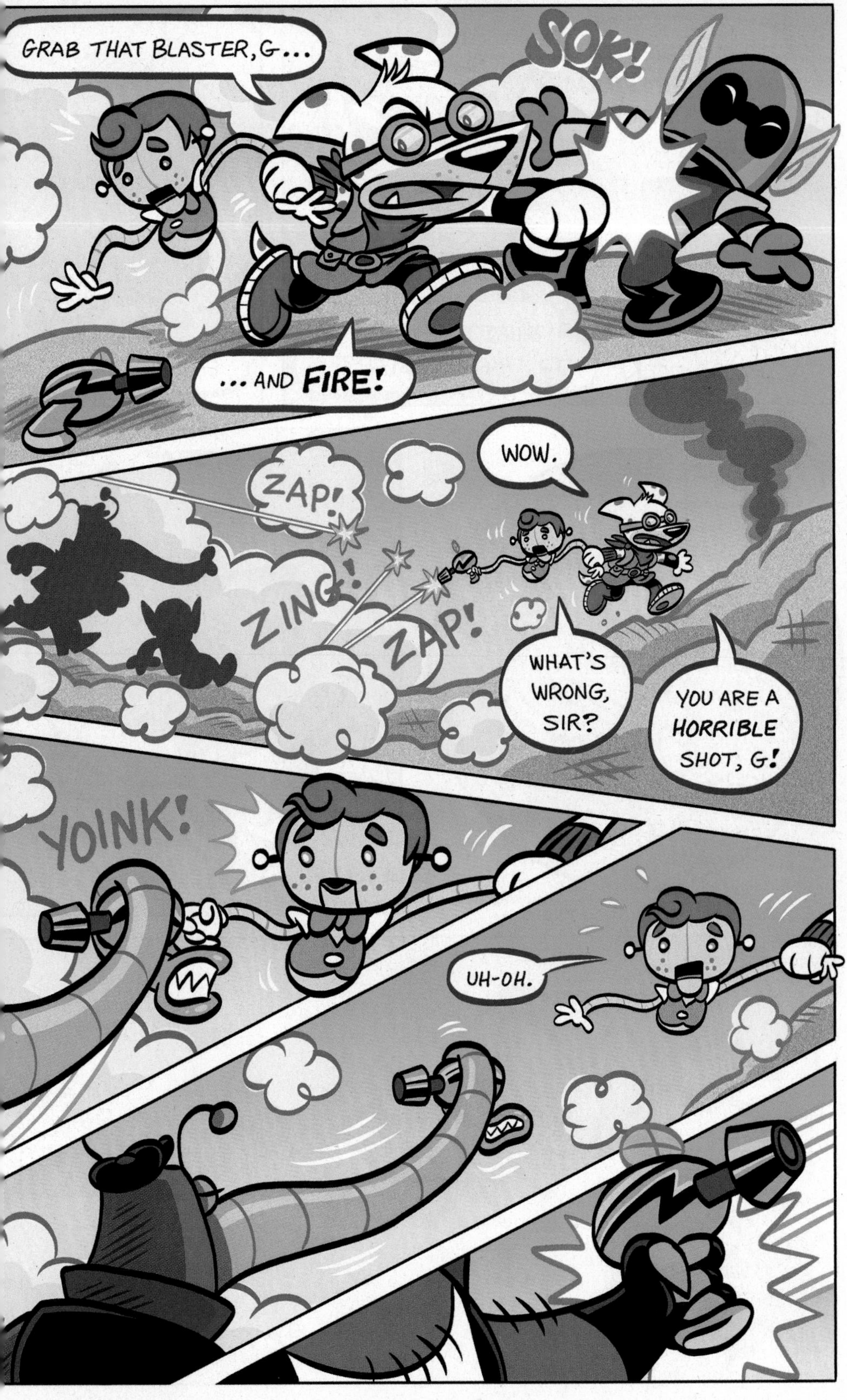
GRAB THAT BLASTER, G...
SOK!
... AND FIRE!
WOW.
ZAP!
ZING!
ZAP!
WHAT'S WRONG, SIR?
YOU ARE A HORRIBLE SHOT, G!
YOINK!
UH-OH.

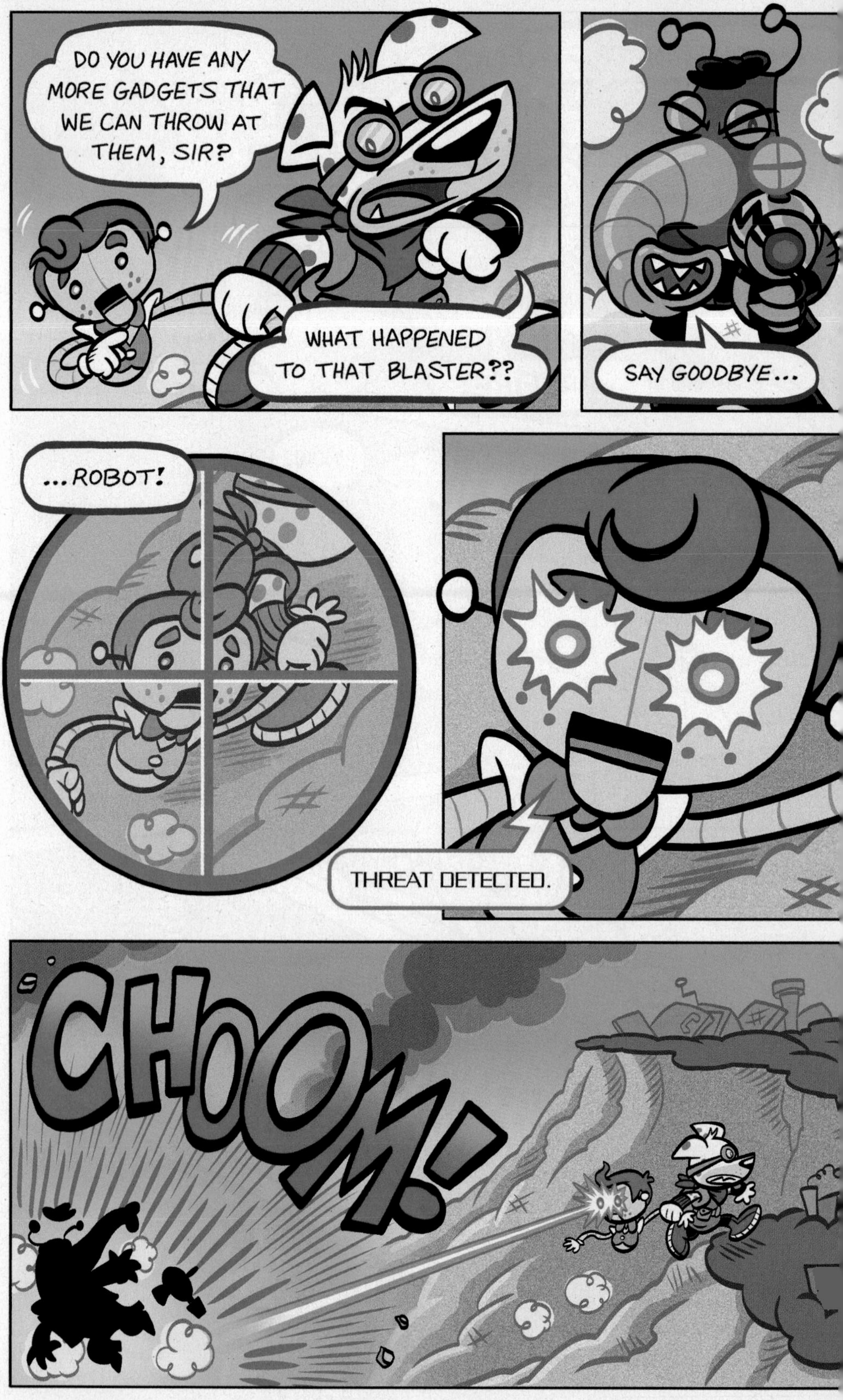
DO YOU HAVE ANY MORE GADGETS THAT WE CAN THROW AT THEM, SIR?
WHAT HAPPENED TO THAT BLASTER??
SAY GOODBYE...
...ROBOT!
THREAT DETECTED.
CHOOM!

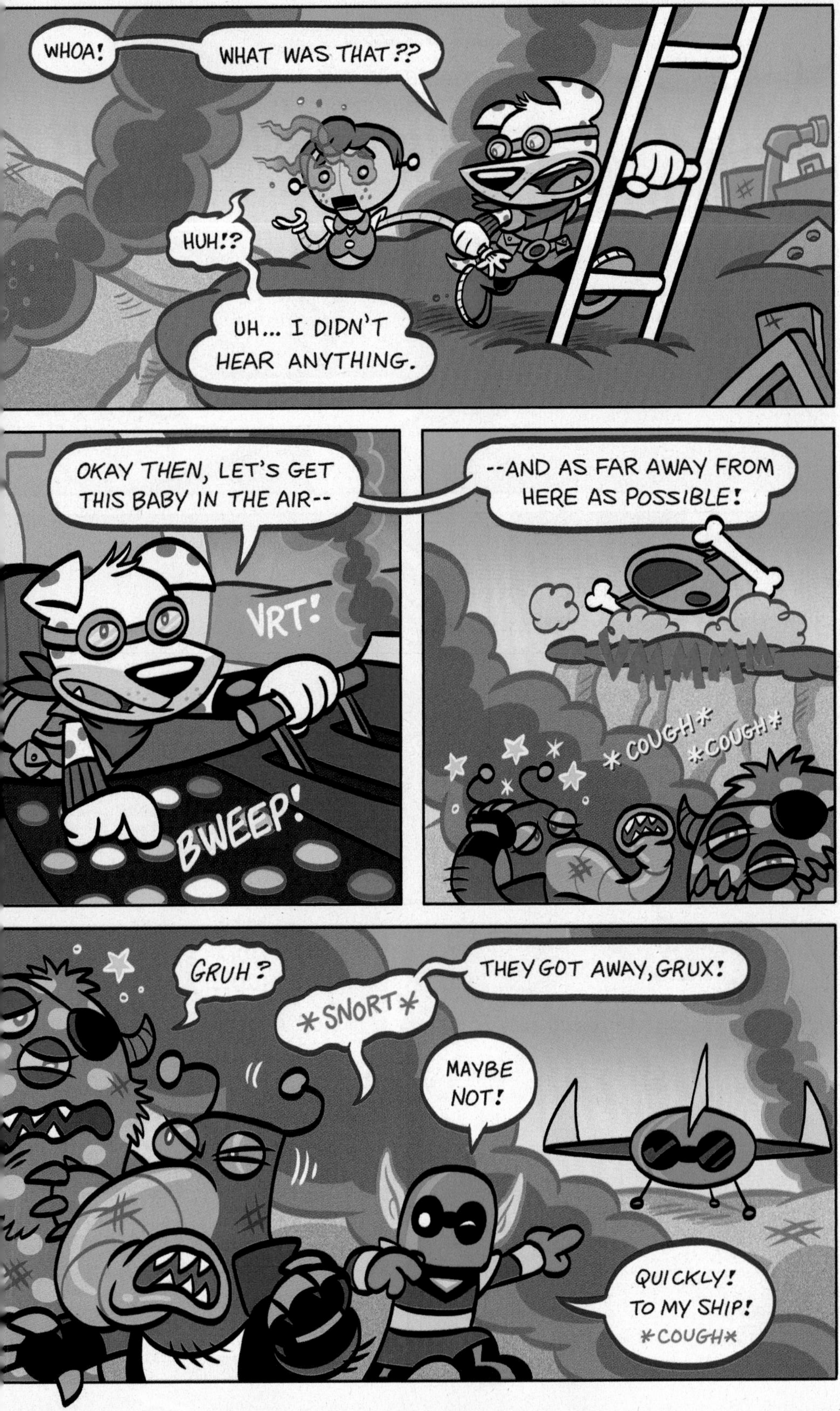
WHOA!
WHAT WAS THAT??
HUH!?
UH... I DIDN'T HEAR ANYTHING.
OKAY THEN, LET'S GET THIS BABY IN THE AIR--
VRT!
BWEEP!
--AND AS FAR AWAY FROM HERE AS POSSIBLE!
VMMMM
COUGH
COUGH
GRUH?
THEY GOT AWAY, GRUX!
SNORT
MAYBE NOT!
QUICKLY! TO MY SHIP! *COUGH*

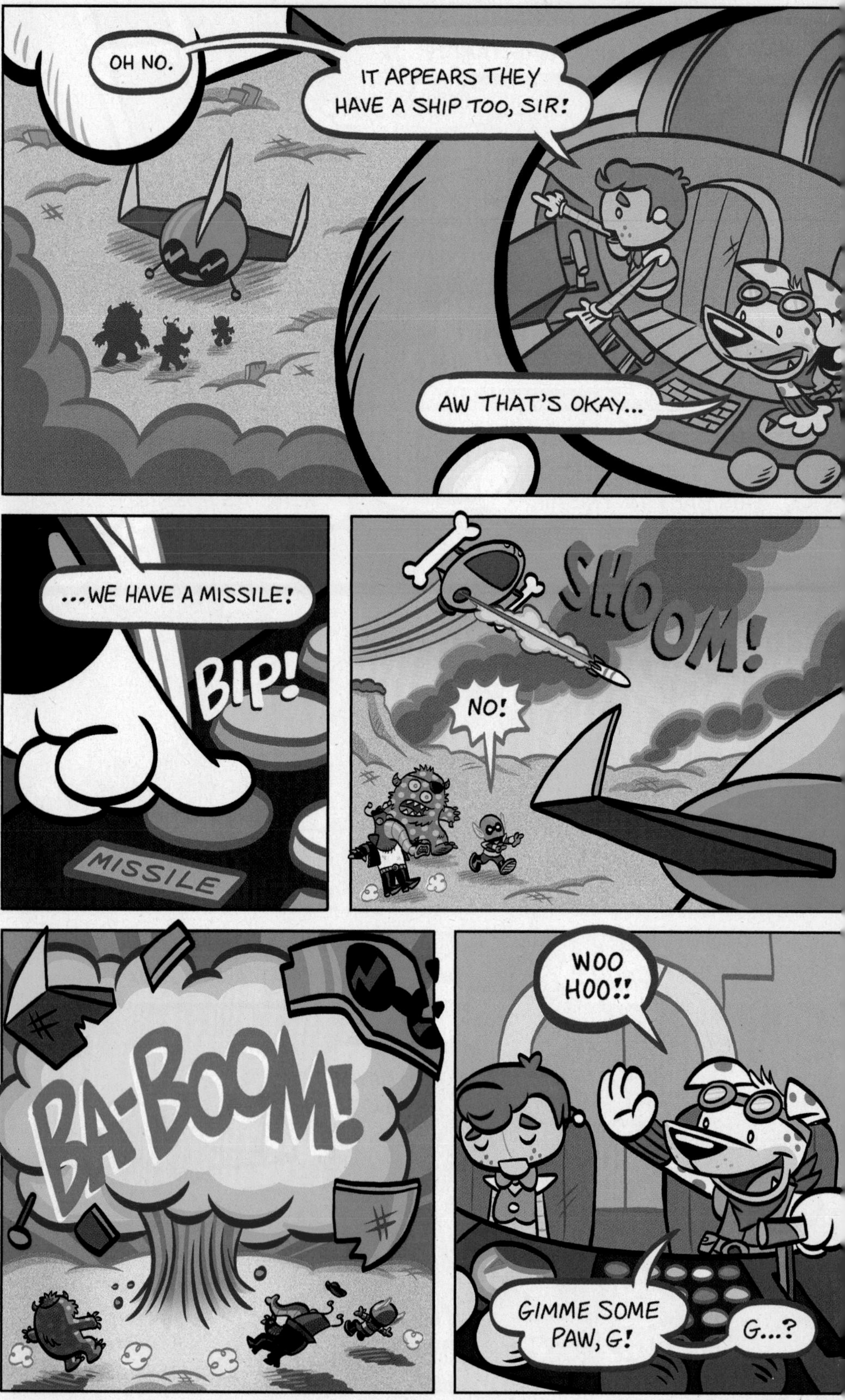
OH NO.
IT APPEARS THEY HAVE A SHIP TOO, SIR!
AW THAT'S OKAY...
...WE HAVE A MISSILE!
BIP!
MISSILE
SHOOM!
NO!
BA-BOOM!
WOO HOO!!
GIMME SOME PAW, G!
G...?

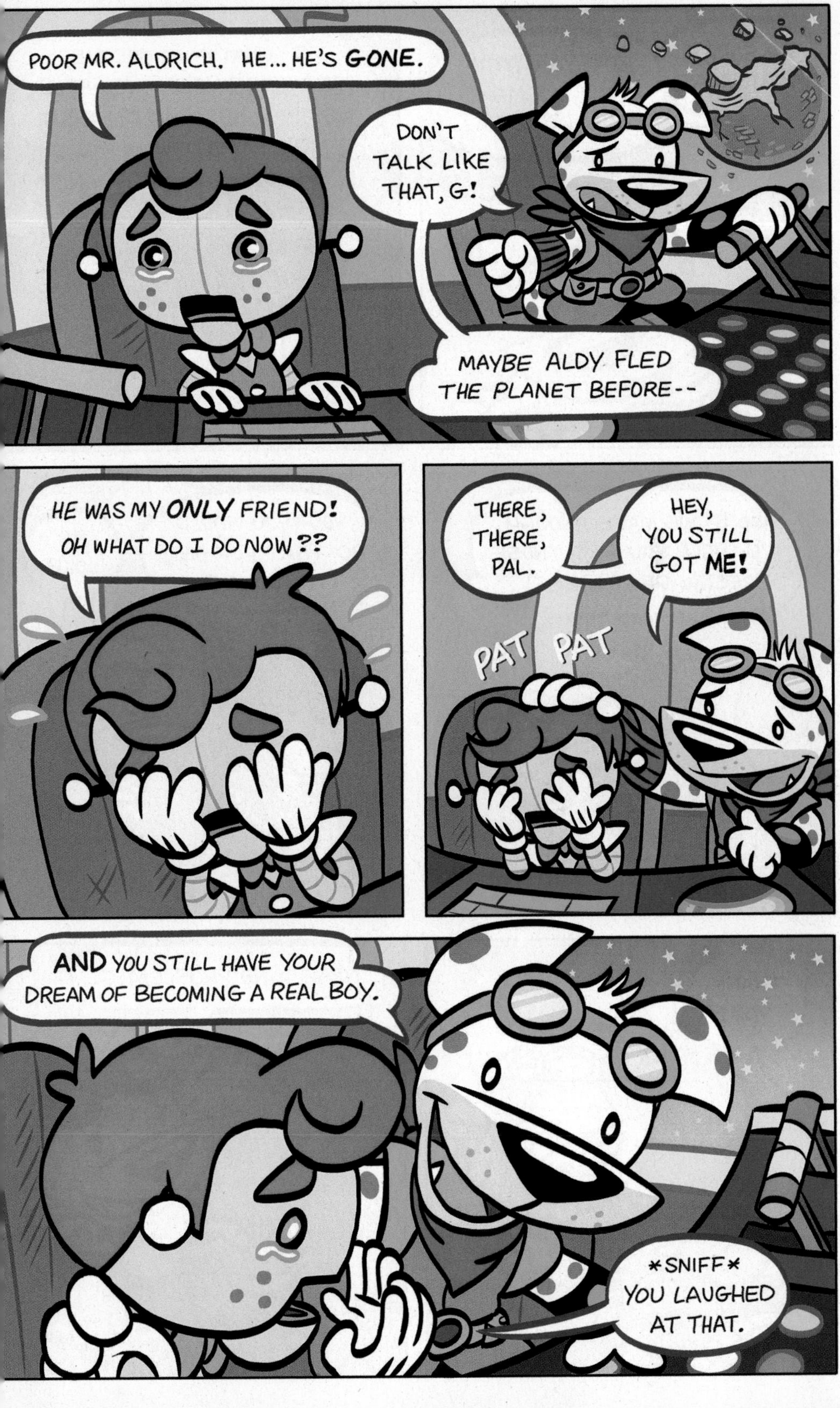
POOR MR. ALDRICH. HE... HE'S GONE.
DON'T TALK LIKE THAT, G!
MAYBE ALDY FLED THE PLANET BEFORE--
HE WAS MY ONLY FRIEND! OH WHAT DO I DO NOW??
THERE, THERE, PAL.
HEY, YOU STILL GOT ME!
PAT PAT
AND YOU STILL HAVE YOUR DREAM OF BECOMING A REAL BOY.
SNIFF YOU LAUGHED AT THAT.

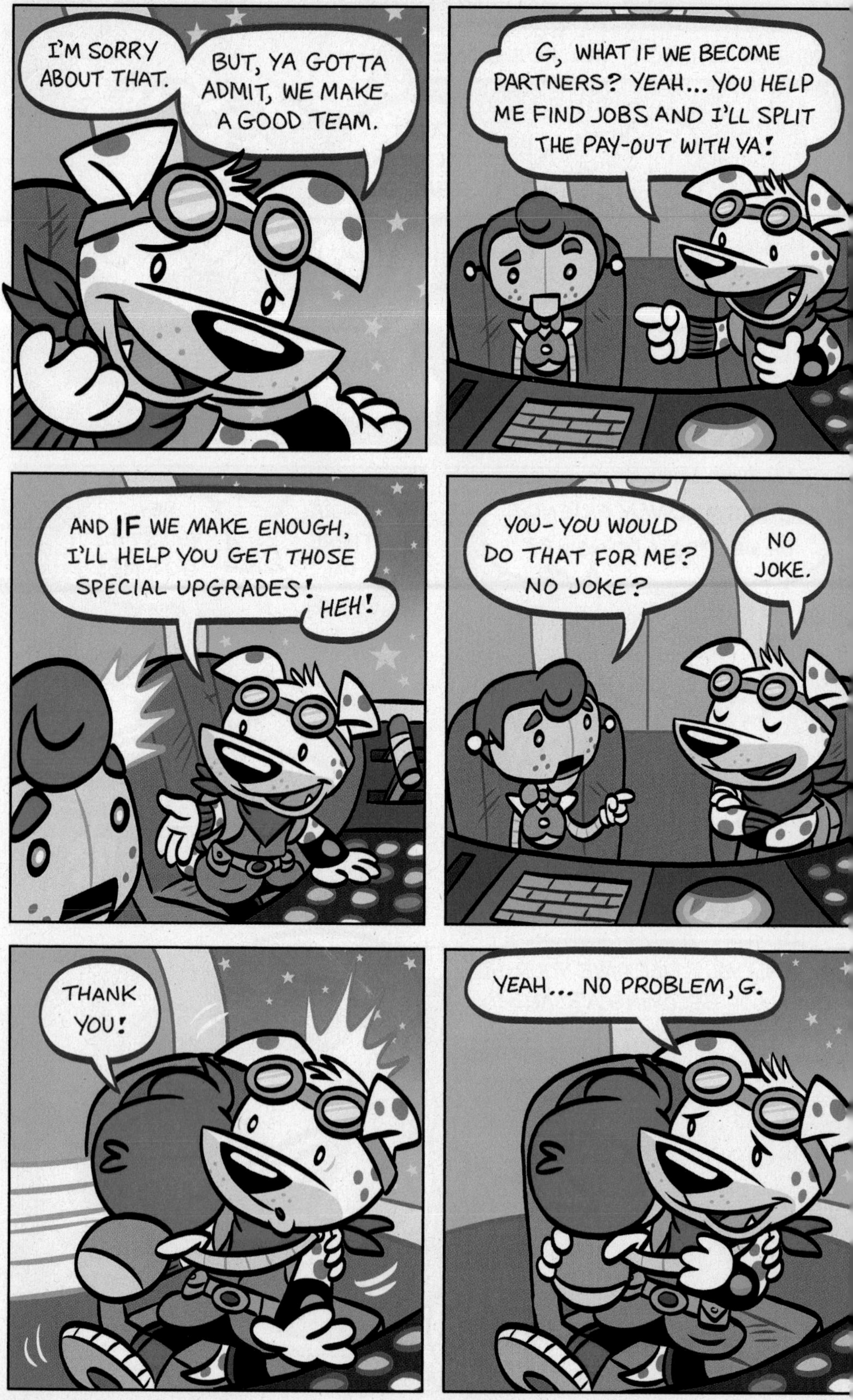

I'M SORRY ABOUT THAT.
BUT, YA GOTTA ADMIT, WE MAKE A GOOD TEAM.
G, WHAT IF WE BECOME PARTNERS? YEAH... YOU HELP ME FIND JOBS AND I'LL SPLIT THE PAY-OUT WITH YA!
AND IF WE MAKE ENOUGH, I'LL HELP YOU GET THOSE SPECIAL UPGRADES!
HEH!
YOU-YOU WOULD DO THAT FOR ME? NO JOKE?
NO JOKE.
THANK YOU!
YEAH... NO PROBLEM, G.

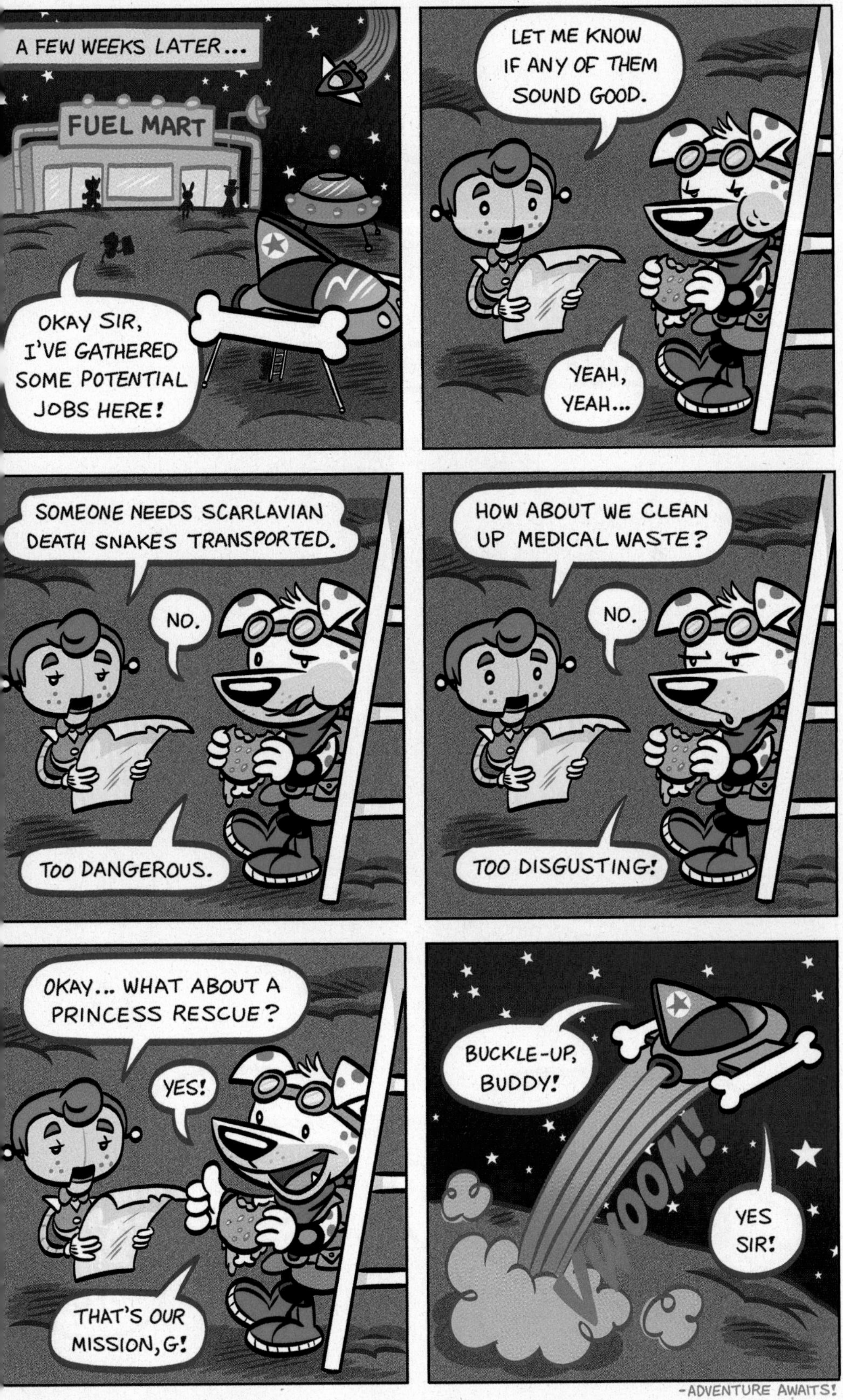
A FEW WEEKS LATER...
FUEL MART
OKAY SIR, I'VE GATHERED SOME POTENTIAL JOBS HERE!
LET ME KNOW IF ANY OF THEM SOUND GOOD.
YEAH, YEAH...
SOMEONE NEEDS SCARLAVIAN DEATH SNAKES TRANSPORTED.
NO.
TOO DANGEROUS.
HOW ABOUT WE CLEAN UP MEDICAL WASTE?
NO.
TOO DISGUSTING!
OKAY... WHAT ABOUT A PRINCESS RESCUE?
YES!
THAT'S OUR MISSION, G!
BUCKLE-UP, BUDDY!
VVOOOM!
YES SIR!

-ADVENTURE AWAITS!

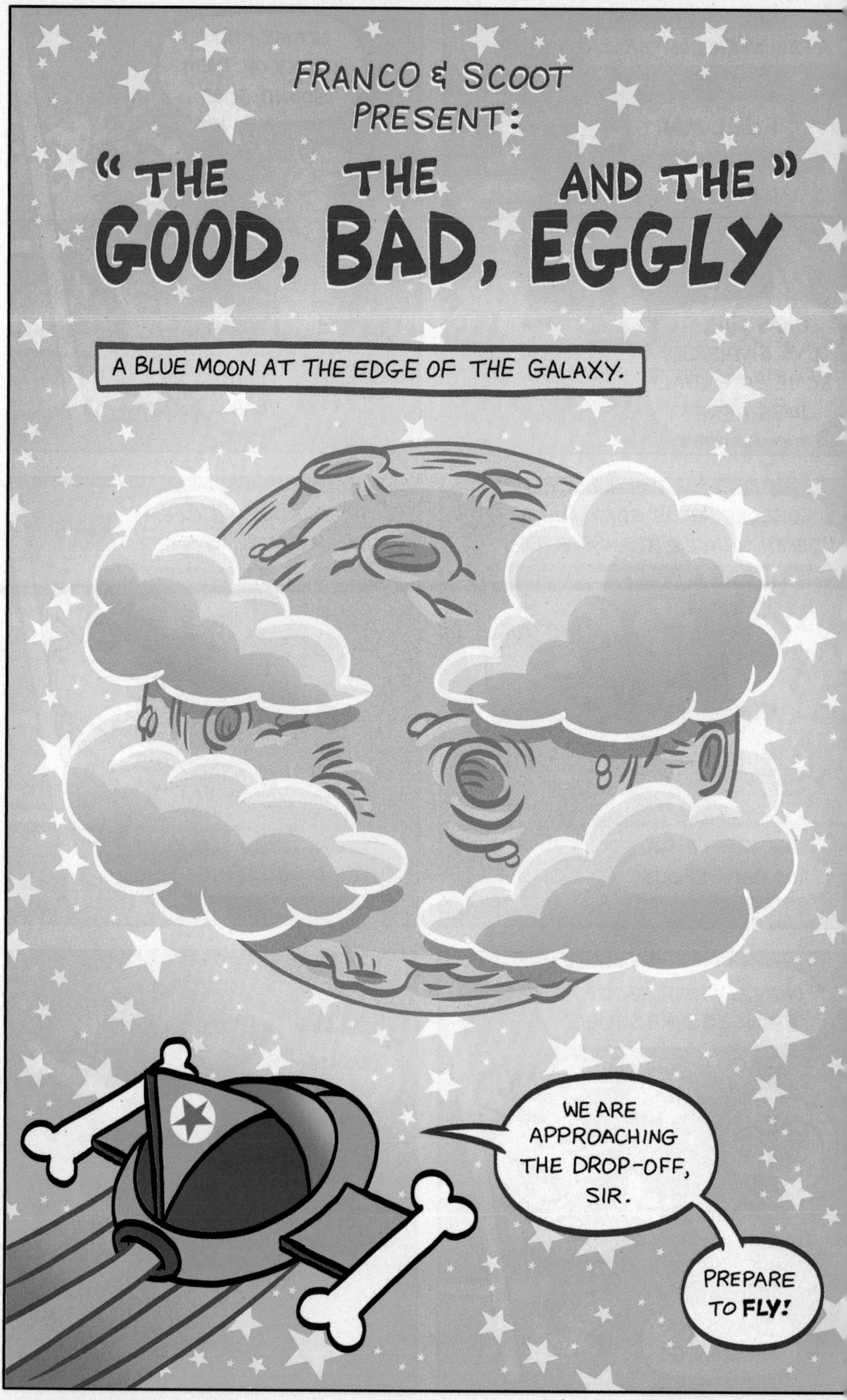
FRANCO & SCOOT PRESENT:
"THE GOOD, THE BAD, AND THE EGGLY"
A BLUE MOON AT THE EDGE OF THE GALAXY.
WE ARE APPROACHING THE DROP-OFF, SIR.
PREPARE TO FLY!

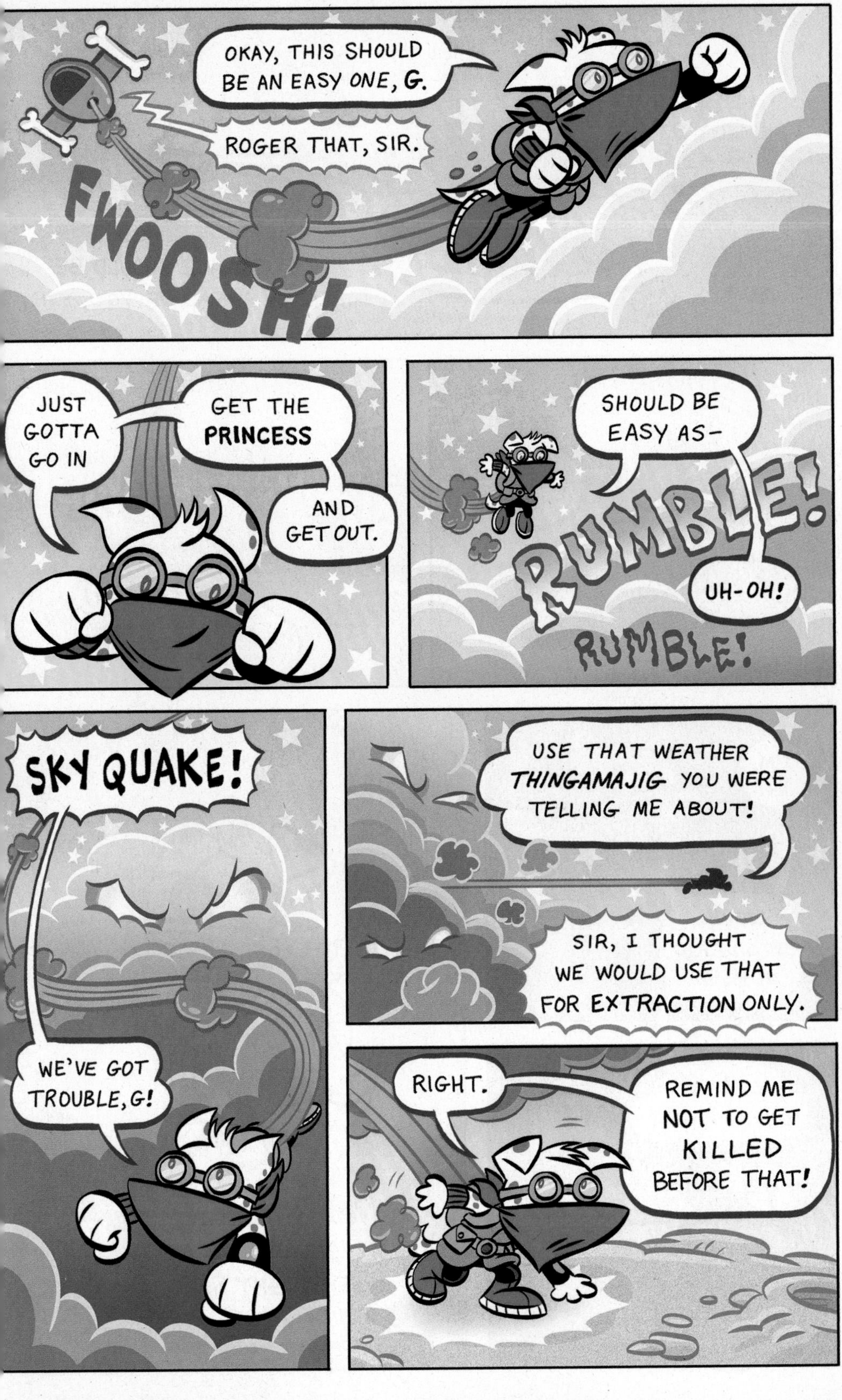

OKAY, THIS SHOULD BE AN EASY ONE, G.
ROGER THAT, SIR.
FWOOSH!
JUST GOTTA GO IN
GET THE PRINCESS
AND GET OUT.
SHOULD BE EASY AS-
RUMBLE!
UH-OH!
RUMBLE!
SKY QUAKE!
WE'VE GOT TROUBLE, G!
USE THAT WEATHER THINGAMAJIG YOU WERE TELLING ME ABOUT!
SIR, I THOUGHT WE WOULD USE THAT FOR EXTRACTION ONLY.
RIGHT.
REMIND ME NOT TO GET KILLED BEFORE THAT!

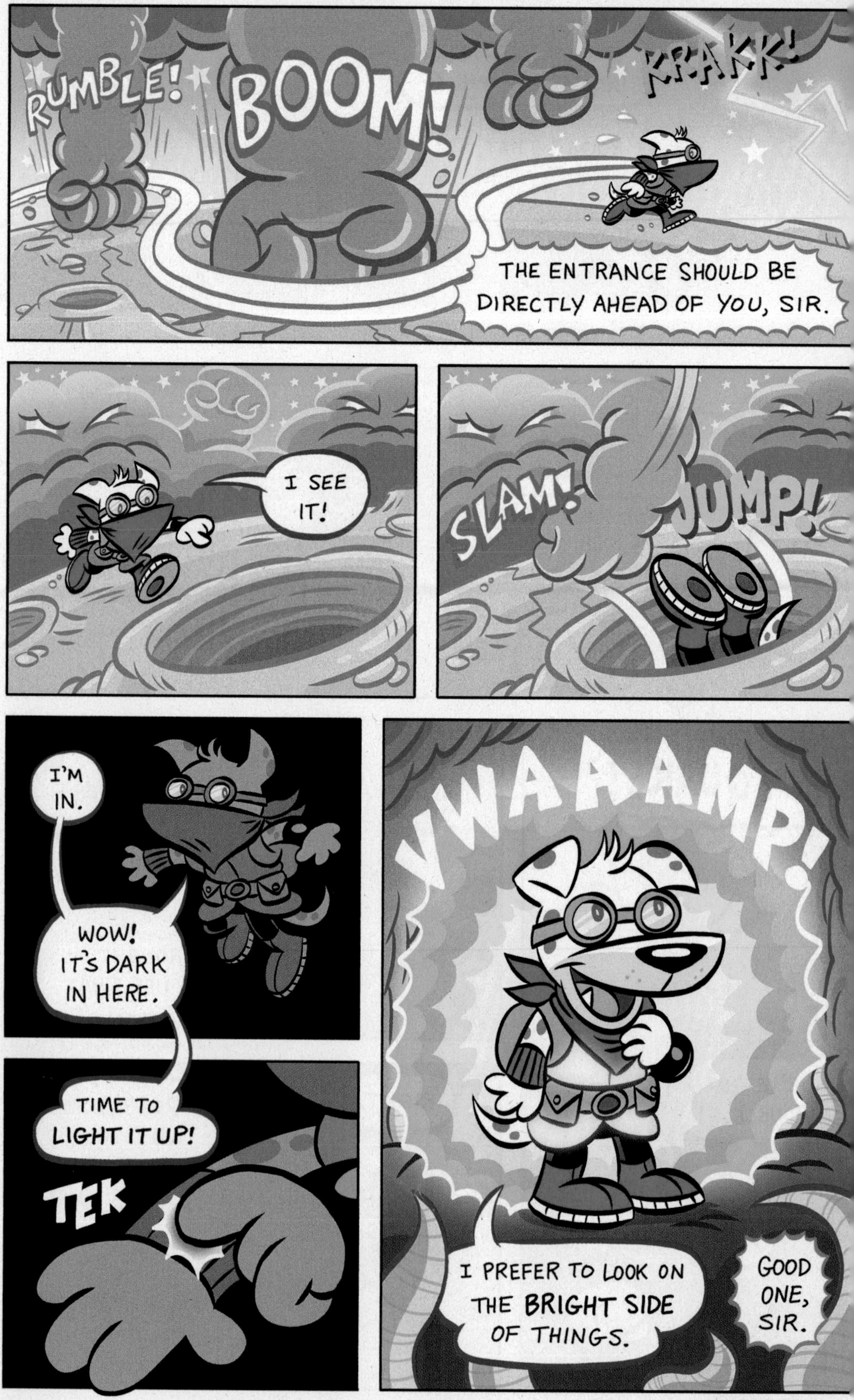
RUMBLE!
BOOM!
KRAKK!
THE ENTRANCE SHOULD BE DIRECTLY AHEAD OF YOU, SIR.
I SEE IT!
SLAM!
JUMP!
I'M IN.
WOW! IT'S DARK IN HERE.
TIME TO LIGHT IT UP!
TEK
VWAAAMP!
I PREFER TO LOOK ON THE BRIGHT SIDE OF THINGS.
GOOD ONE, SIR.

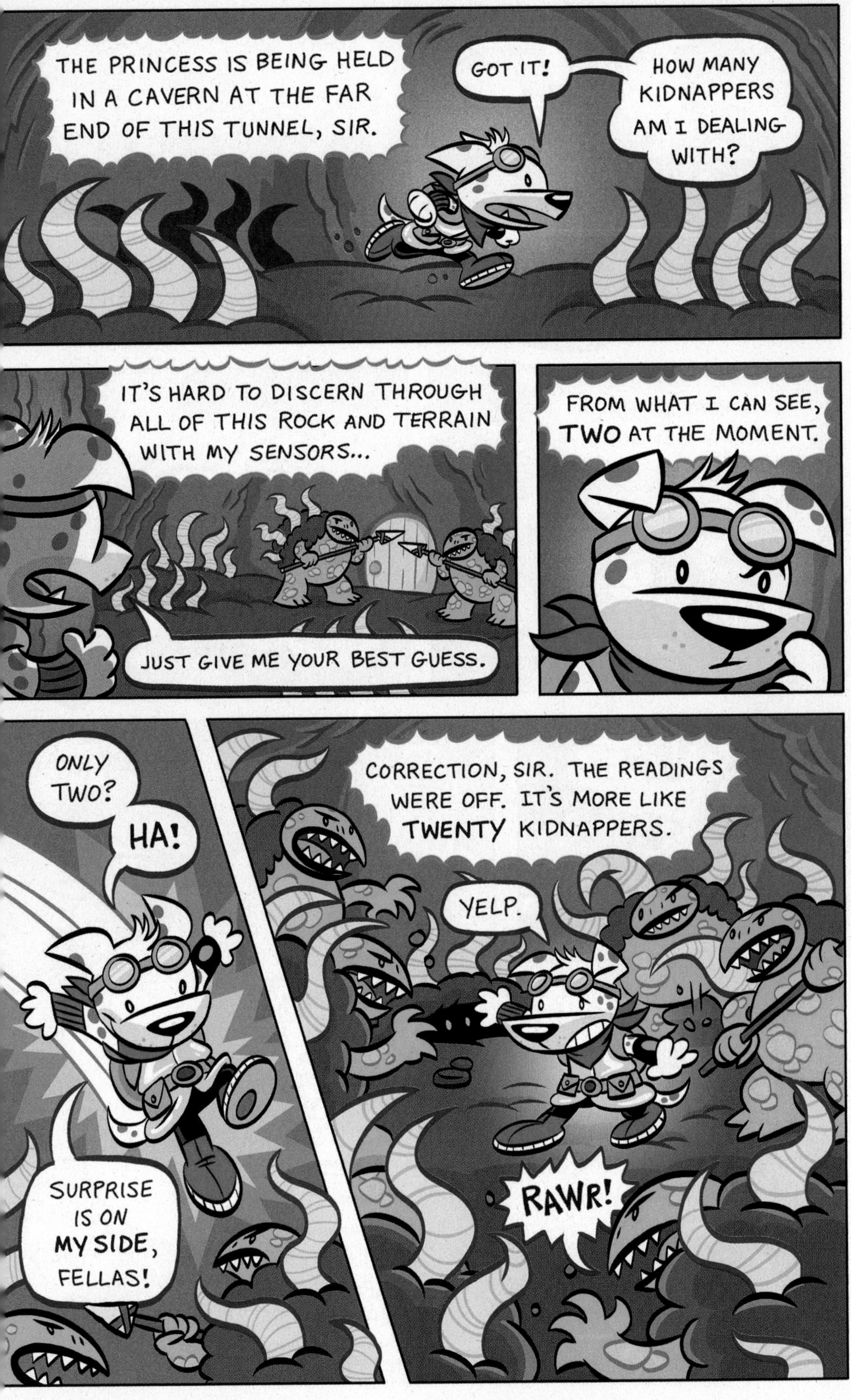
THE PRINCESS IS BEING HELD IN A CAVERN AT THE FAR END OF THIS TUNNEL, SIR.
GOT IT!
HOW MANY KIDNAPPERS AM I DEALING WITH?
IT'S HARD TO DISCERN THROUGH ALL OF THIS ROCK AND TERRAIN WITH MY SENSORS...
JUST GIVE ME YOUR BEST GUESS.
FROM WHAT I CAN SEE, TWO AT THE MOMENT.
ONLY TWO?
HA!
SURPRISE IS ON MY SIDE, FELLAS!
CORRECTION, SIR. THE READINGS WERE OFF. IT'S MORE LIKE TWENTY KIDNAPPERS.
YELP.
RAWR!

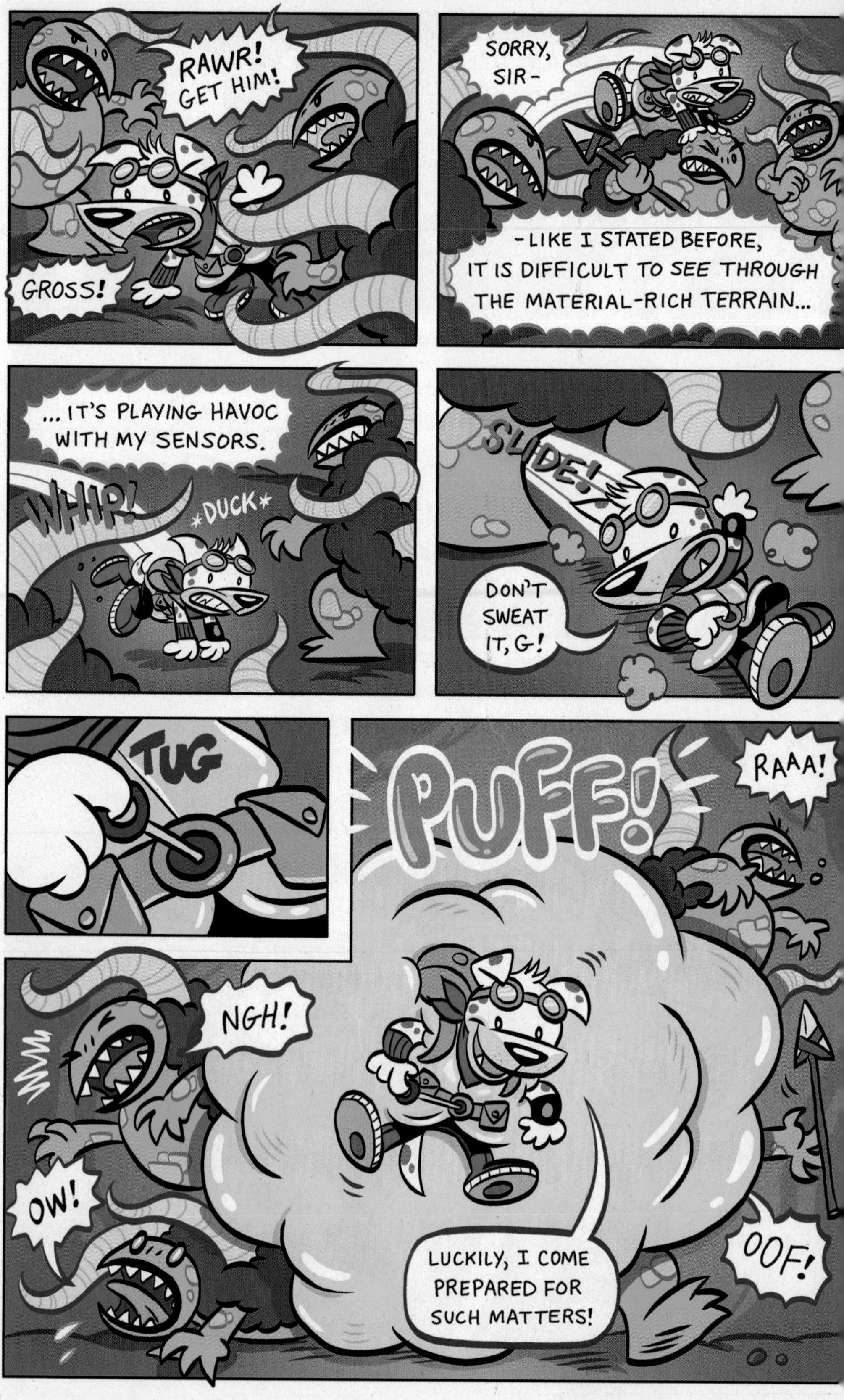
RAWR! GET HIM!
GROSS!
SORRY, SIR-
-LIKE I STATED BEFORE, IT IS DIFFICULT TO SEE THROUGH THE MATERIAL-RICH TERRAIN...
... IT'S PLAYING HAVOC WITH MY SENSORS.
WHIP!
DUCK
SLIDE!
DON'T SWEAT IT, G!
TUG
PUFF!
RAAA!
NGH!
OW!
OOF!
LUCKILY, I COME PREPARED FOR SUCH MATTERS!

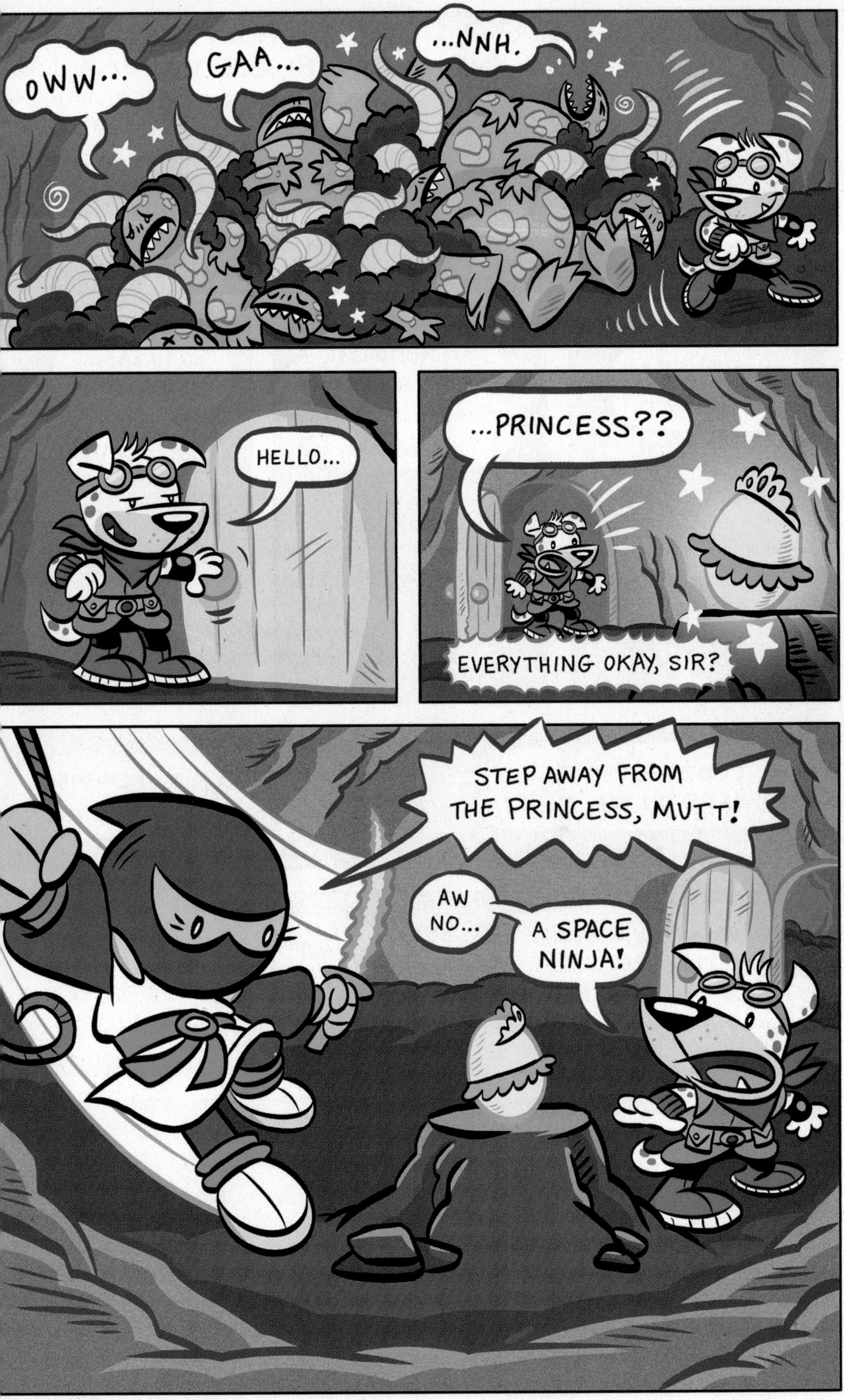
OWW...
GAA...
...NNH.
HELLO...
...PRINCESS??
EVERYTHING OKAY, SIR?
STEP AWAY FROM THE PRINCESS, MUTT!
AW NO...
A SPACE NINJA!

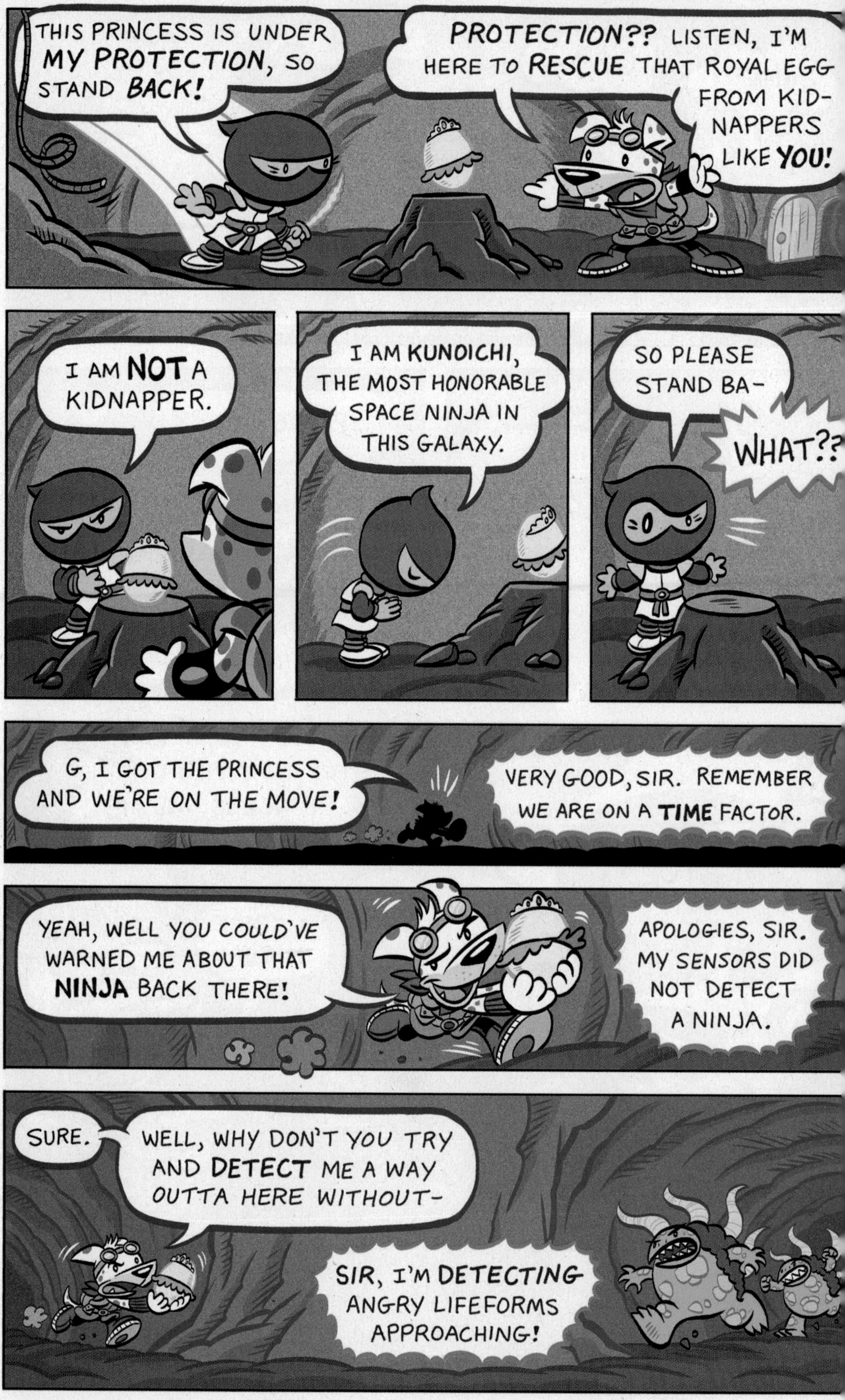
THIS PRINCESS IS UNDER MY PROTECTION, SO STAND BACK!
PROTECTION?? LISTEN, I'M HERE TO RESCUE THAT ROYAL EGG FROM KID-NAPPERS LIKE YOU!
I AM NOT A KIDNAPPER.
I AM KUNOICHI, THE MOST HONORABLE SPACE NINJA IN THIS GALAXY.
SO PLEASE STAND BA-
WHAT??
G, I GOT THE PRINCESS AND WE'RE ON THE MOVE!
VERY GOOD, SIR. REMEMBER WE ARE ON A TIME FACTOR.
YEAH, WELL YOU COULD'VE WARNED ME ABOUT THAT NINJA BACK THERE!
APOLOGIES, SIR. MY SENSORS DID NOT DETECT A NINJA.
SURE.
WELL, WHY DON'T YOU TRY AND DETECT ME A WAY OUTTA HERE WITHOUT-
SIR, I'M DETECTING ANGRY LIFEFORMS APPROACHING!

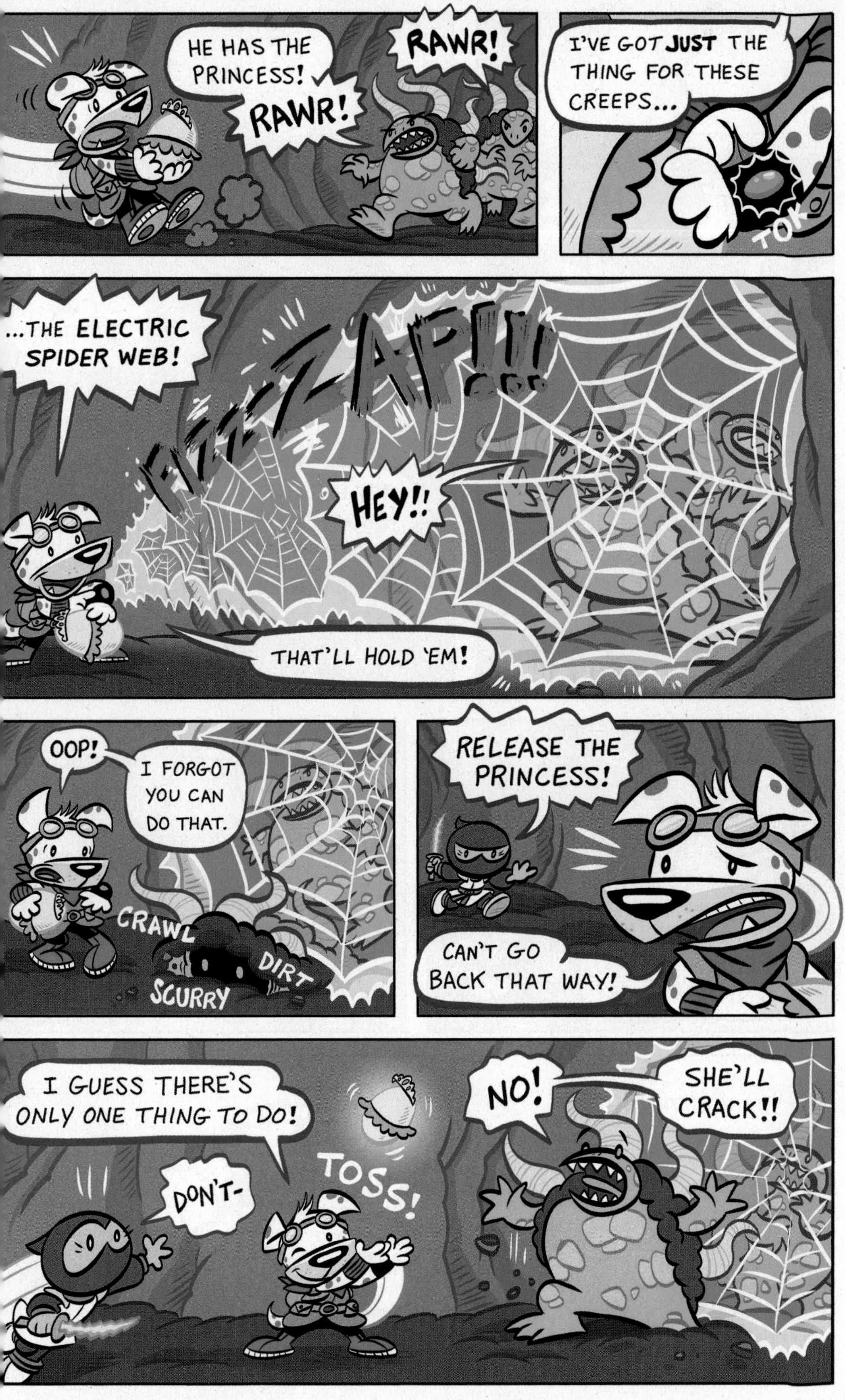
HE HAS THE PRINCESS!
RAWR!
RAWR!
I'VE GOT JUST THE THING FOR THESE CREEPS...
TOK
...THE ELECTRIC SPIDER WEB!
FIZZZ-ZAP!!!
HEY!!
THAT'LL HOLD 'EM!
OOP!
I FORGOT YOU CAN DO THAT.
CRAWL
DIRT
SCURRY
RELEASE THE PRINCESS!
CAN'T GO BACK THAT WAY!
I GUESS THERE'S ONLY ONE THING TO DO!
DON'T-
TOSS!
NO!
SHE'LL CRACK!!

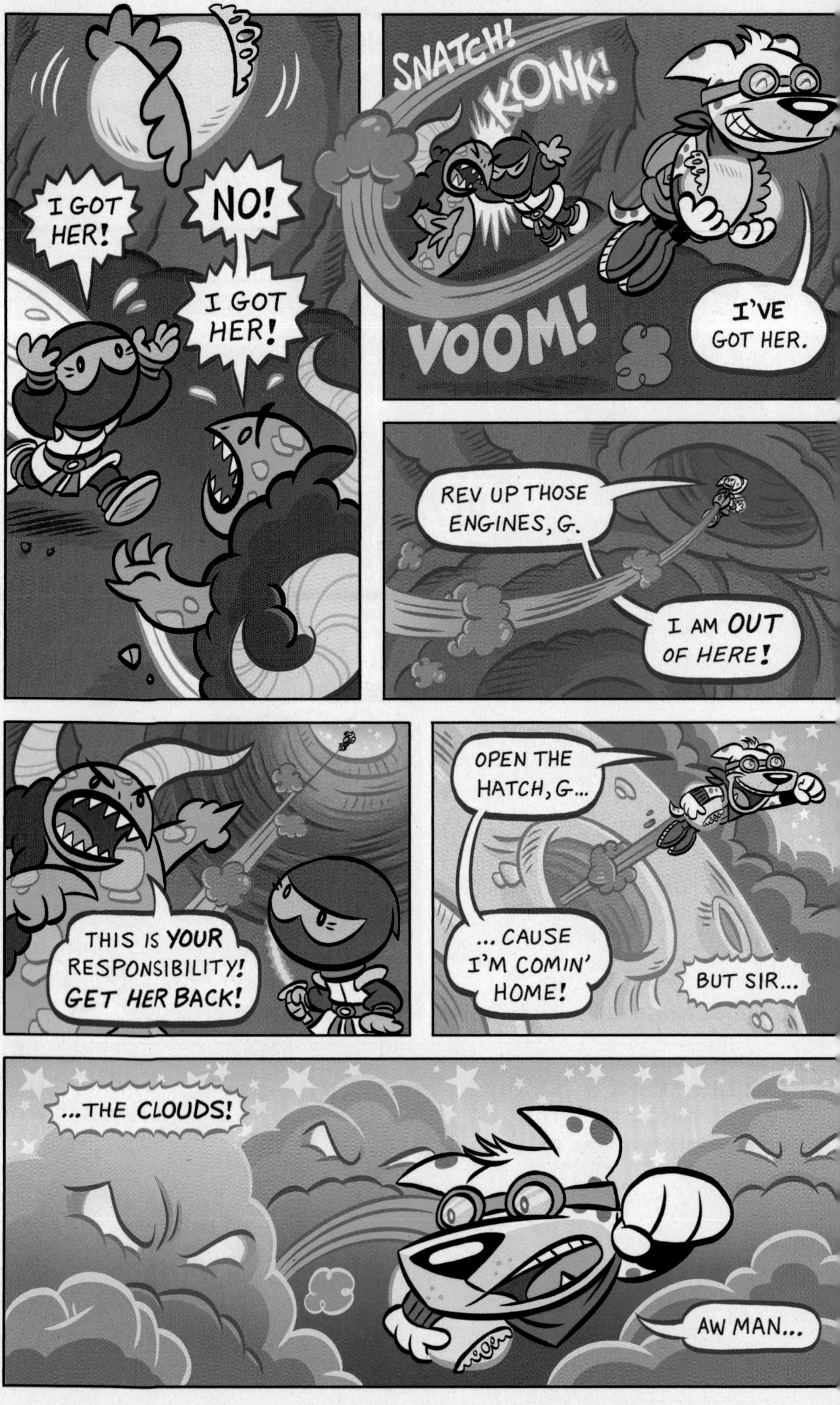
I GOT HER!
NO!
I GOT HER!
SNATCH!
KONK!
VOOM!
I'VE GOT HER.
REV UP THOSE ENGINES, G.
I AM OUT OF HERE!
THIS IS YOUR RESPONSIBILITY! GET HER BACK!
OPEN THE HATCH, G...
... CAUSE I'M COMIN' HOME!
BUT SIR...
...THE CLOUDS!
AW MAN...

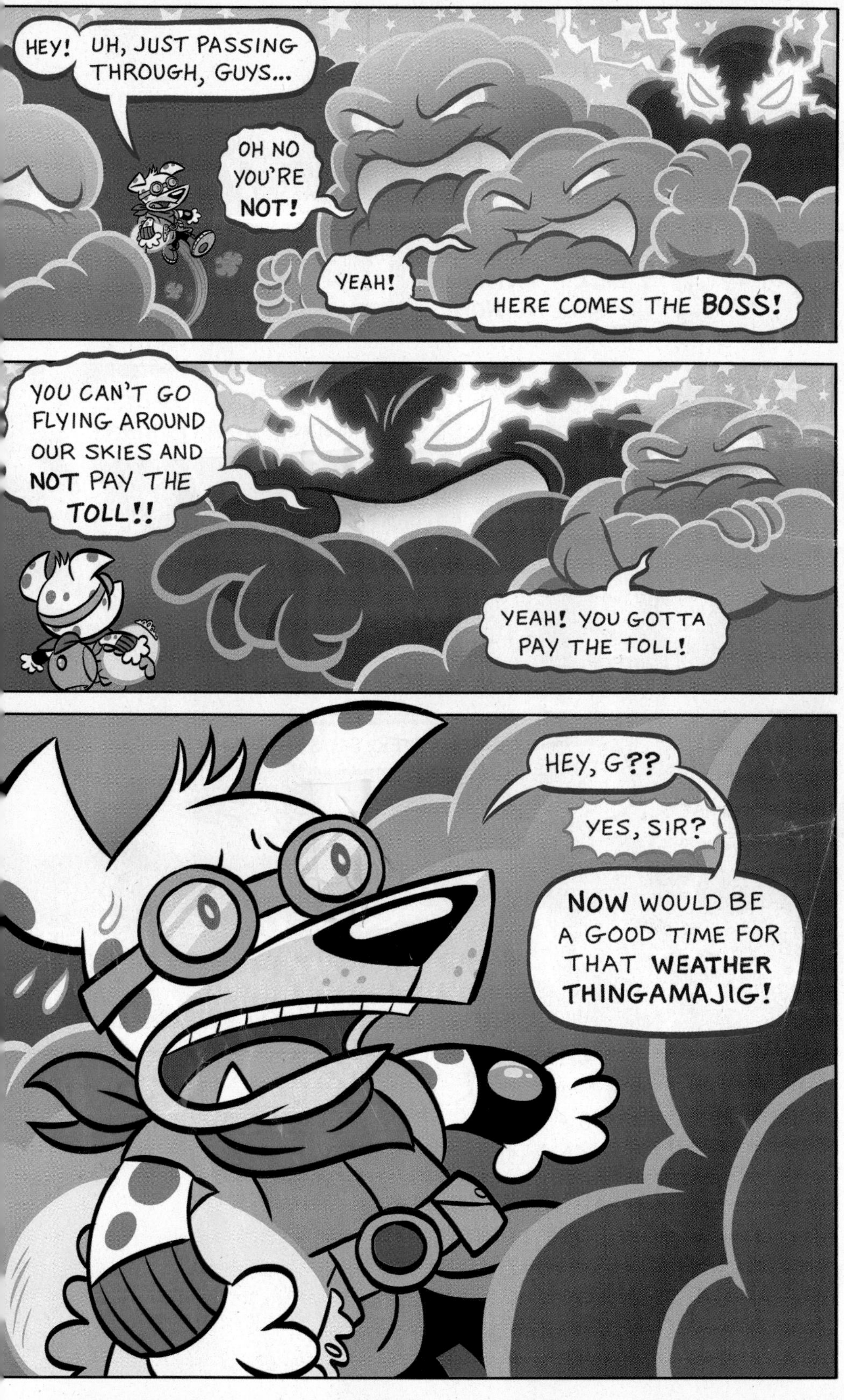
HEY!
UH, JUST PASSING THROUGH, GUYS...
OH NO YOU'RE **NOT!**
YEAH!
HERE COMES THE **BOSS!**
YOU CAN'T GO FLYING AROUND OUR SKIES AND **NOT** PAY THE **TOLL!!**
YEAH! YOU GOTTA PAY THE TOLL!
HEY, G??
YES, SIR?
NOW WOULD BE A GOOD TIME FOR THAT **WEATHER THINGAMAJIG!**

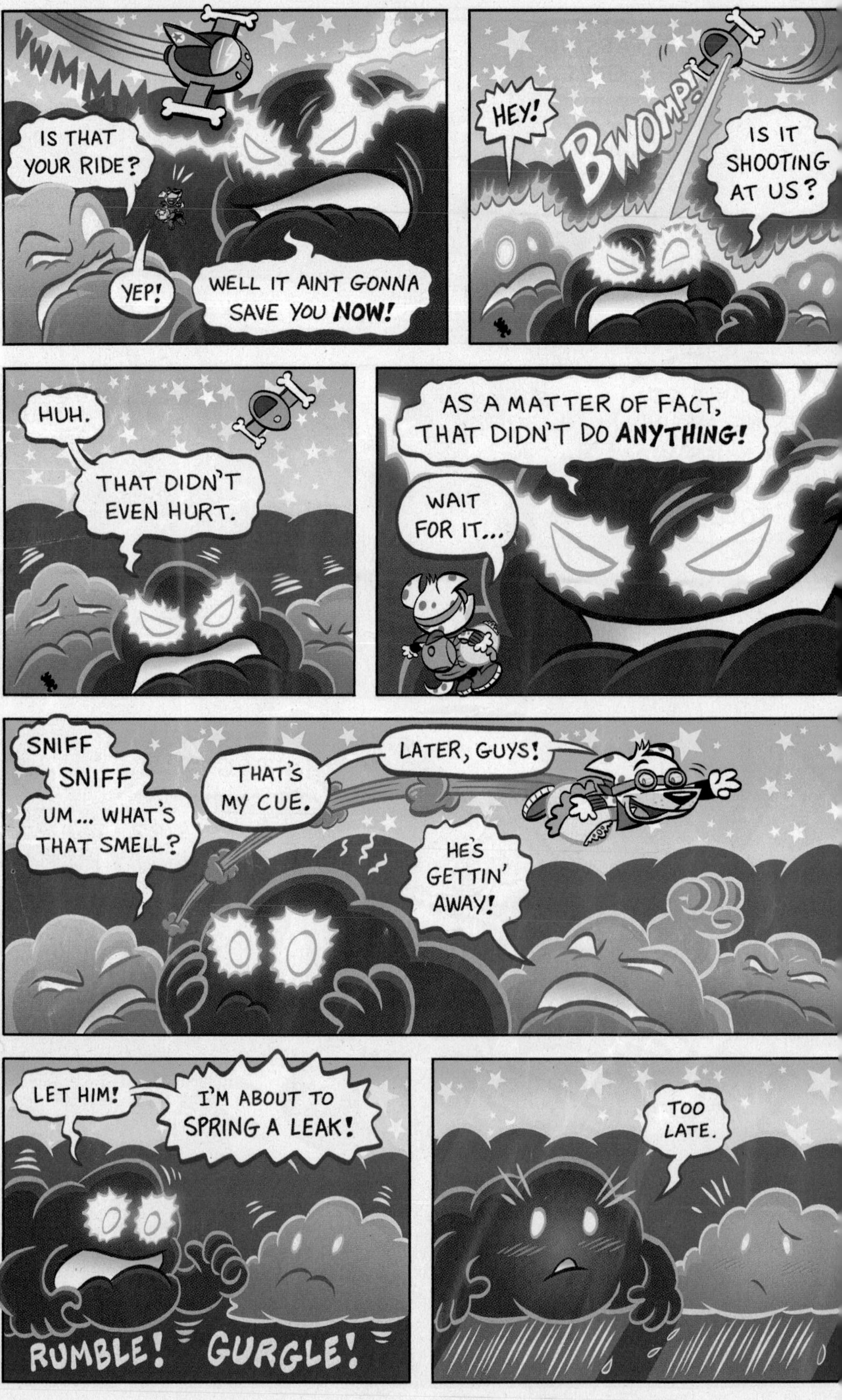
VWMMMM
IS THAT YOUR RIDE?
YEP!
WELL IT AINT GONNA SAVE YOU NOW!
HEY!
BWOMP!
IS IT SHOOTING AT US?
HUH.
THAT DIDN'T EVEN HURT.
AS A MATTER OF FACT, THAT DIDN'T DO ANYTHING!
WAIT FOR IT...
SNIFF SNIFF
UM... WHAT'S THAT SMELL?
THAT'S MY CUE.
LATER, GUYS!
HE'S GETTIN' AWAY!
LET HIM!
I'M ABOUT TO SPRING A LEAK!
RUMBLE! GURGLE!
TOO LATE.

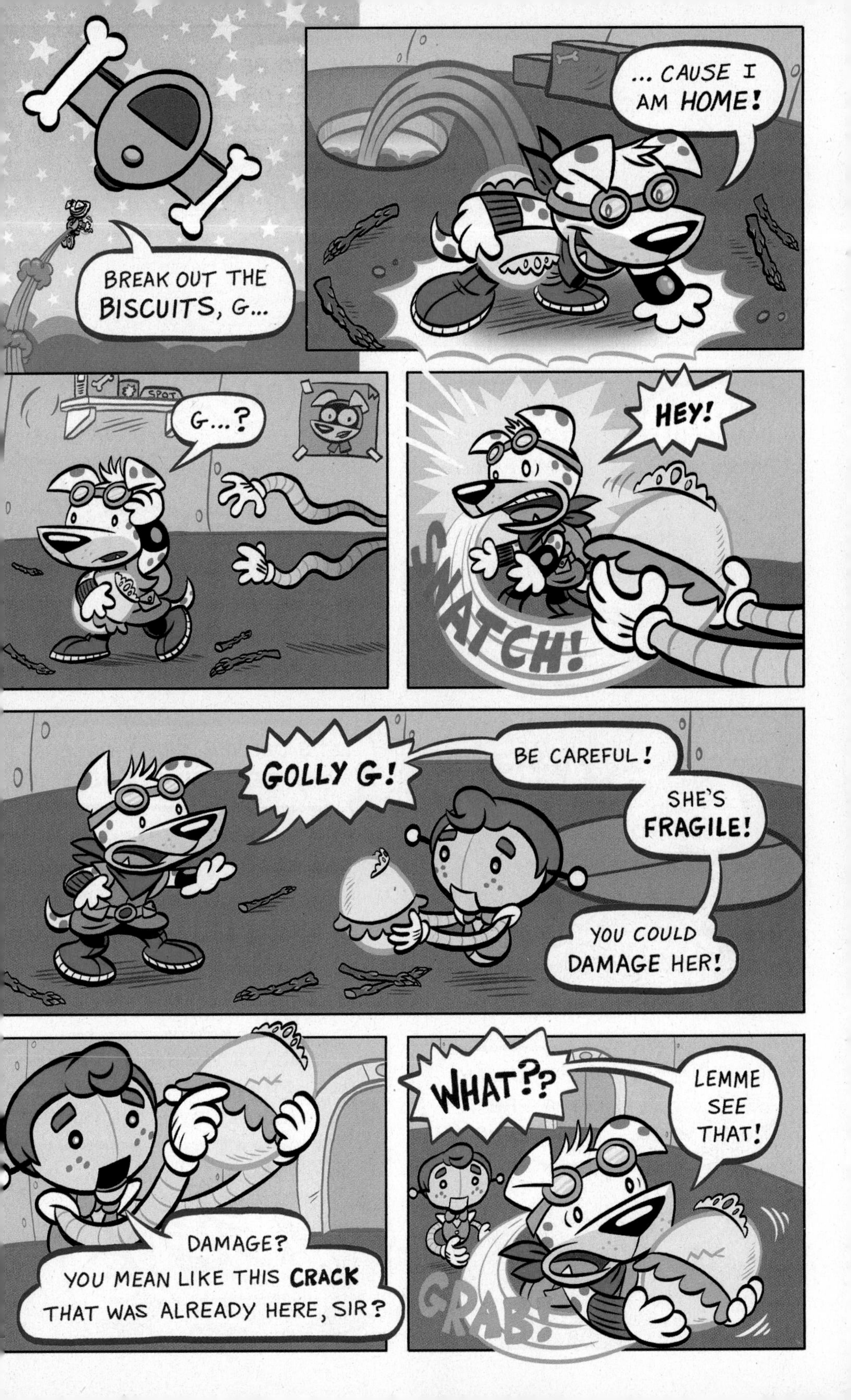
BREAK OUT THE BISCUITS, G...
... CAUSE I AM HOME!
SPOT
G...?
HEY!
SWATCH!
GOLLY G!
BE CAREFUL!
SHE'S FRAGILE!
YOU COULD DAMAGE HER!
DAMAGE? YOU MEAN LIKE THIS CRACK THAT WAS ALREADY HERE, SIR?
WHAT??
LEMME SEE THAT!
GRAB!

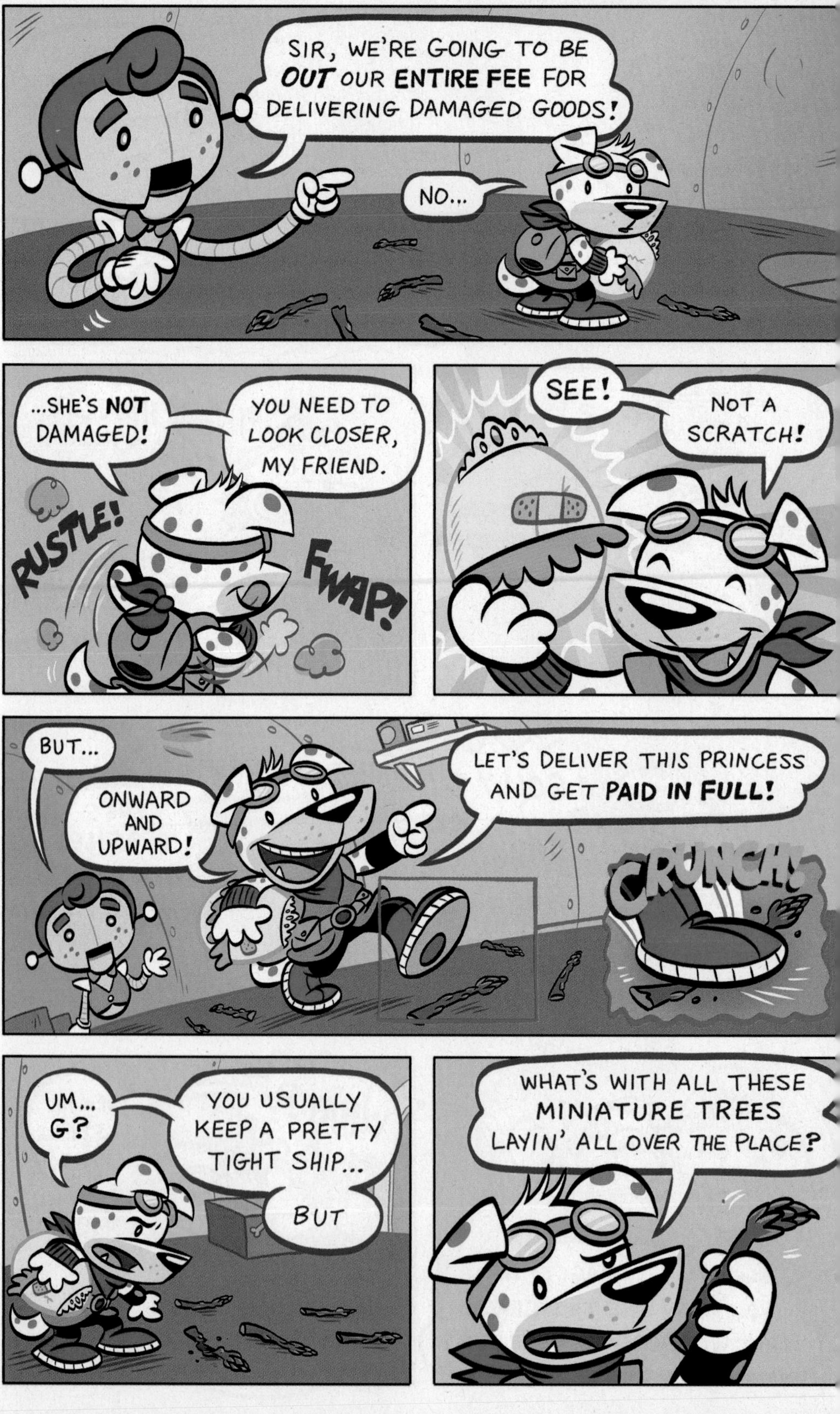
SIR, WE'RE GOING TO BE OUT OUR ENTIRE FEE FOR DELIVERING DAMAGED GOODS!
NO...
...SHE'S NOT DAMAGED!
YOU NEED TO LOOK CLOSER, MY FRIEND.
RUSTLE!
FWAP!
SEE!
NOT A SCRATCH!
BUT...
ONWARD AND UPWARD!
LET'S DELIVER THIS PRINCESS AND GET PAID IN FULL!
CRUNCH!
UM... G?
YOU USUALLY KEEP A PRETTY TIGHT SHIP...
BUT
WHAT'S WITH ALL THESE MINIATURE TREES LAYIN' ALL OVER THE PLACE?

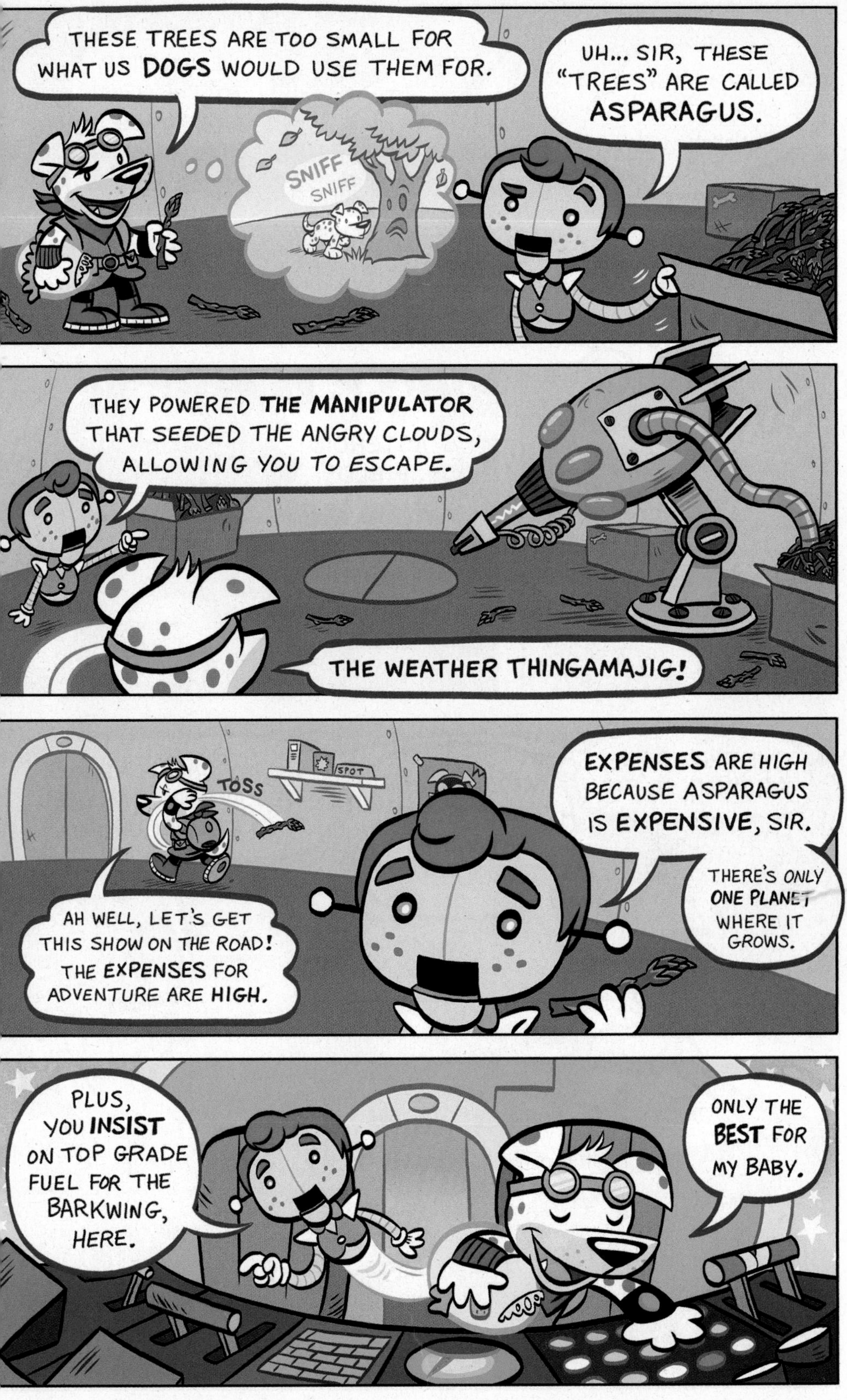
THESE TREES ARE TOO SMALL FOR WHAT US DOGS WOULD USE THEM FOR.
SNIFF SNIFF
UH... SIR, THESE "TREES" ARE CALLED ASPARAGUS.
THEY POWERED THE MANIPULATOR THAT SEEDED THE ANGRY CLOUDS, ALLOWING YOU TO ESCAPE.
THE WEATHER THINGAMAJIG!
TOSS
SPOT
AH WELL, LET'S GET THIS SHOW ON THE ROAD! THE EXPENSES FOR ADVENTURE ARE HIGH.
EXPENSES ARE HIGH BECAUSE ASPARAGUS IS EXPENSIVE, SIR.
THERE'S ONLY ONE PLANET WHERE IT GROWS.
PLUS, YOU INSIST ON TOP GRADE FUEL FOR THE BARKWING, HERE.
ONLY THE BEST FOR MY BABY.

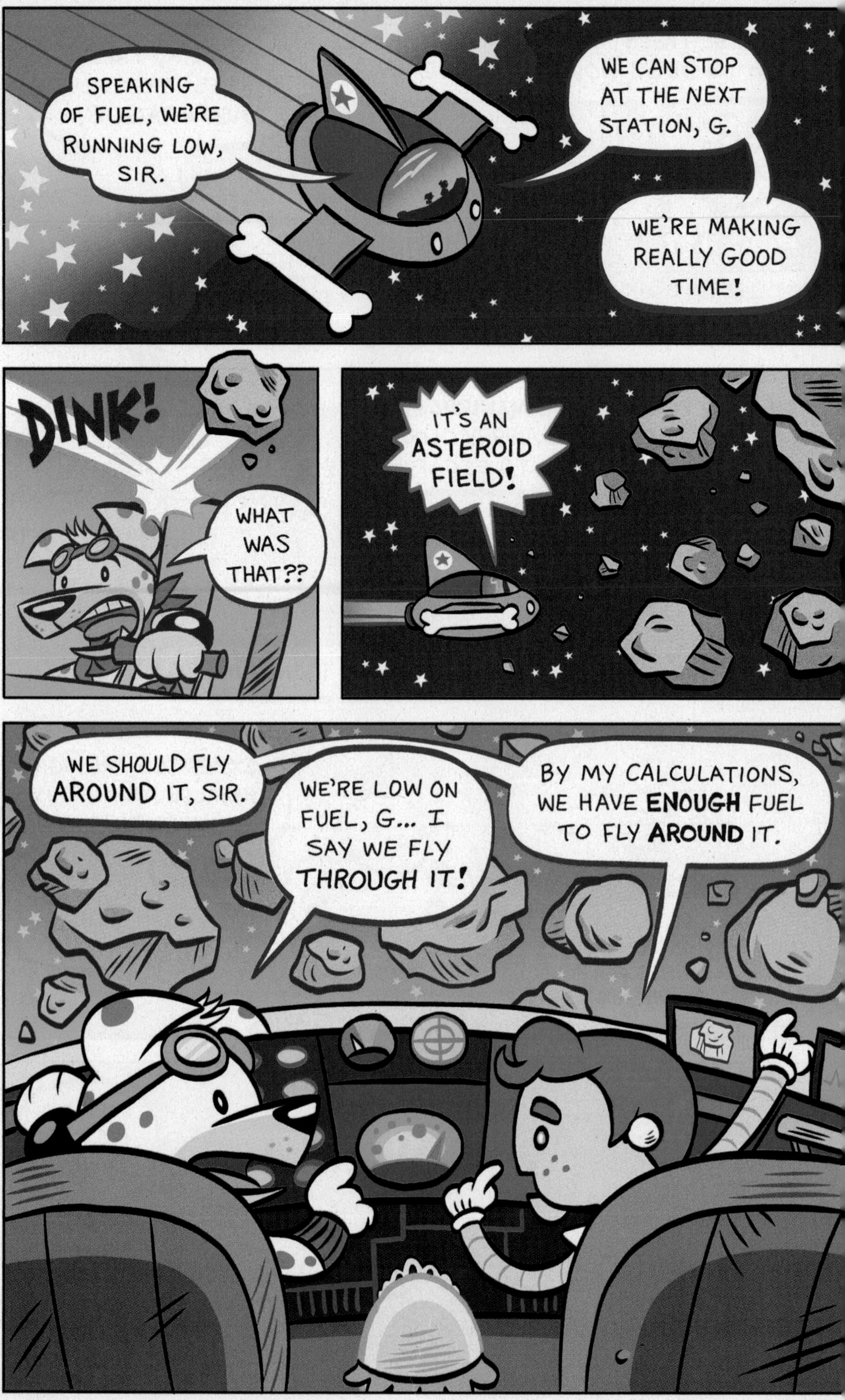
SPEAKING OF FUEL, WE'RE RUNNING LOW, SIR.
WE CAN STOP AT THE NEXT STATION, G.
WE'RE MAKING REALLY GOOD TIME!
DINK!
WHAT WAS THAT??
IT'S AN ASTEROID FIELD!
WE SHOULD FLY AROUND IT, SIR.
WE'RE LOW ON FUEL, G... I SAY WE FLY THROUGH IT!
BY MY CALCULATIONS, WE HAVE ENOUGH FUEL TO FLY AROUND IT.

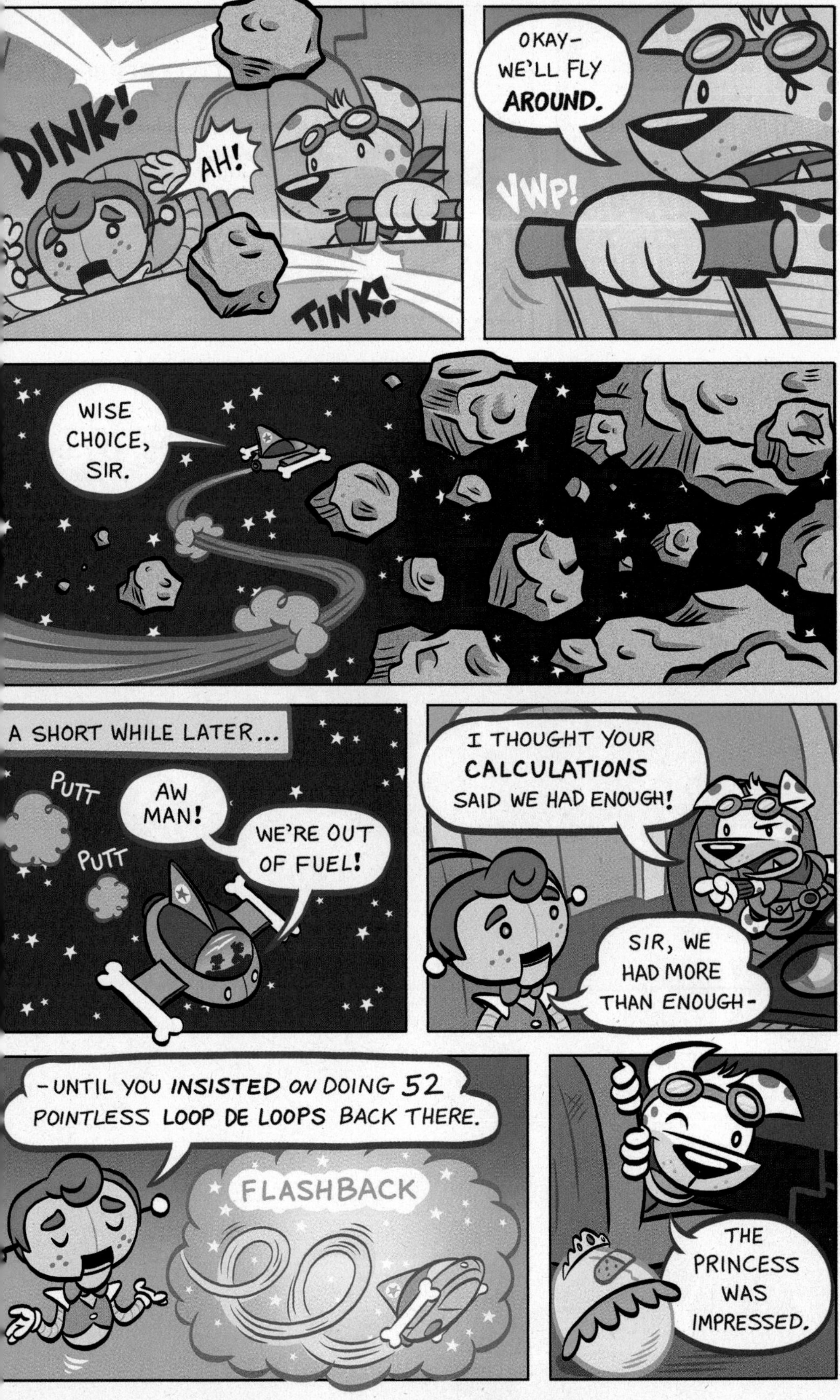
DINK!
AH!
TINK!
OKAY- WE'LL FLY AROUND.
VWP!
WISE CHOICE, SIR.
A SHORT WHILE LATER...
PUTT
PUTT
AW MAN!
WE'RE OUT OF FUEL!
I THOUGHT YOUR CALCULATIONS SAID WE HAD ENOUGH!
SIR, WE HAD MORE THAN ENOUGH-
-UNTIL YOU INSISTED ON DOING 52 POINTLESS LOOP DE LOOPS BACK THERE.
FLASHBACK
THE PRINCESS WAS IMPRESSED.

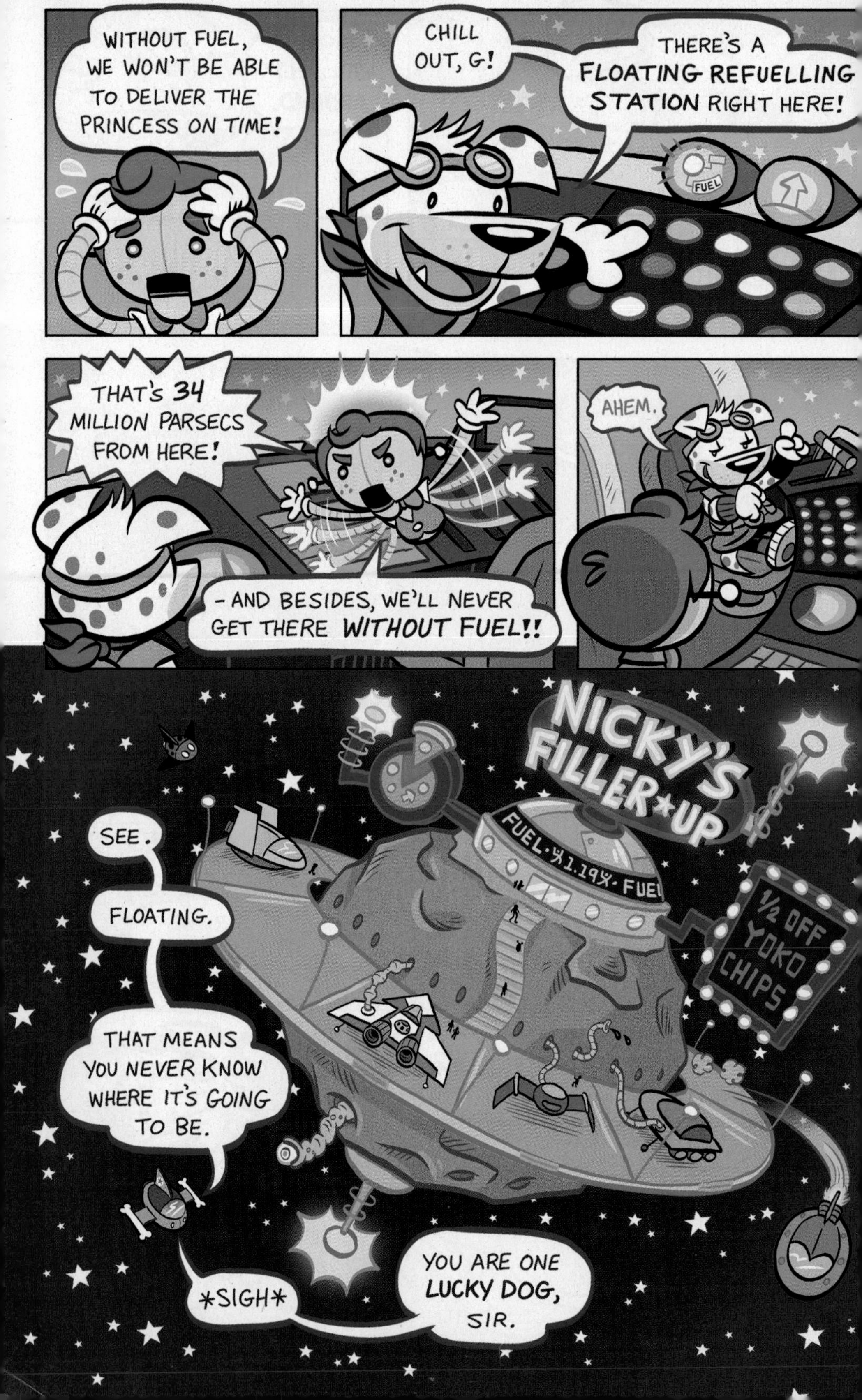
WITHOUT FUEL, WE WON'T BE ABLE TO DELIVER THE PRINCESS ON TIME!
CHILL OUT, G!
THERE'S A FLOATING REFUELLING STATION RIGHT HERE!
FUEL
THAT'S 34 MILLION PARSECS FROM HERE!
- AND BESIDES, WE'LL NEVER GET THERE WITHOUT FUEL!!
AHEM.
NICKY'S FILLER*UP
1/2 OFF YOKO CHIPS
SEE.
FLOATING.
THAT MEANS YOU NEVER KNOW WHERE IT'S GOING TO BE.
SIGH
YOU ARE ONE LUCKY DOG, SIR.

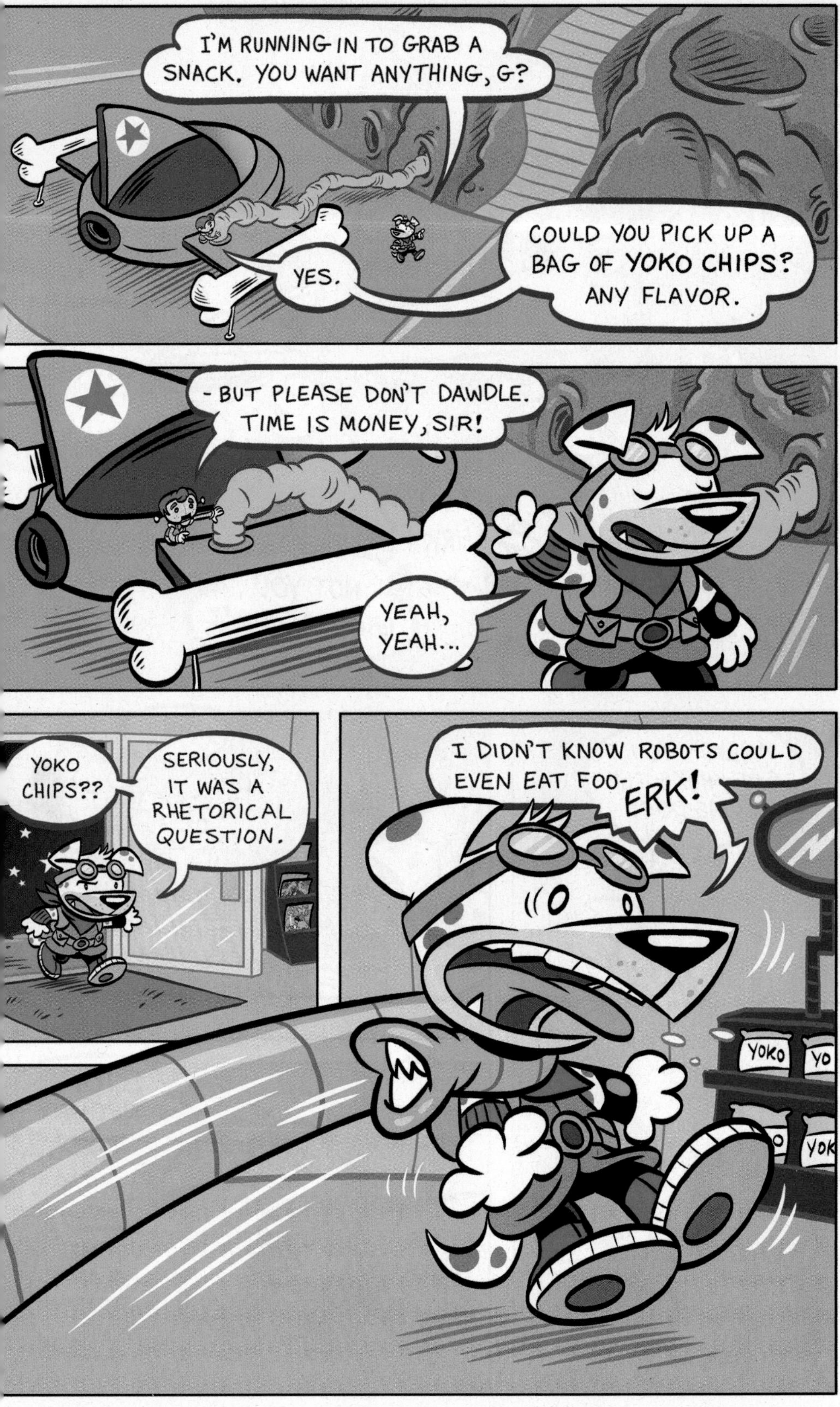
I'M RUNNING IN TO GRAB A SNACK. YOU WANT ANYTHING, G?
YES.
COULD YOU PICK UP A BAG OF YOKO CHIPS? ANY FLAVOR.
- BUT PLEASE DON'T DAWDLE. TIME IS MONEY, SIR!
YEAH, YEAH...
YOKO CHIPS??
SERIOUSLY, IT WAS A RHETORICAL QUESTION.
I DIDN'T KNOW ROBOTS COULD EVEN EAT FOO-
ERK!
YOKO
YO
YOK

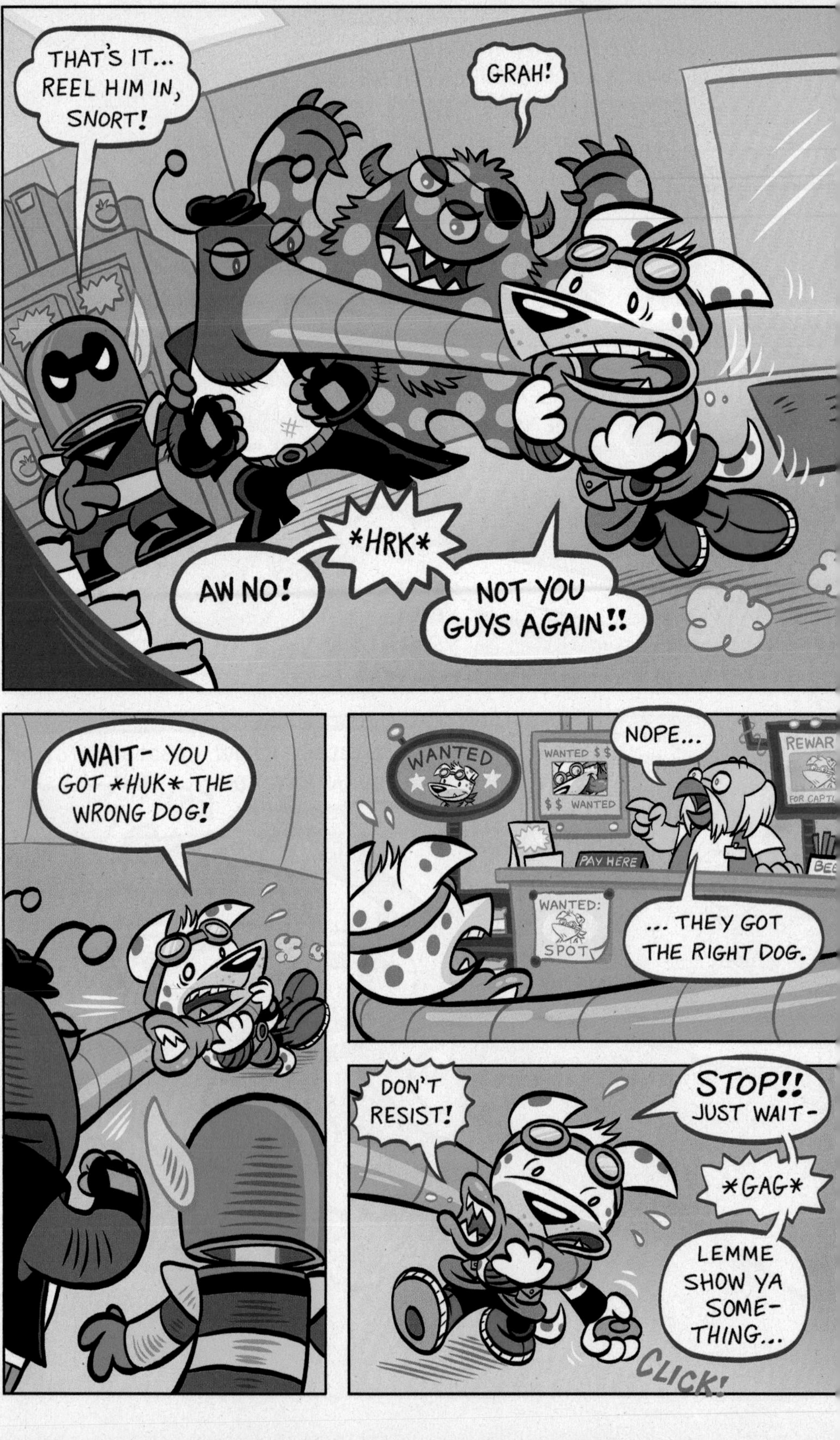
THAT'S IT... REEL HIM IN, SNORT!
GRAH!
HRK
AW NO!
NOT YOU GUYS AGAIN!!
WAIT- YOU GOT *HUK* THE WRONG DOG!
WANTED
WANTED $ $
$ $ WANTED
PAY HERE
WANTED: SPOT
NOPE...
... THEY GOT THE RIGHT DOG.
DON'T RESIST!
STOP!! JUST WAIT-
GAG
LEMME SHOW YA SOME-THING...
CLICK!

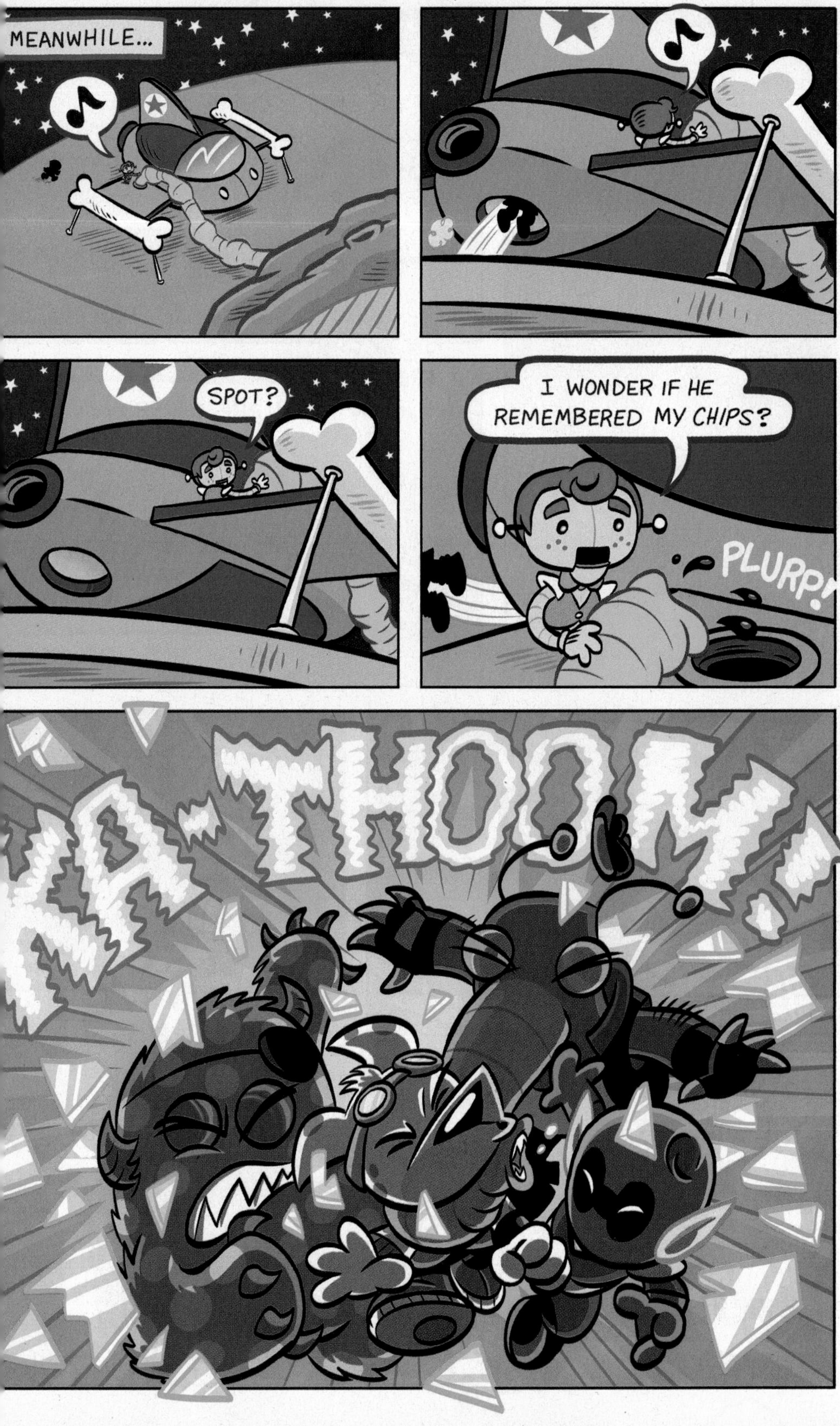

MEANWHILE...
SPOT?
I WONDER IF HE REMEMBERED MY CHIPS?
PLURP!
A-THOOM!!

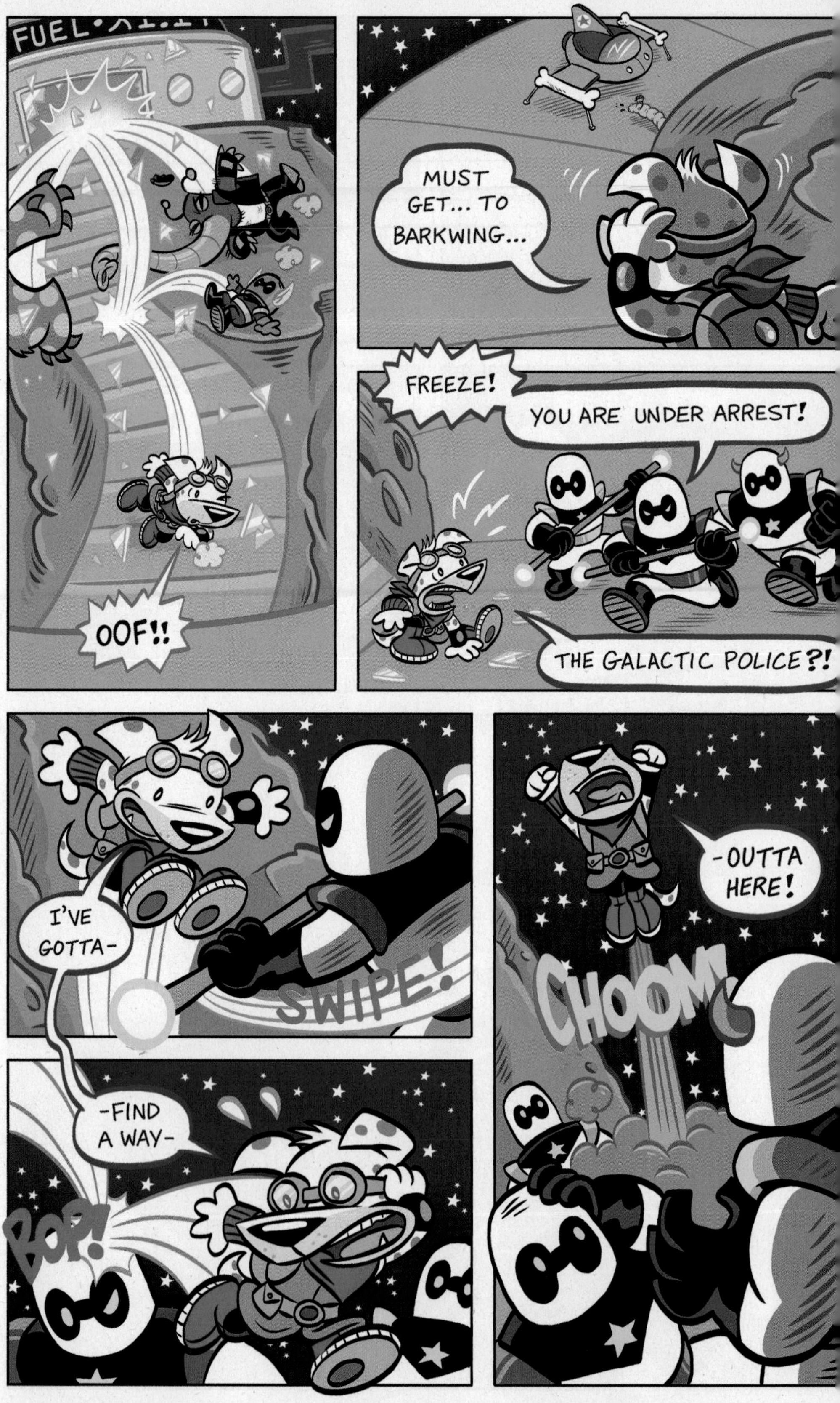
FUEL
OOF!!
MUST GET... TO BARKWING...
FREEZE!
YOU ARE UNDER ARREST!
THE GALACTIC POLICE?!
I'VE GOTTA-
SWIPE!
-FIND A WAY-
BOP!
-OUTTA HERE!
CHOOM!

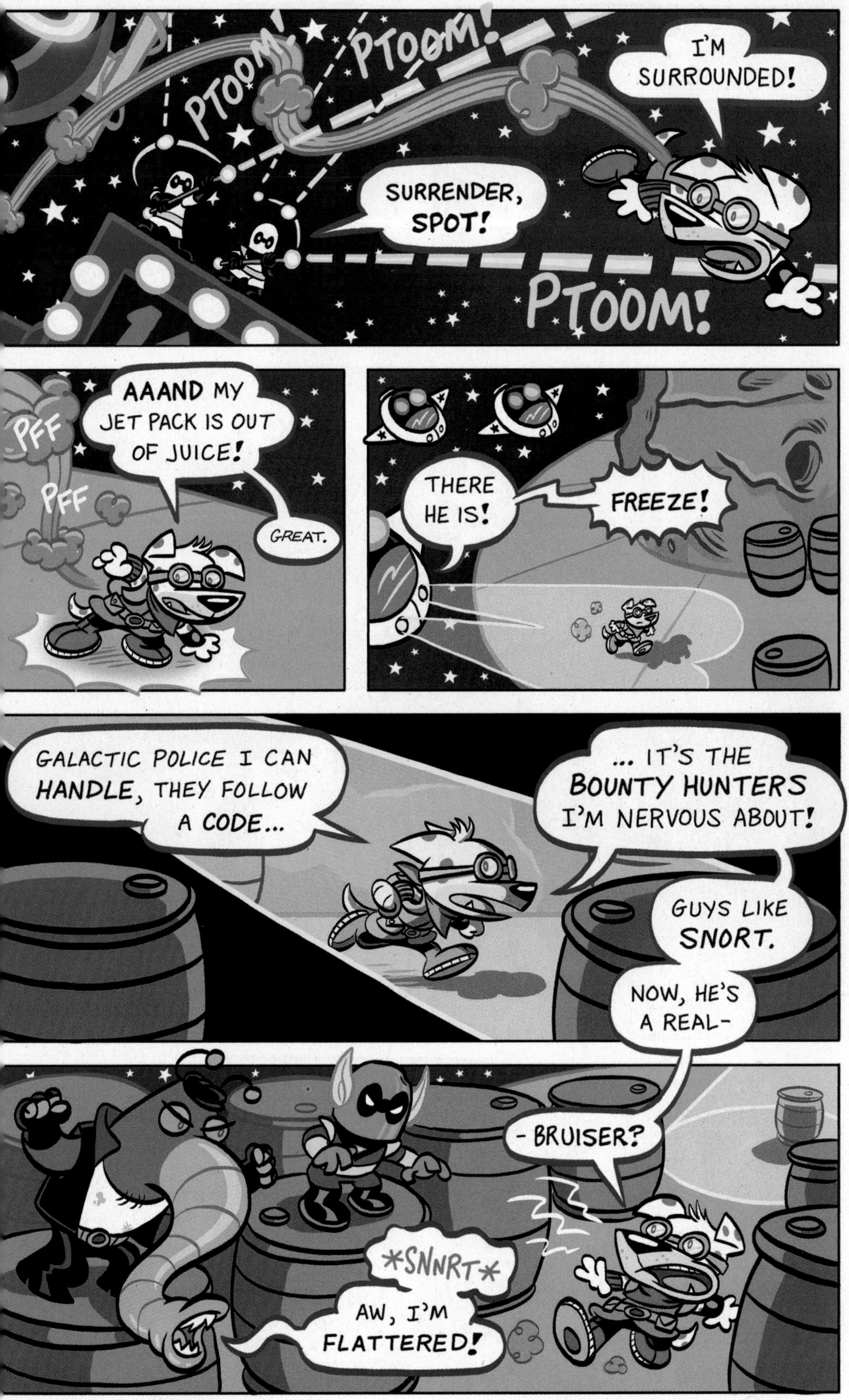
PTOOM!
PTOOM!
I'M SURROUNDED!
SURRENDER, SPOT!
PTOOM!
AAAND MY JET PACK IS OUT OF JUICE!
PFF
PFF
GREAT.
THERE HE IS!
FREEZE!
GALACTIC POLICE I CAN HANDLE, THEY FOLLOW A CODE...
... IT'S THE BOUNTY HUNTERS I'M NERVOUS ABOUT!
GUYS LIKE SNORT.
NOW, HE'S A REAL-
- BRUISER?
SNNRT
AW, I'M FLATTERED!

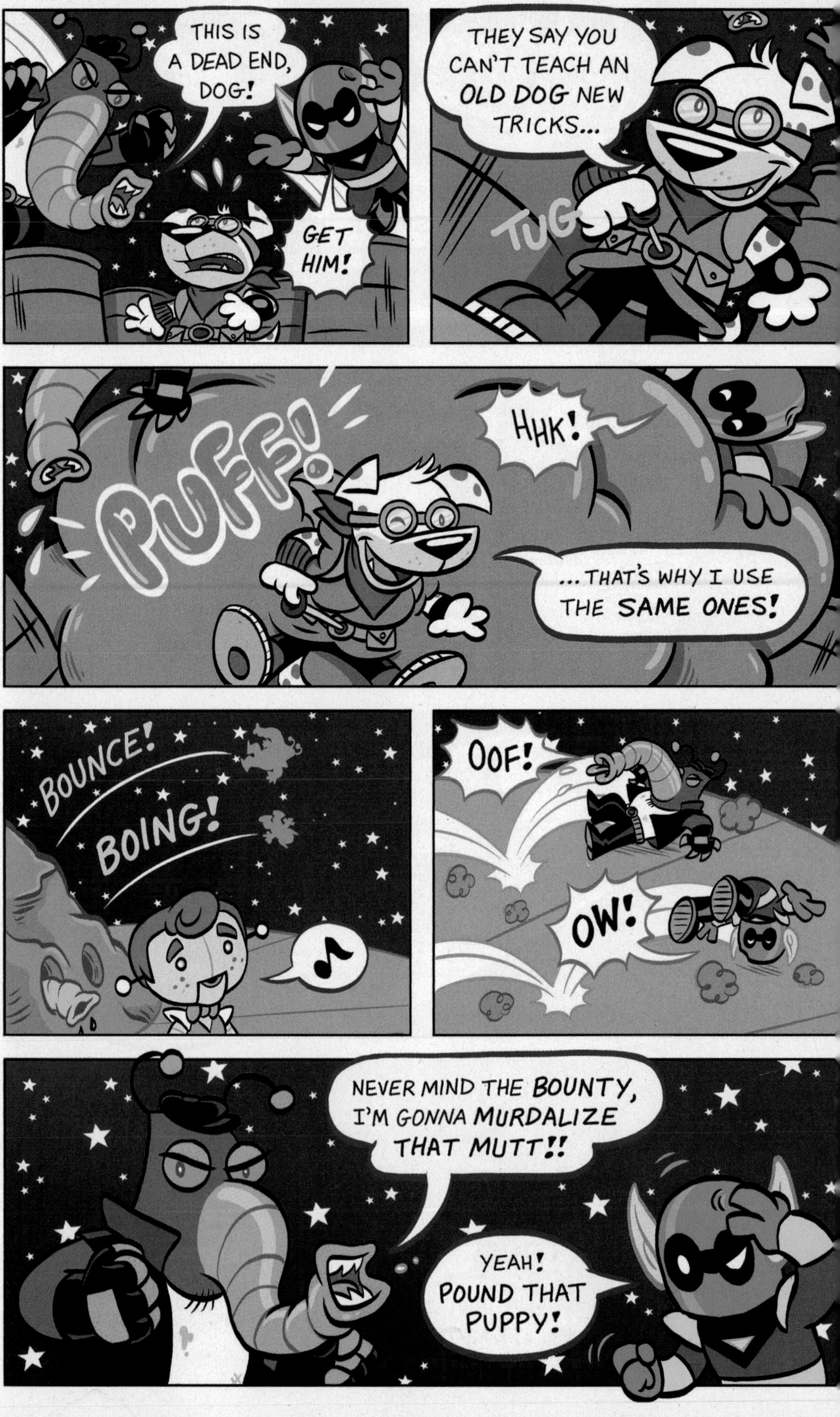
THIS IS A DEAD END, DOG!
GET HIM!
THEY SAY YOU CAN'T TEACH AN OLD DOG NEW TRICKS...
TUG
PUFF!
HHK!
...THAT'S WHY I USE THE SAME ONES!
BOUNCE!
BOING!
♪
OOF!
OW!
NEVER MIND THE BOUNTY, I'M GONNA MURDALIZE THAT MUTT!!
YEAH! POUND THAT PUPPY!

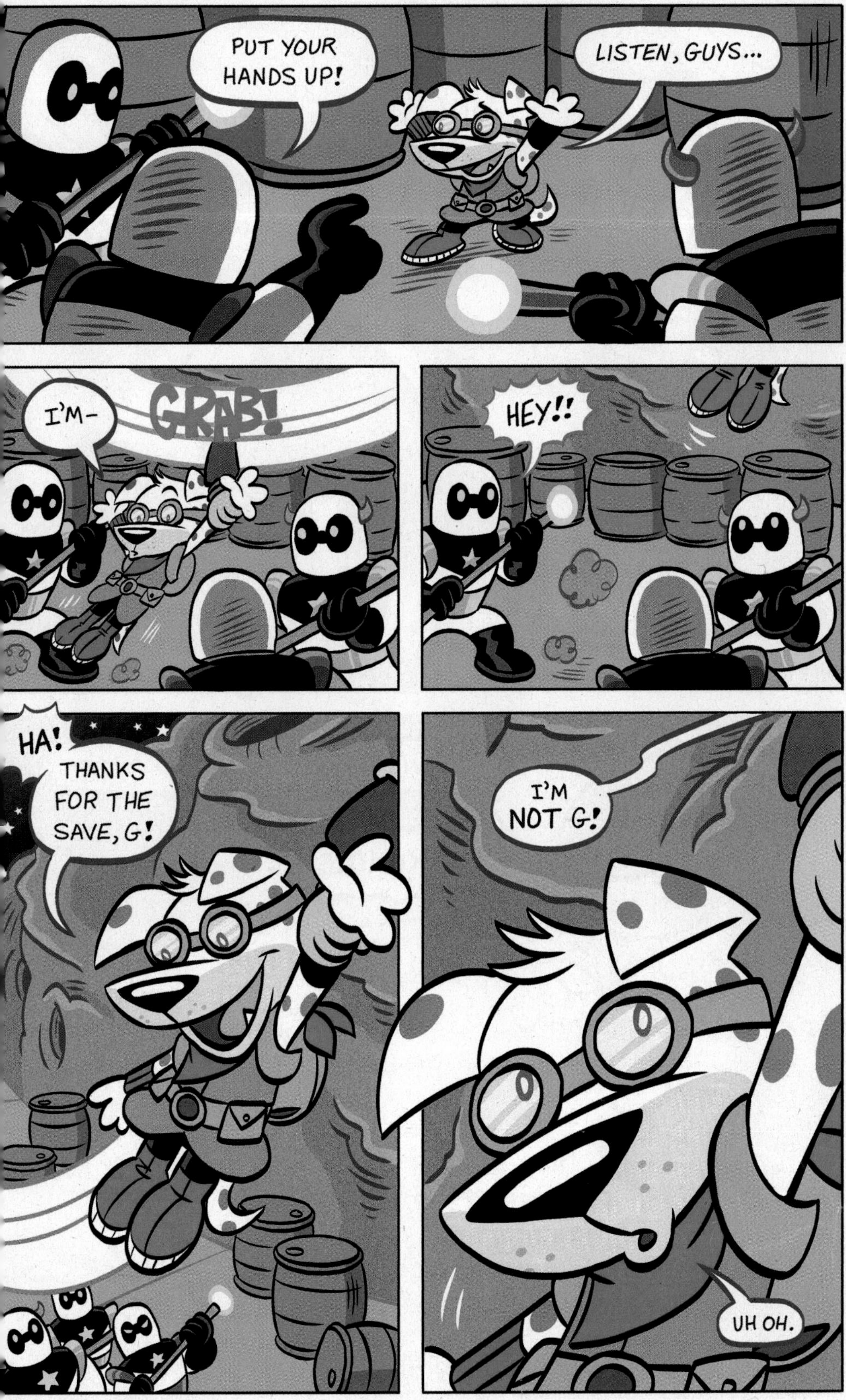
PUT YOUR HANDS UP!
LISTEN, GUYS...
I'M-
GRAB!
HEY!!
HA!
THANKS FOR THE SAVE, G!
I'M NOT G!
UH OH.

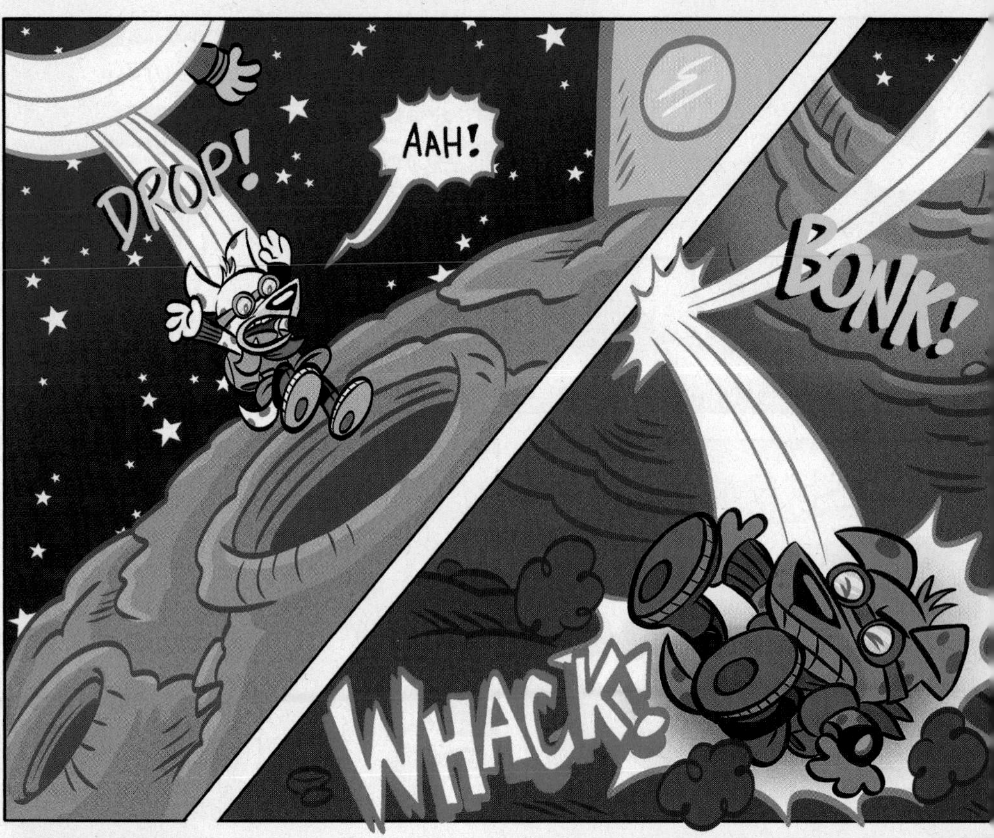
DROP!
AAH!
BONK!
WHACK!

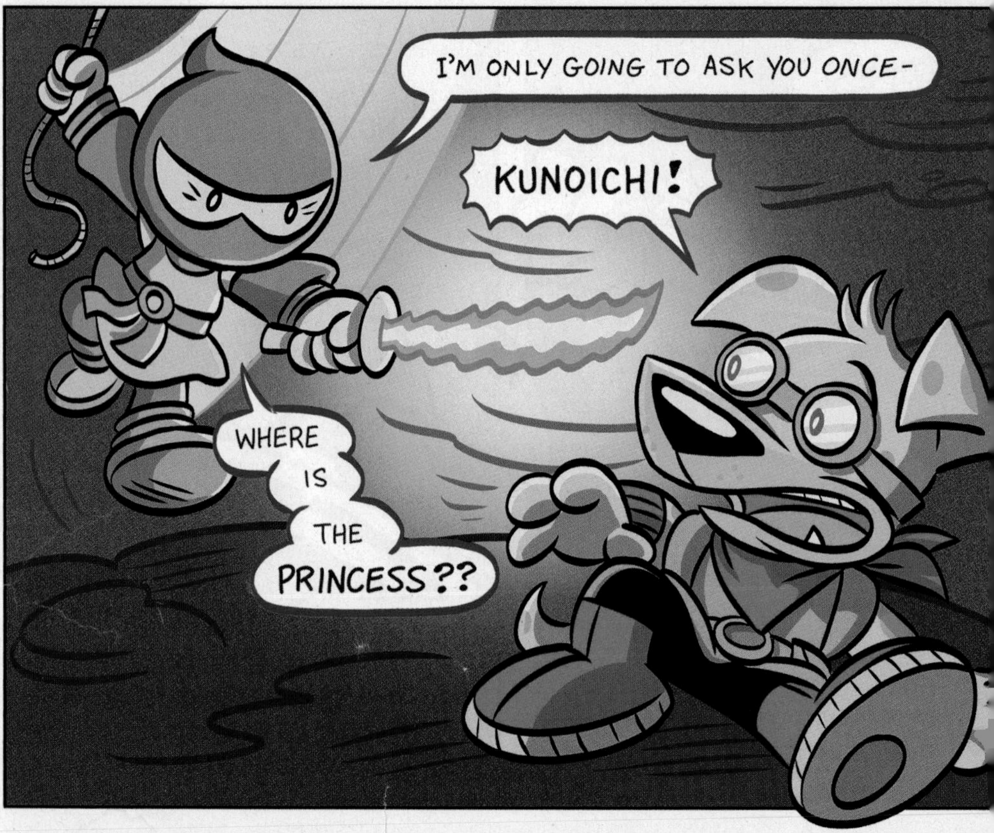
I'M ONLY GOING TO ASK YOU ONCE-
KUNOICHI!
WHERE IS THE PRINCESS??

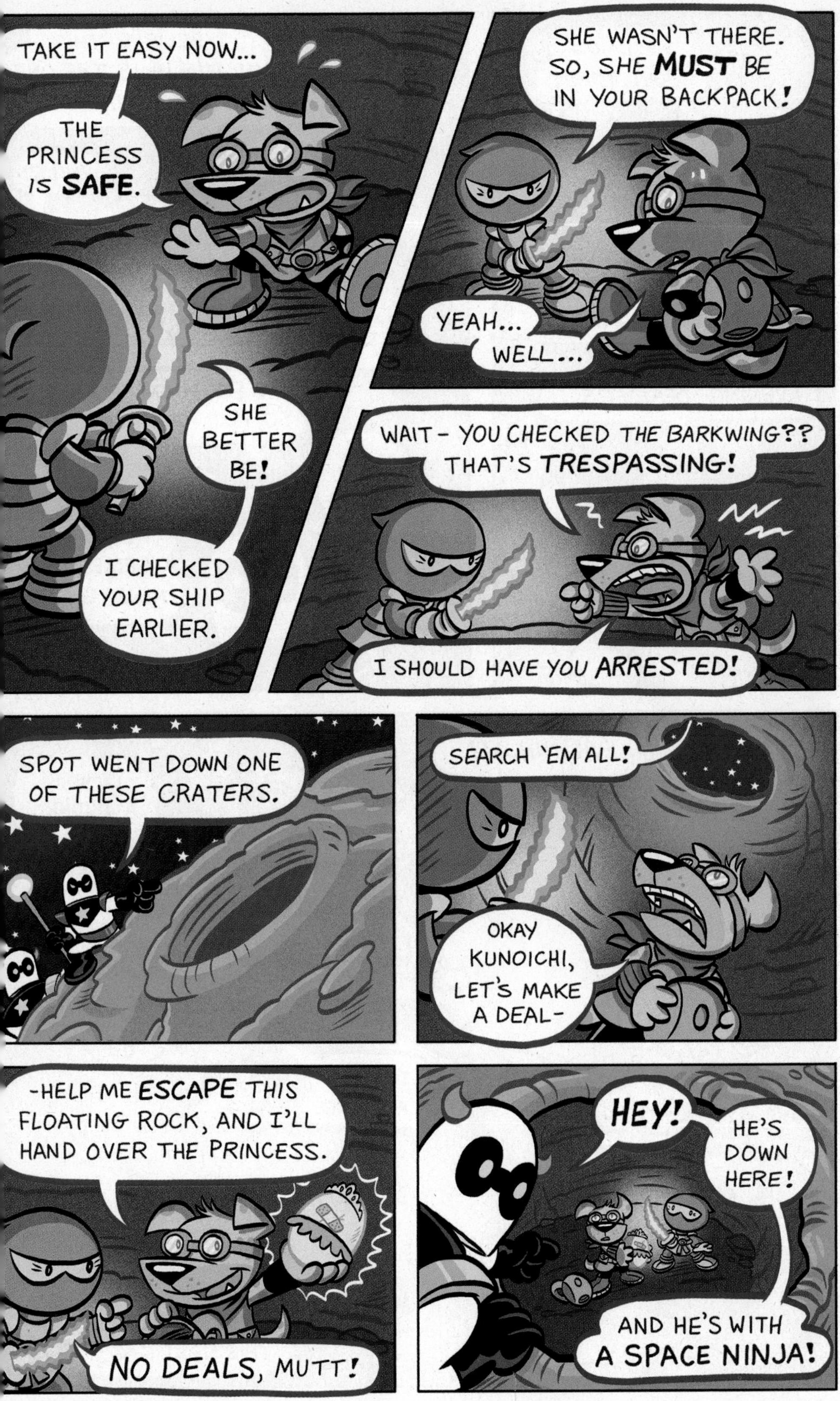
TAKE IT EASY NOW...
THE PRINCESS IS SAFE.
SHE BETTER BE!
I CHECKED YOUR SHIP EARLIER.
SHE WASN'T THERE. SO, SHE MUST BE IN YOUR BACKPACK!
YEAH... WELL...
WAIT - YOU CHECKED THE BARKWING?? THAT'S TRESPASSING!
I SHOULD HAVE YOU ARRESTED!
SPOT WENT DOWN ONE OF THESE CRATERS.
SEARCH 'EM ALL!
OKAY KUNOICHI, LET'S MAKE A DEAL-
-HELP ME ESCAPE THIS FLOATING ROCK, AND I'LL HAND OVER THE PRINCESS.
NO DEALS, MUTT!
HEY!
HE'S DOWN HERE!
AND HE'S WITH A SPACE NINJA!

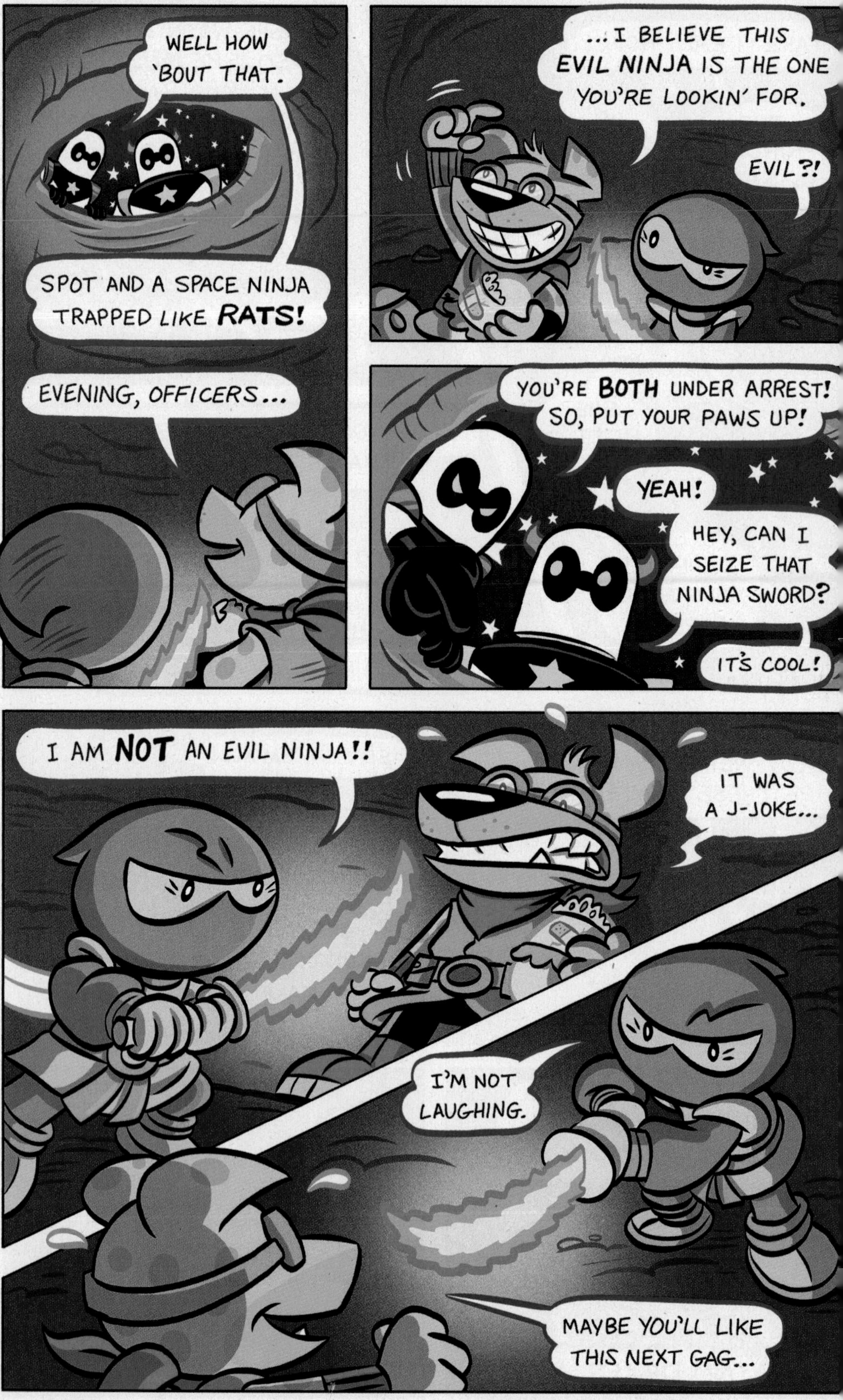
WELL HOW 'BOUT THAT.
SPOT AND A SPACE NINJA TRAPPED LIKE RATS!
EVENING, OFFICERS...
...I BELIEVE THIS EVIL NINJA IS THE ONE YOU'RE LOOKIN' FOR.
EVIL?!
YOU'RE BOTH UNDER ARREST! SO, PUT YOUR PAWS UP!
YEAH!
HEY, CAN I SEIZE THAT NINJA SWORD?
IT'S COOL!
I AM NOT AN EVIL NINJA!!
IT WAS A J-JOKE...
I'M NOT LAUGHING.
MAYBE YOU'LL LIKE THIS NEXT GAG...

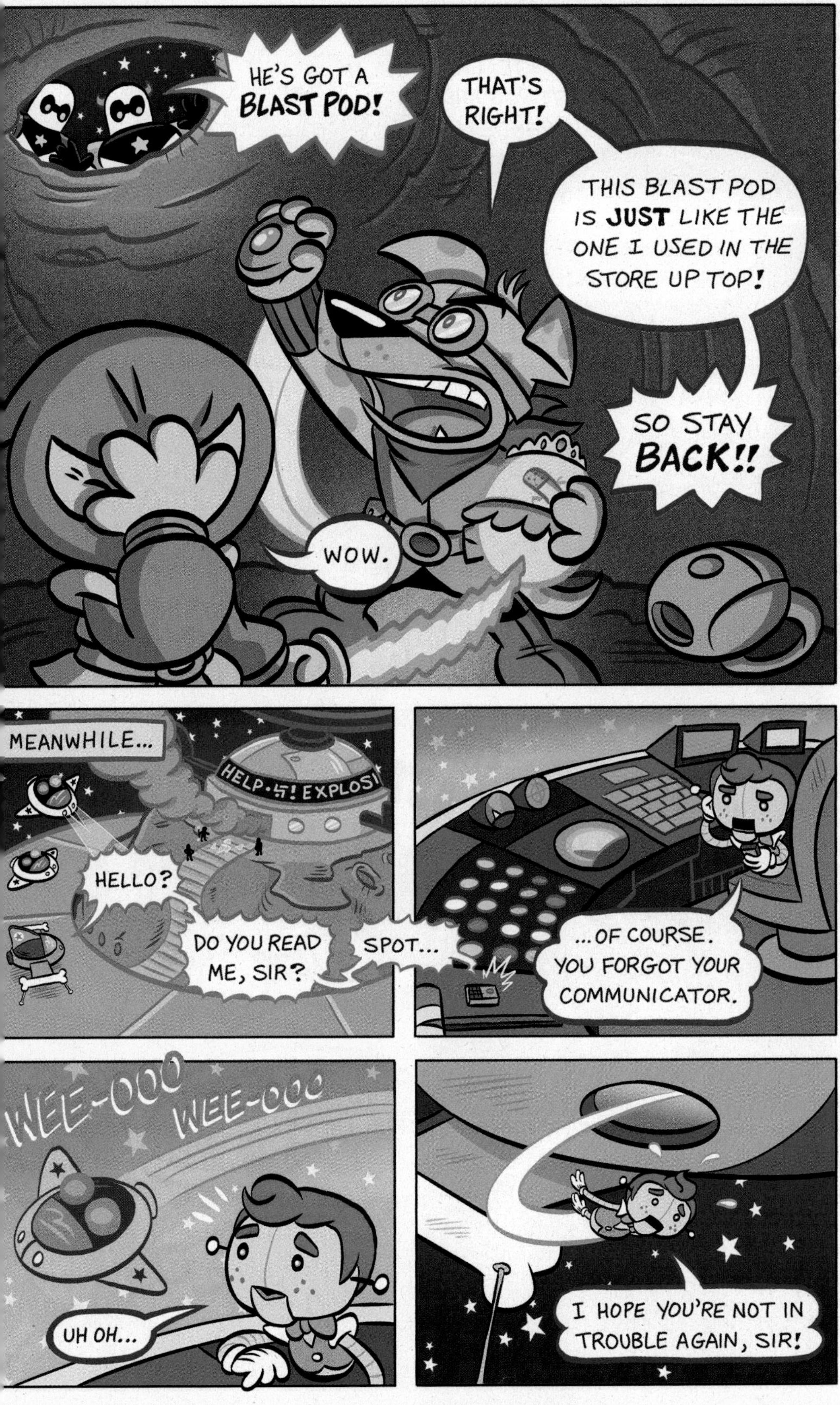

HE'S GOT A BLAST POD!
THAT'S RIGHT!
THIS BLAST POD IS JUST LIKE THE ONE I USED IN THE STORE UP TOP!
SO STAY BACK!!
WOW.
MEANWHILE...
HELLO?
DO YOU READ ME, SIR?
SPOT...
...OF COURSE. YOU FORGOT YOUR COMMUNICATOR.
WEE-OOO WEE-OOO
UH OH...
I HOPE YOU'RE NOT IN TROUBLE AGAIN, SIR!

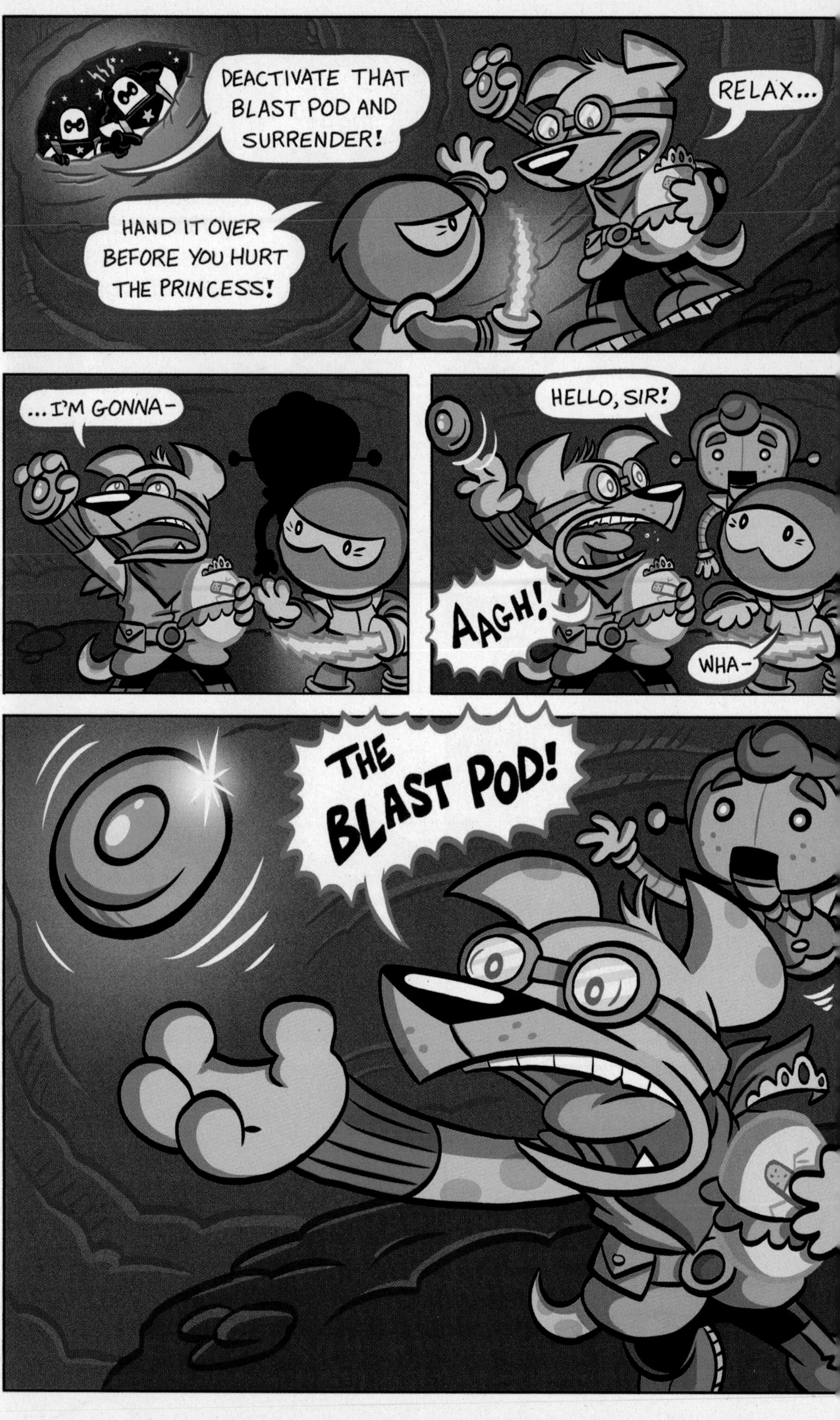
DEACTIVATE THAT BLAST POD AND SURRENDER!
RELAX...
HAND IT OVER BEFORE YOU HURT THE PRINCESS!
...I'M GONNA-
HELLO, SIR!
AAGH!
WHA-
THE BLAST POD!

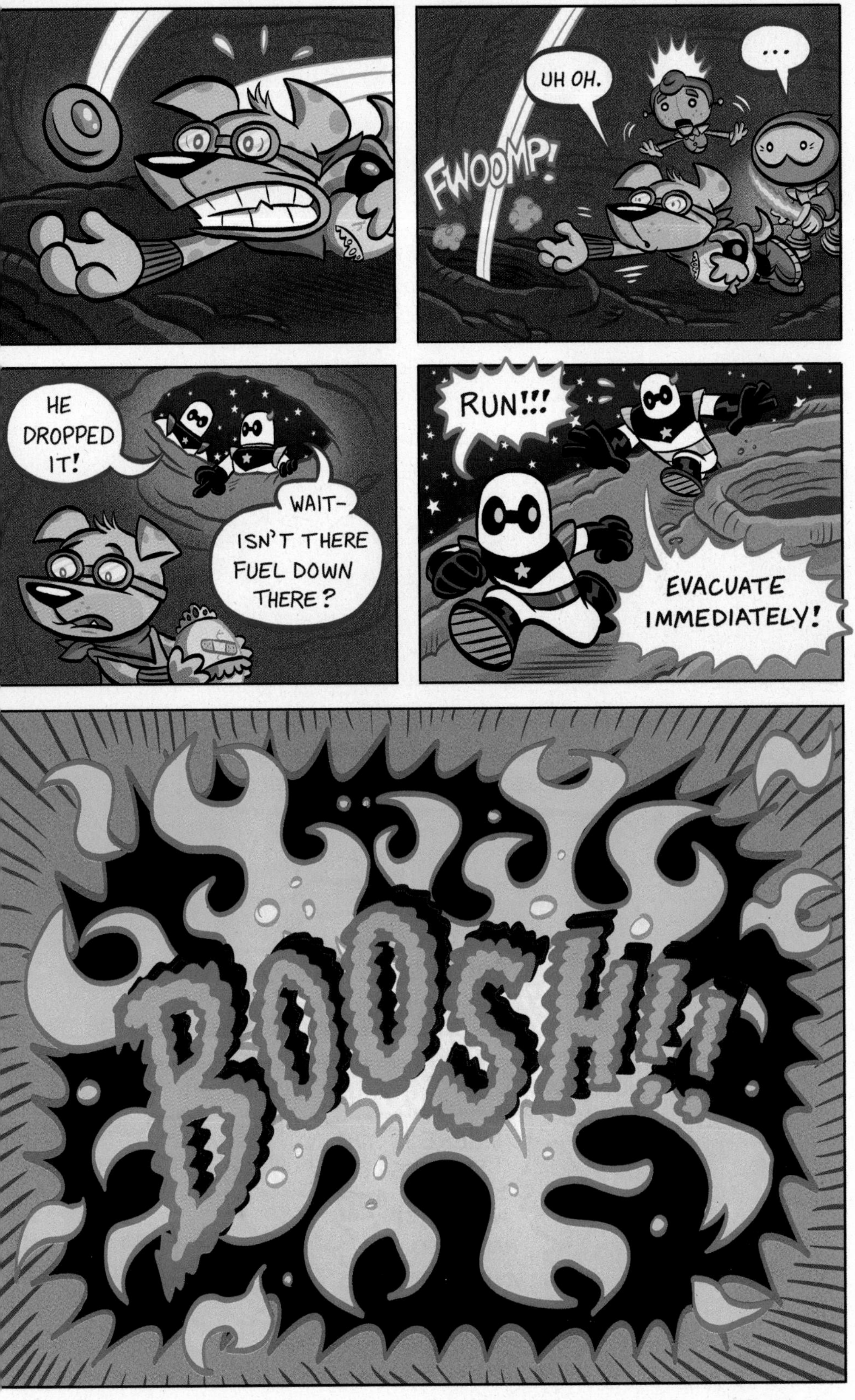
UH OH.
...
FWOOMP!
HE DROPPED IT!
WAIT- ISN'T THERE FUEL DOWN THERE?
RUN!!!
EVACUATE IMMEDIATELY!
BOOSH!!

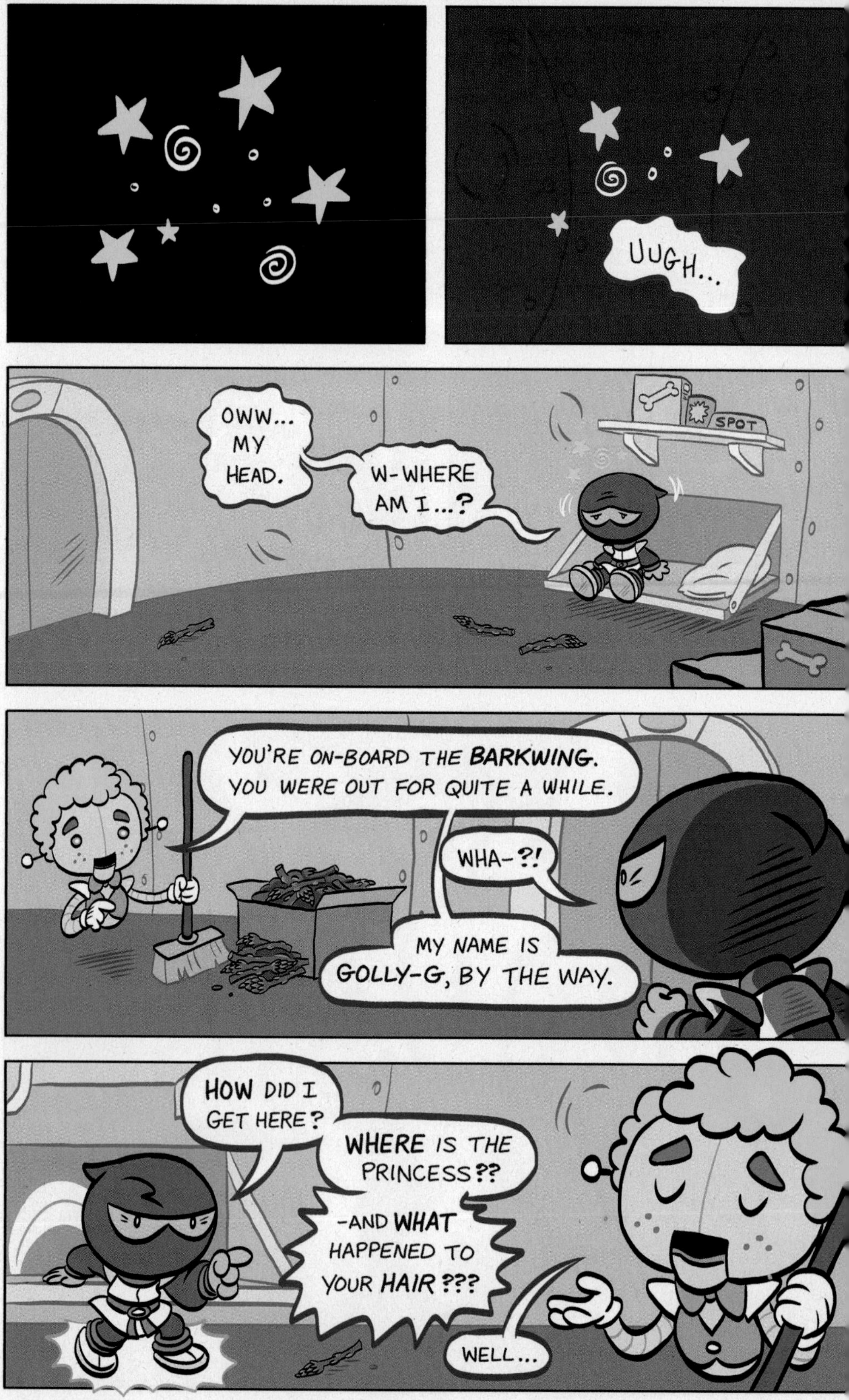
UUGH...
OWW... MY HEAD.
W-WHERE AM I...?
SPOT
YOU'RE ON-BOARD THE BARKWING. YOU WERE OUT FOR QUITE A WHILE.
WHA-?!
MY NAME IS GOLLY-G, BY THE WAY.
HOW DID I GET HERE?
WHERE IS THE PRINCESS??
-AND WHAT HAPPENED TO YOUR HAIR???
WELL...

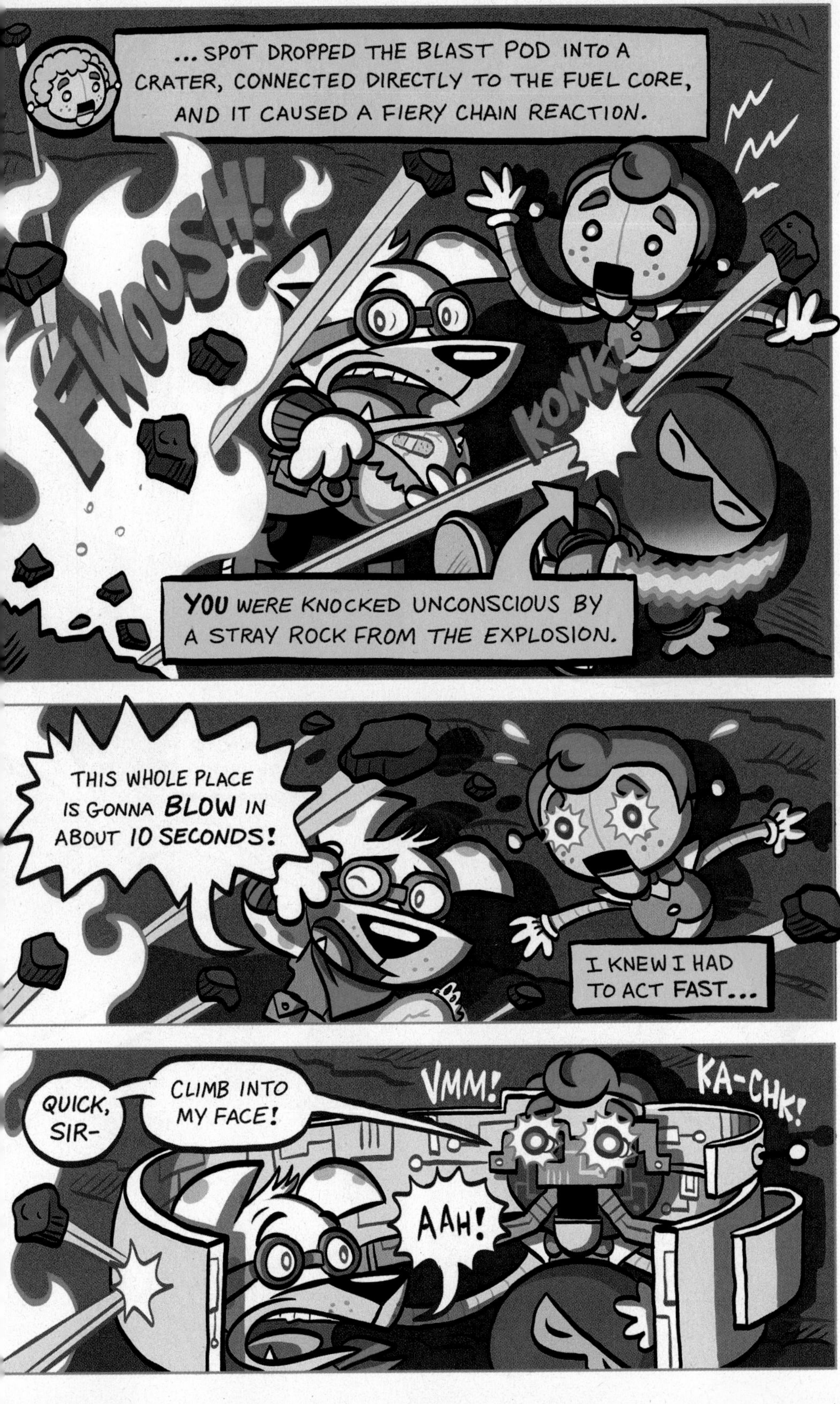
...SPOT DROPPED THE BLAST POD INTO A CRATER, CONNECTED DIRECTLY TO THE FUEL CORE, AND IT CAUSED A FIERY CHAIN REACTION.
FWOOSH!
KONK!
YOU WERE KNOCKED UNCONSCIOUS BY A STRAY ROCK FROM THE EXPLOSION.
THIS WHOLE PLACE IS GONNA BLOW IN ABOUT 10 SECONDS!
I KNEW I HAD TO ACT FAST...
QUICK, SIR-
CLIMB INTO MY FACE!
VMM!
KA-CHK!
AAH!

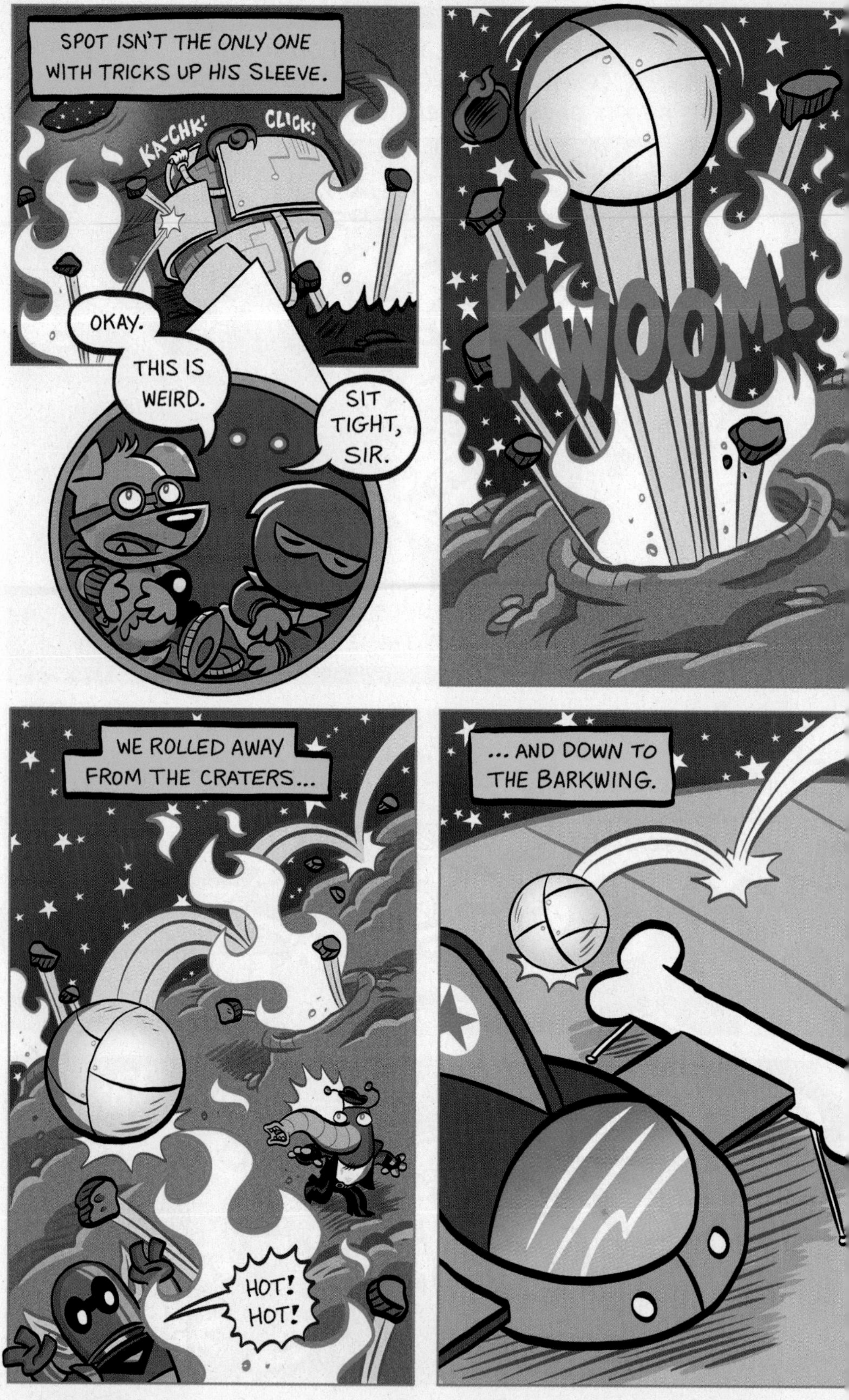
SPOT ISN'T THE ONLY ONE WITH TRICKS UP HIS SLEEVE.
KA-CHK!
CLICK!
OKAY.
THIS IS WEIRD.
SIT TIGHT, SIR.
KWOOM!
WE ROLLED AWAY FROM THE CRATERS...
HOT! HOT!
... AND DOWN TO THE BARKWING.

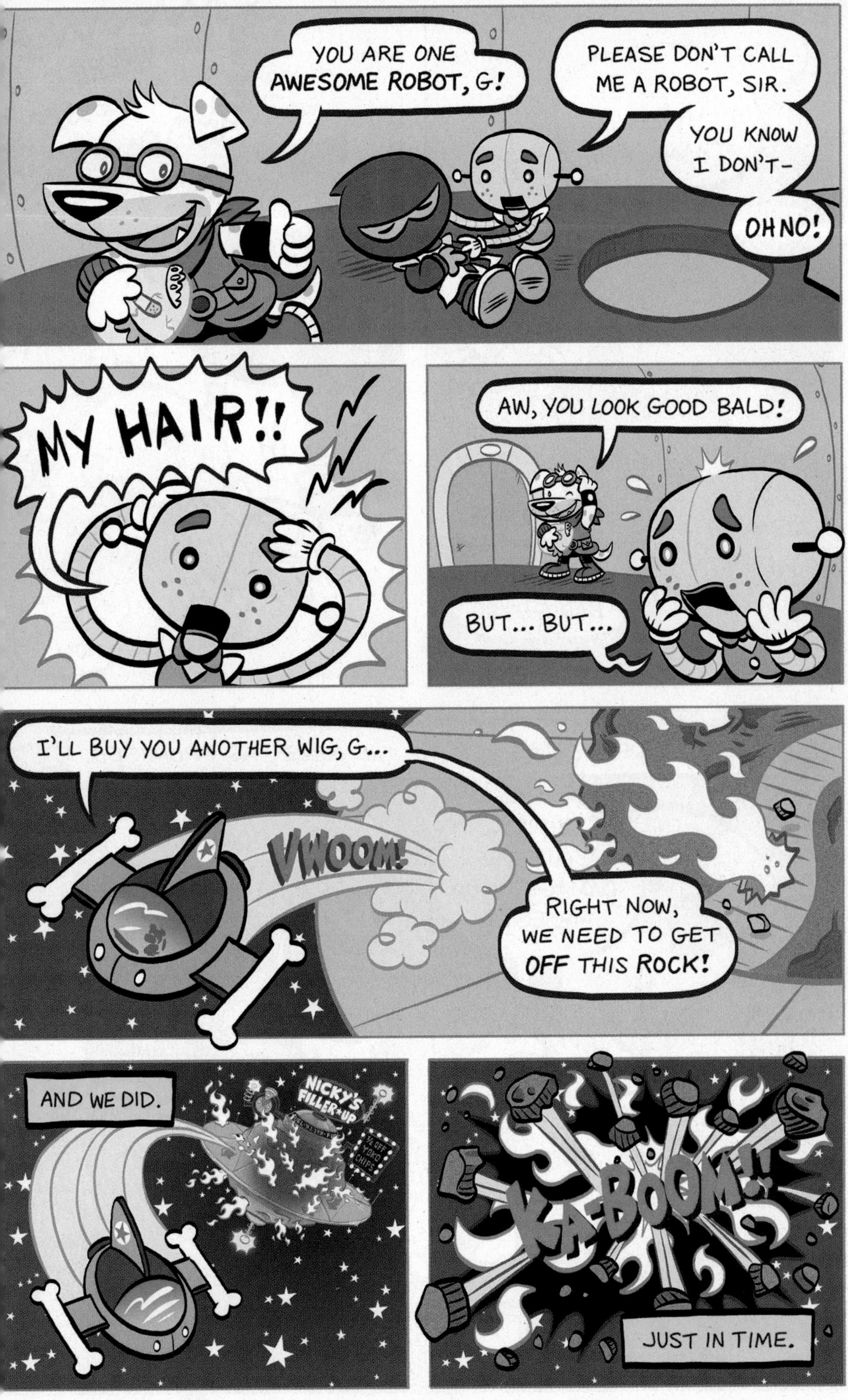
YOU ARE ONE AWESOME ROBOT, G!
PLEASE DON'T CALL ME A ROBOT, SIR.
YOU KNOW I DON'T-
OH NO!
MY HAIR!!
AW, YOU LOOK GOOD BALD!
BUT... BUT...
I'LL BUY YOU ANOTHER WIG, G...
VWOOM!
RIGHT NOW, WE NEED TO GET OFF THIS ROCK!
AND WE DID.
NICKY'S FILLER-UP
JUST IN TIME.
KA-BOOM!!

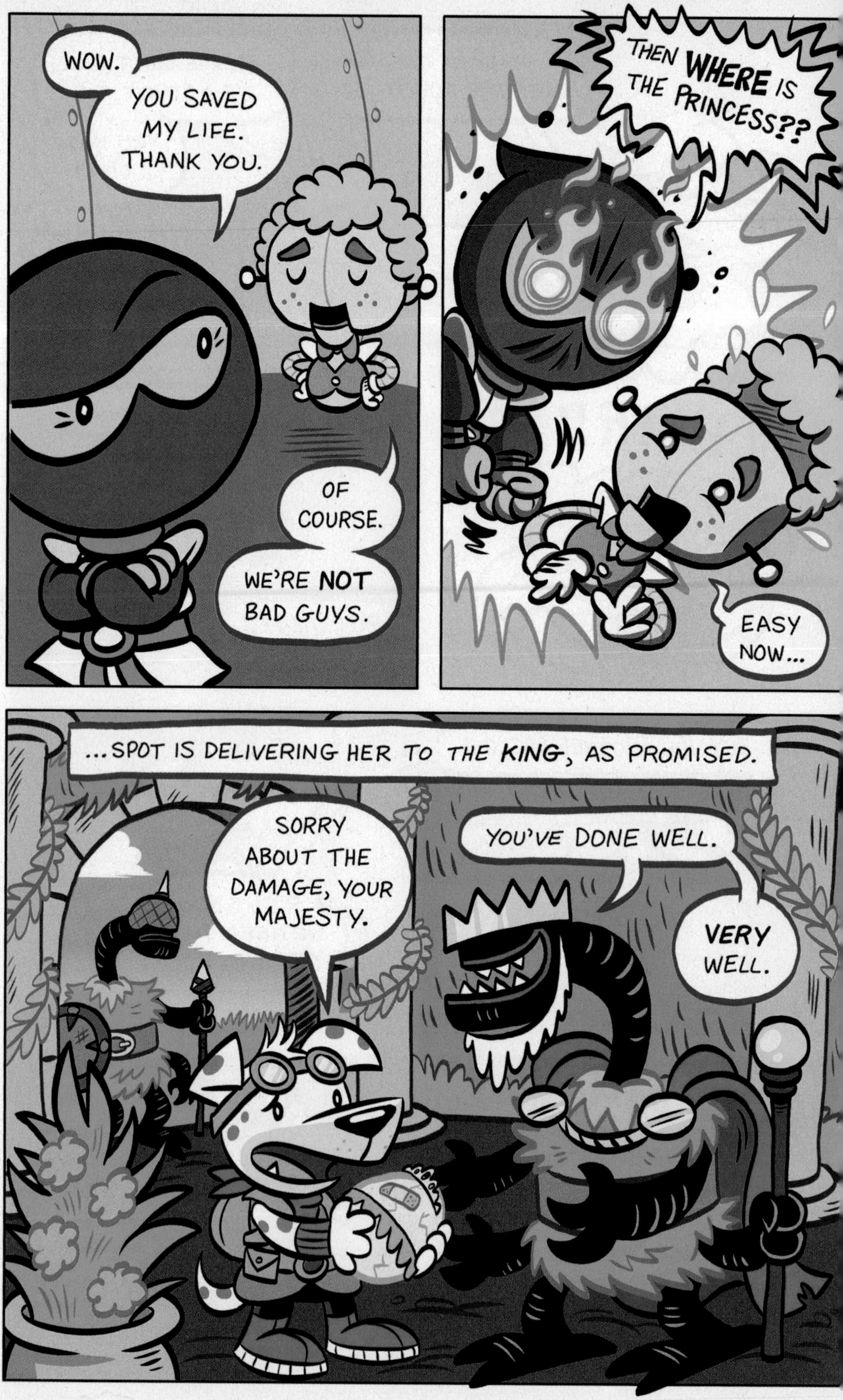
WOW.
YOU SAVED MY LIFE. THANK YOU.
OF COURSE.
WE'RE **NOT** BAD GUYS.
THEN **WHERE** IS THE PRINCESS??
EASY NOW...
...SPOT IS DELIVERING HER TO THE **KING**, AS PROMISED.
SORRY ABOUT THE DAMAGE, YOUR MAJESTY.
YOU'VE DONE WELL.
VERY WELL.

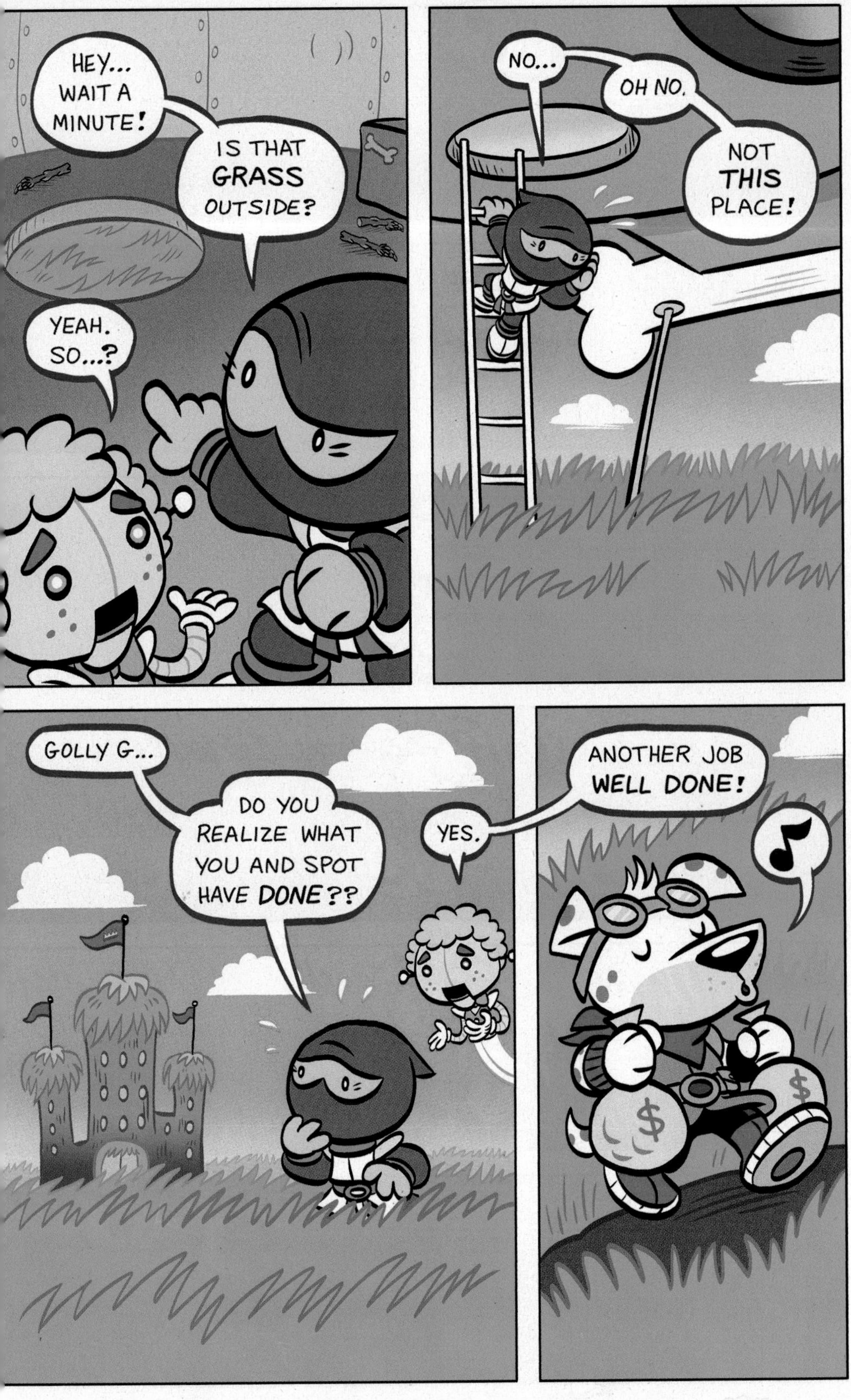
HEY... WAIT A MINUTE!
IS THAT GRASS OUTSIDE?
YEAH. SO...?
NO...
OH NO.
NOT THIS PLACE!
GOLLY G...
DO YOU REALIZE WHAT YOU AND SPOT HAVE DONE??
YES.
ANOTHER JOB WELL DONE!

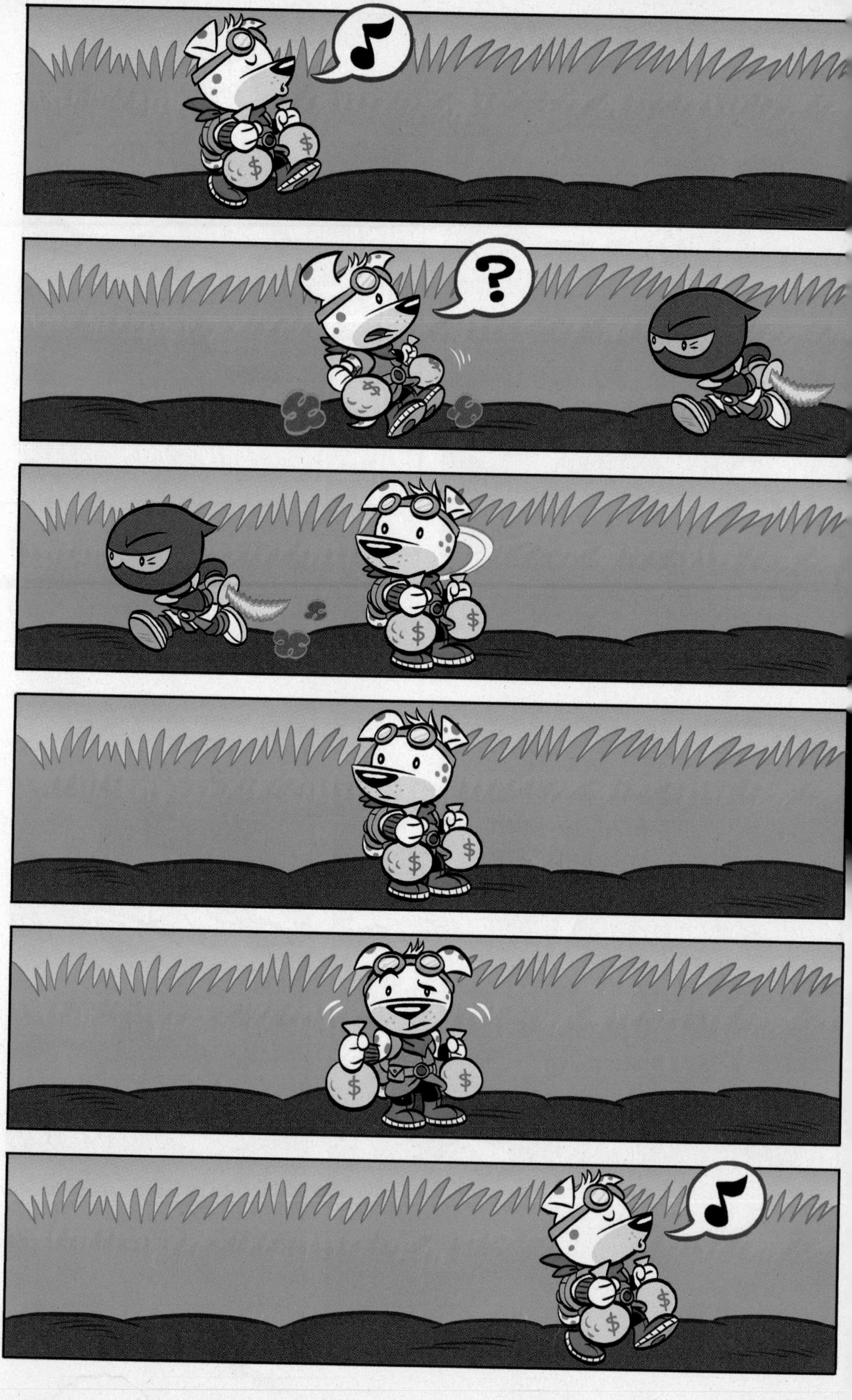
?

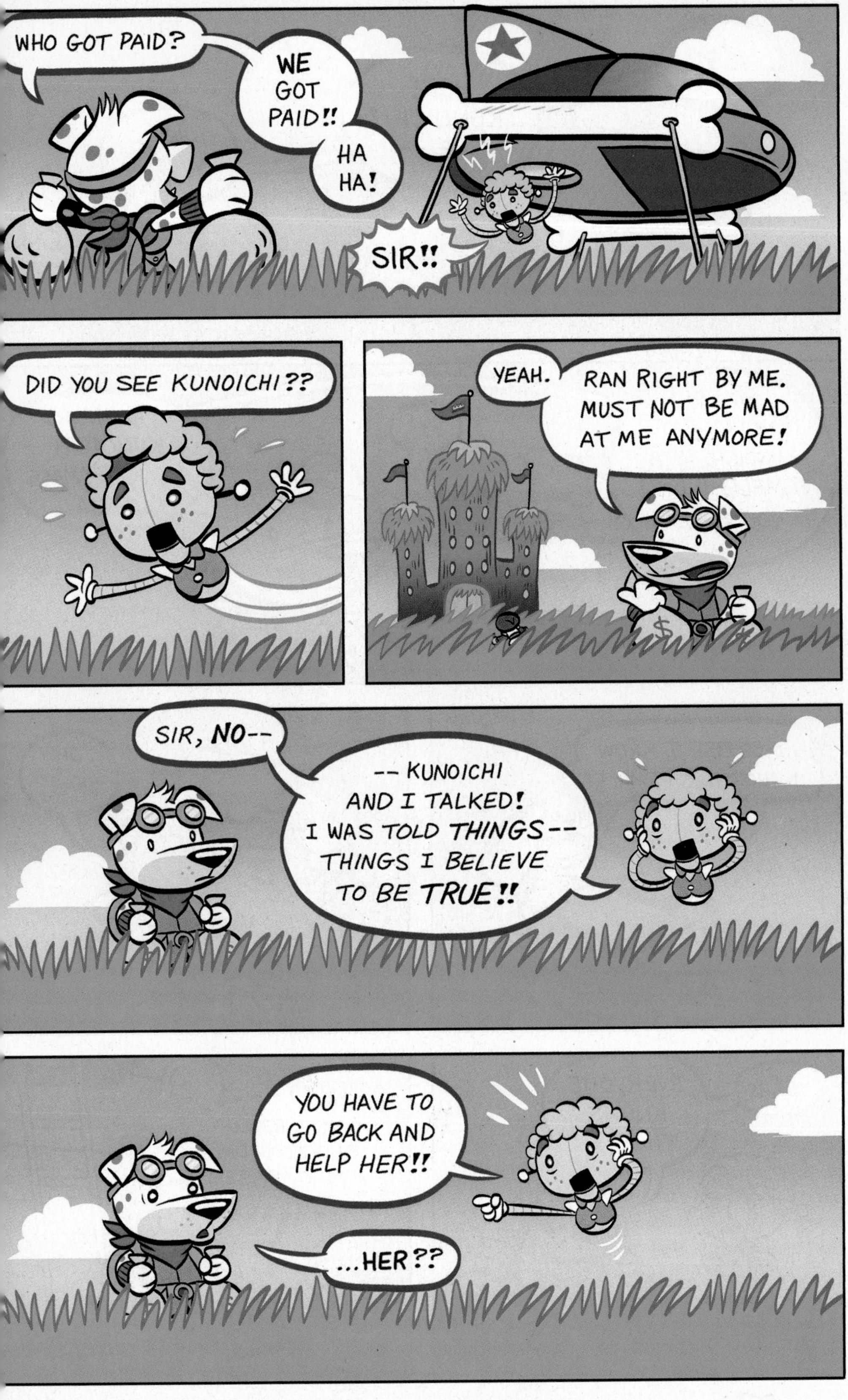
WHO GOT PAID?
WE GOT PAID!!
HA HA!
SIR!!
DID YOU SEE KUNOICHI??
YEAH.
RAN RIGHT BY ME. MUST NOT BE MAD AT ME ANYMORE!
SIR, NO--
-- KUNOICHI AND I TALKED! I WAS TOLD THINGS-- THINGS I BELIEVE TO BE TRUE!!
YOU HAVE TO GO BACK AND HELP HER!!
...HER??

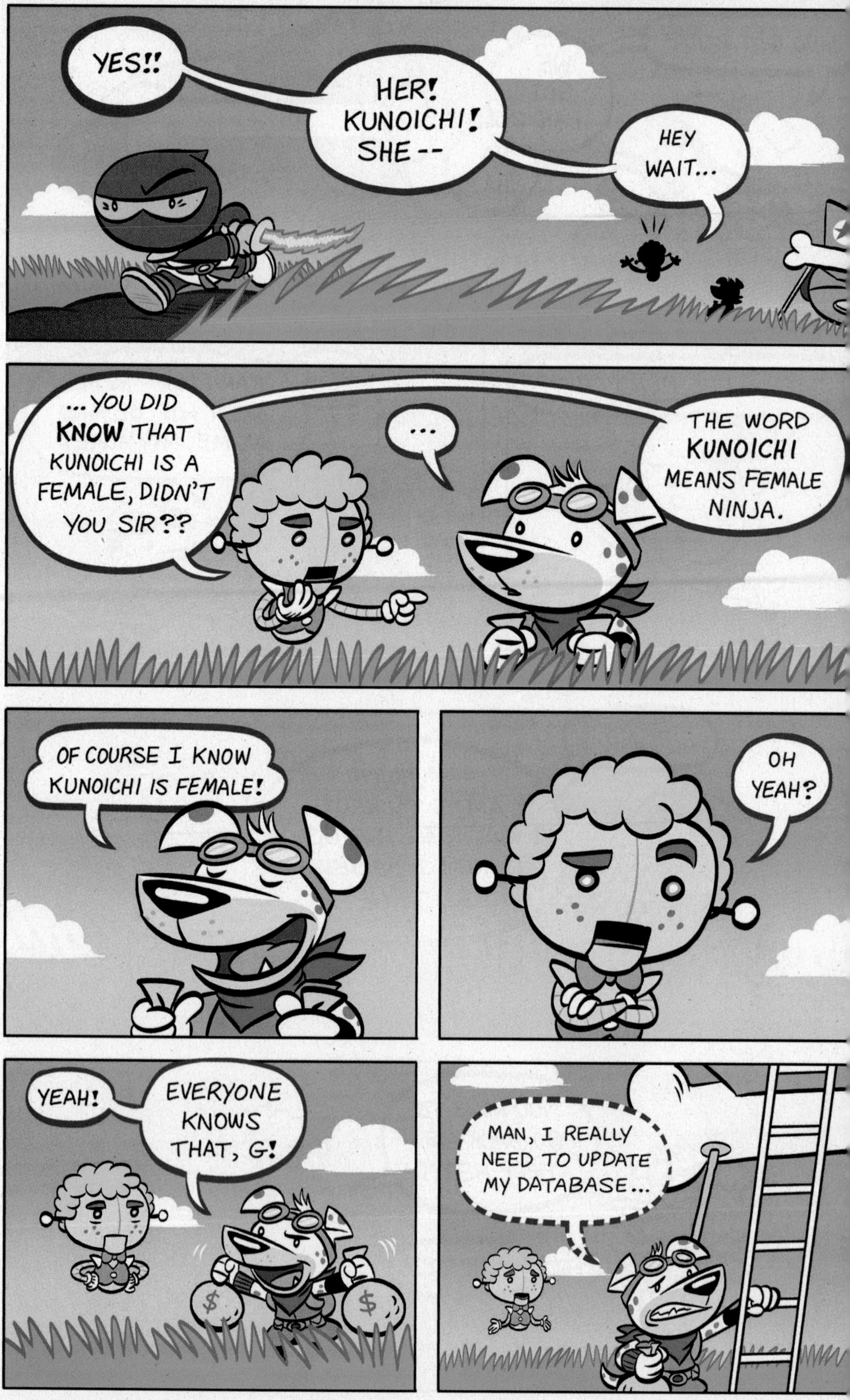
YES!!
HER! KUNOICHI! SHE--
HEY WAIT...
...YOU DID KNOW THAT KUNOICHI IS A FEMALE, DIDN'T YOU SIR??
...
THE WORD KUNOICHI MEANS FEMALE NINJA.
OF COURSE I KNOW KUNOICHI IS FEMALE!
OH YEAH?
YEAH!
EVERYONE KNOWS THAT, G!
MAN, I REALLY NEED TO UPDATE MY DATABASE...

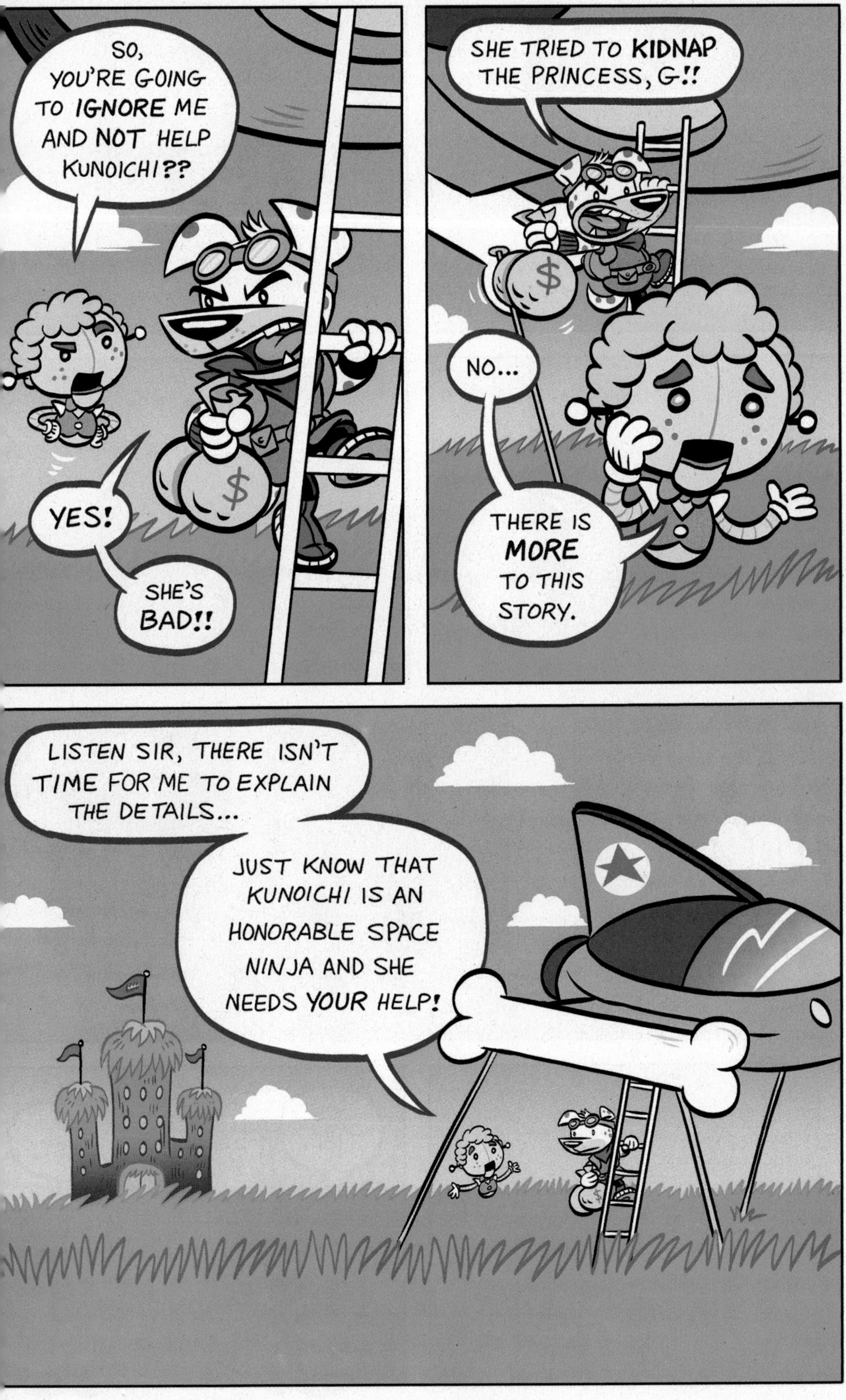
SO, YOU'RE GOING TO IGNORE ME AND NOT HELP KUNOICHI??
YES!
SHE'S BAD!!
SHE TRIED TO KIDNAP THE PRINCESS, G!!
NO...
THERE IS MORE TO THIS STORY.
LISTEN SIR, THERE ISN'T TIME FOR ME TO EXPLAIN THE DETAILS...
JUST KNOW THAT KUNOICHI IS AN HONORABLE SPACE NINJA AND SHE NEEDS YOUR HELP!

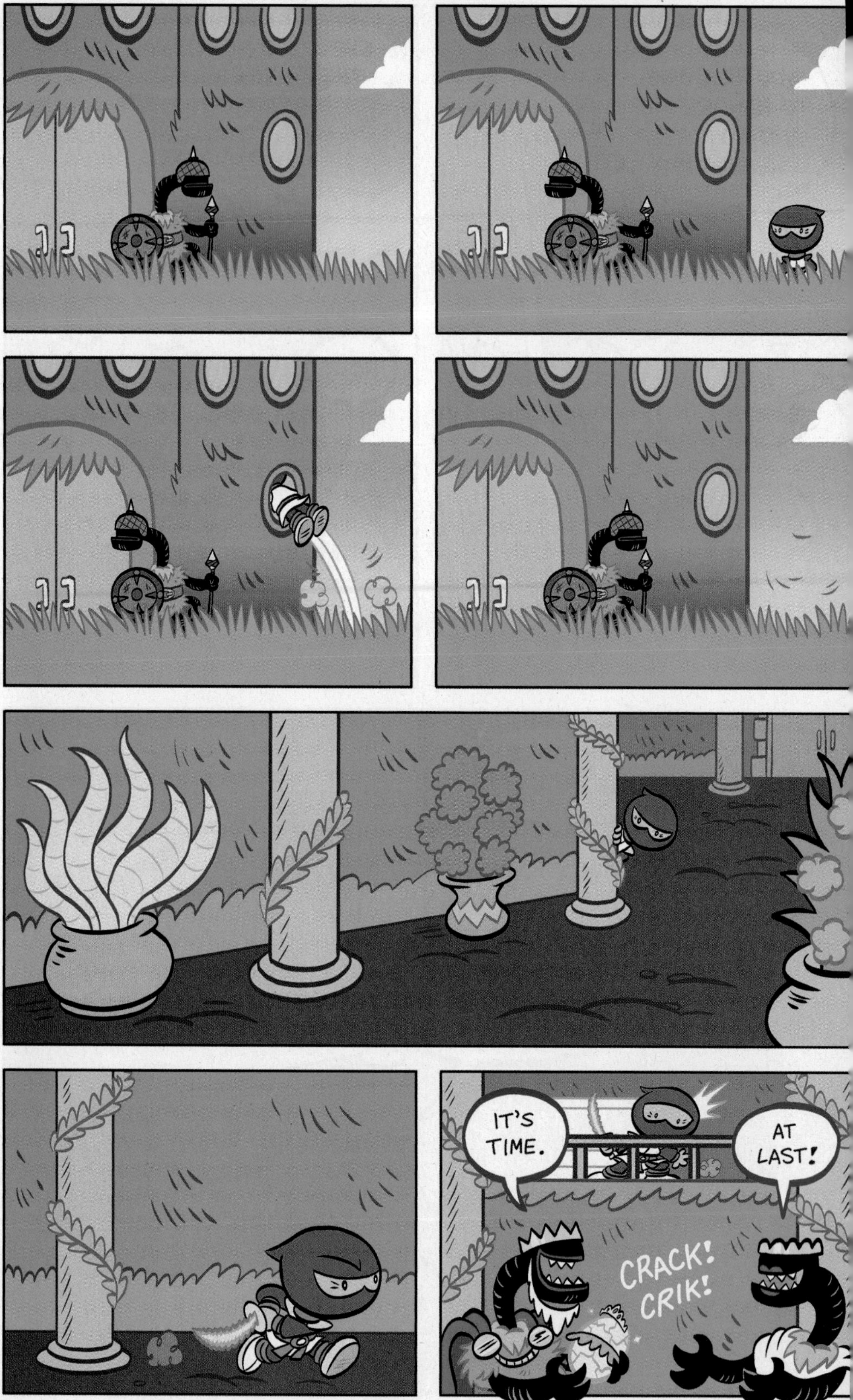
IT'S TIME.
AT LAST!
CRACK!
CRIK!

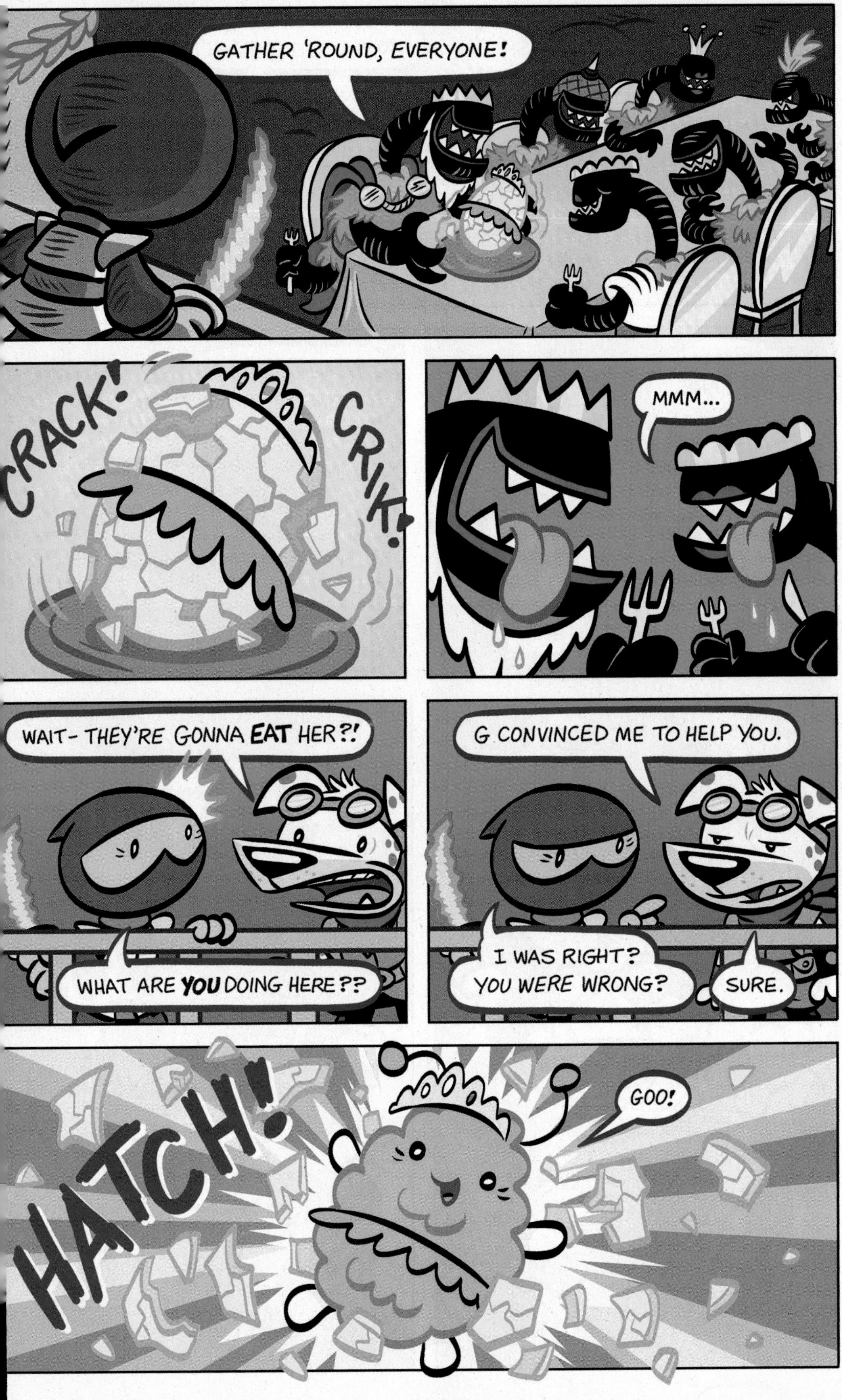
GATHER 'ROUND, EVERYONE!
CRACK!
CRIK!
MMM...
WAIT- THEY'RE GONNA **EAT** HER?!
WHAT ARE **YOU** DOING HERE??
G CONVINCED ME TO HELP YOU.
I WAS RIGHT? YOU WERE WRONG?
SURE.
HATCH!
GOO!

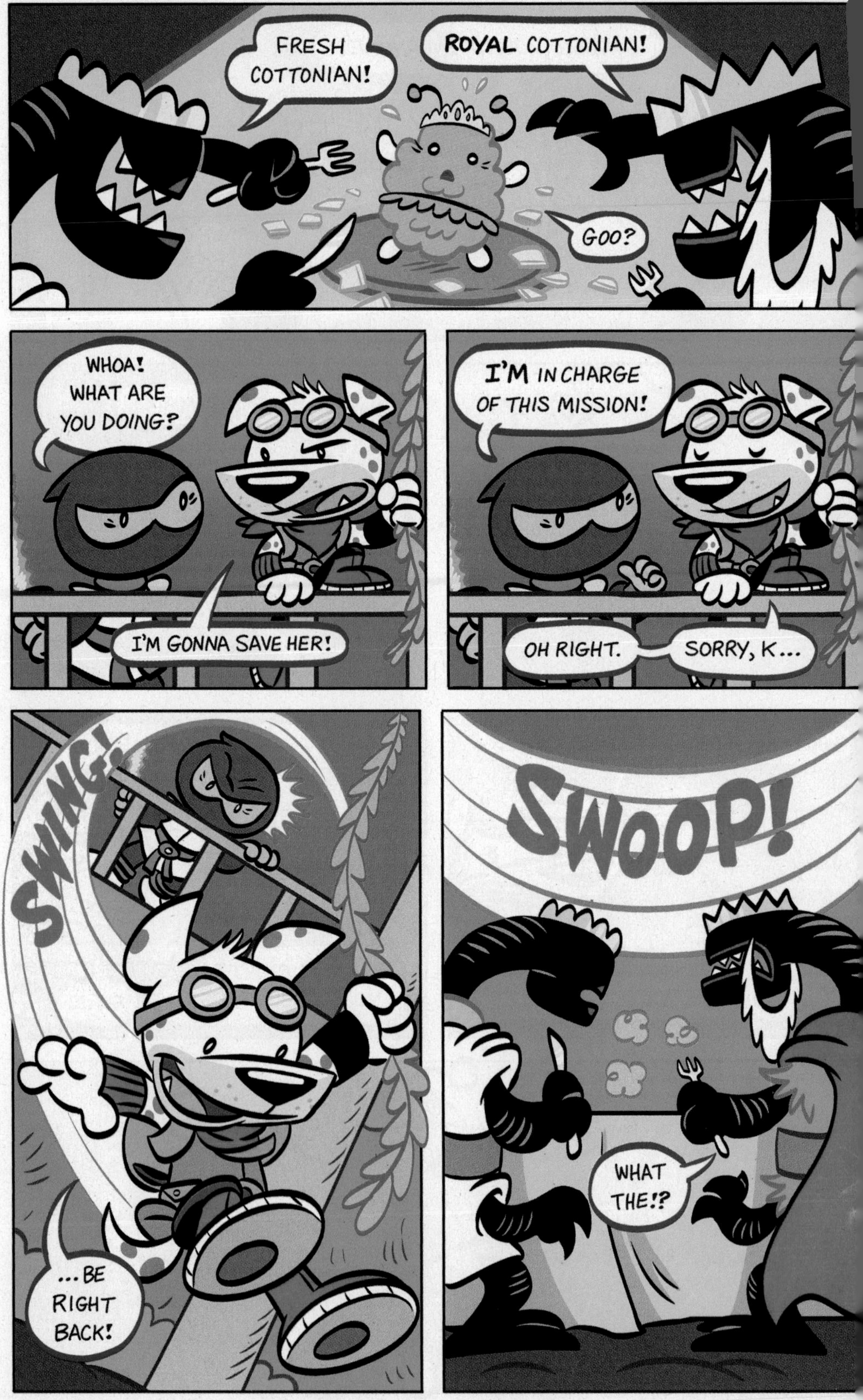
FRESH COTTONIAN!
ROYAL COTTONIAN!
GOO?
WHOA! WHAT ARE YOU DOING?
I'M GONNA SAVE HER!
I'M IN CHARGE OF THIS MISSION!
OH RIGHT.
SORRY, K...
SWING!
...BE RIGHT BACK!
SWOOP!
WHAT THE!?

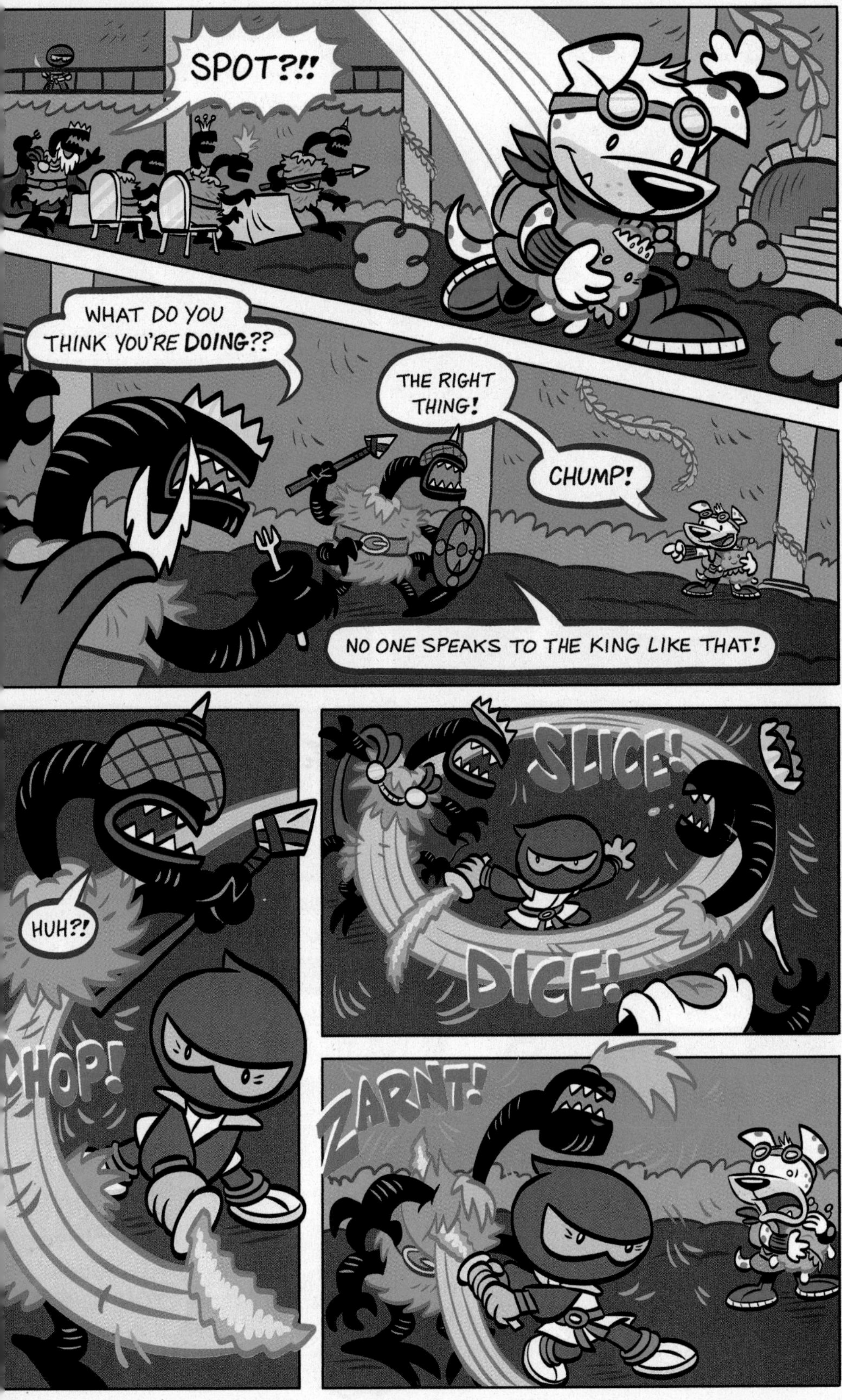

SPOT?!!
WHAT DO YOU THINK YOU'RE DOING??
THE RIGHT THING!
CHUMP!
NO ONE SPEAKS TO THE KING LIKE THAT!
HUH?!
CHOP!
SLICE!
DICE!
ZARNT!

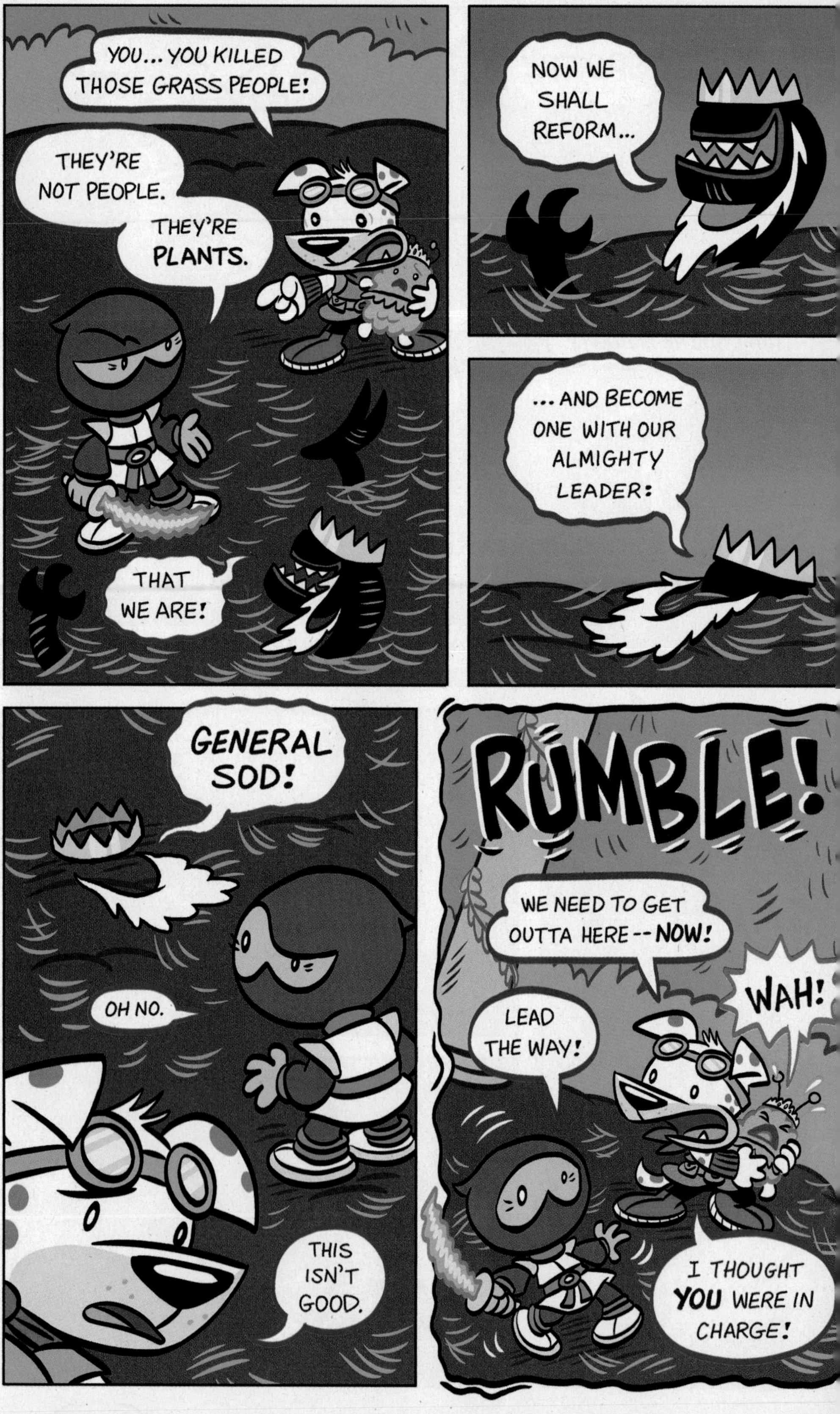
YOU... YOU KILLED THOSE GRASS PEOPLE!
THEY'RE NOT PEOPLE.
THEY'RE PLANTS.
THAT WE ARE!
NOW WE SHALL REFORM...
...AND BECOME ONE WITH OUR ALMIGHTY LEADER:
GENERAL SOD!
OH NO.
THIS ISN'T GOOD.
RUMBLE!
WE NEED TO GET OUTTA HERE--NOW!
WAH!
LEAD THE WAY!
I THOUGHT YOU WERE IN CHARGE!

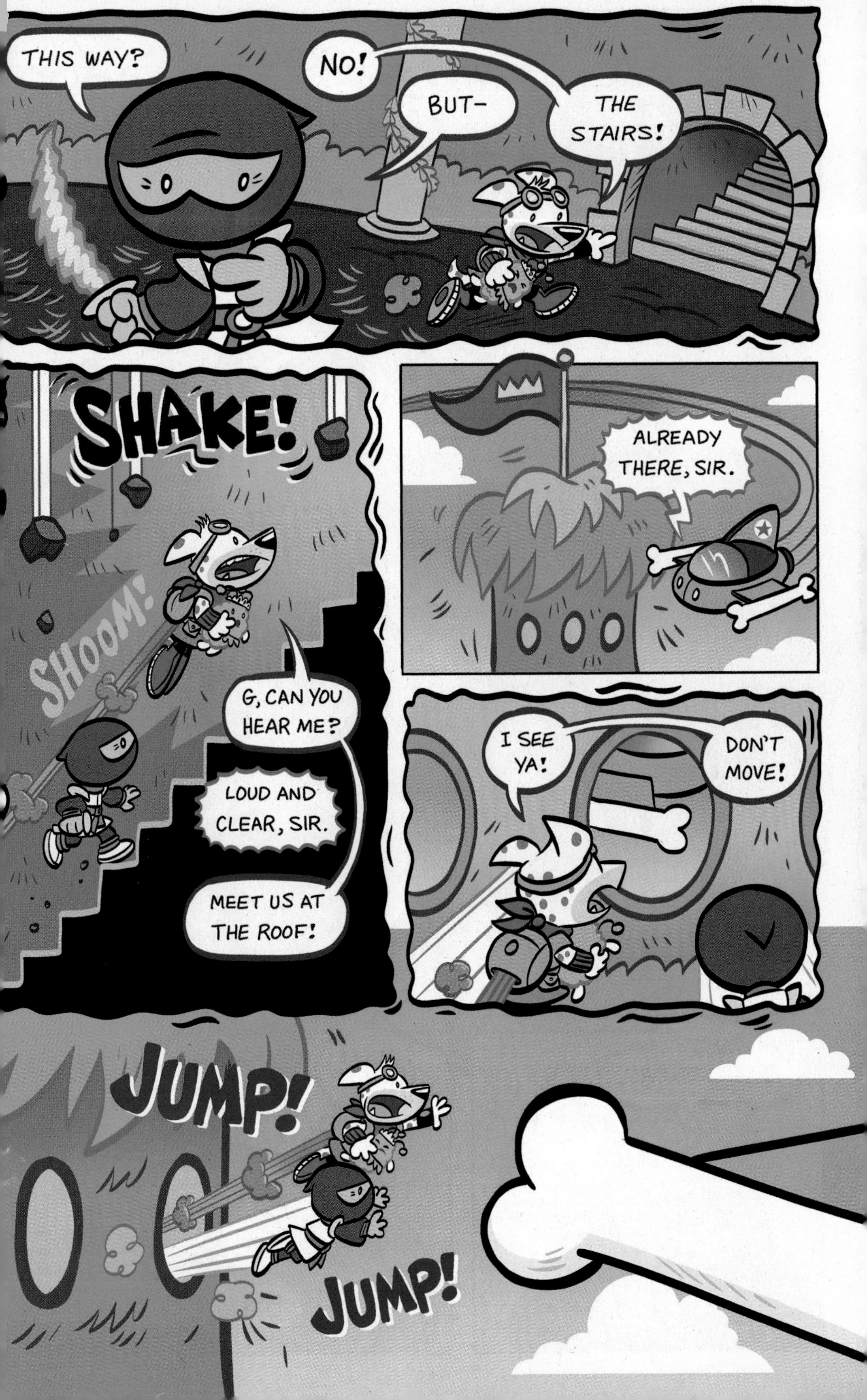
THIS WAY?
NO!
BUT-
THE STAIRS!
SHAKE!
SHOOM!
G, CAN YOU HEAR ME?
LOUD AND CLEAR, SIR.
MEET US AT THE ROOF!
ALREADY THERE, SIR.
I SEE YA!
DON'T MOVE!
JUMP!
JUMP!

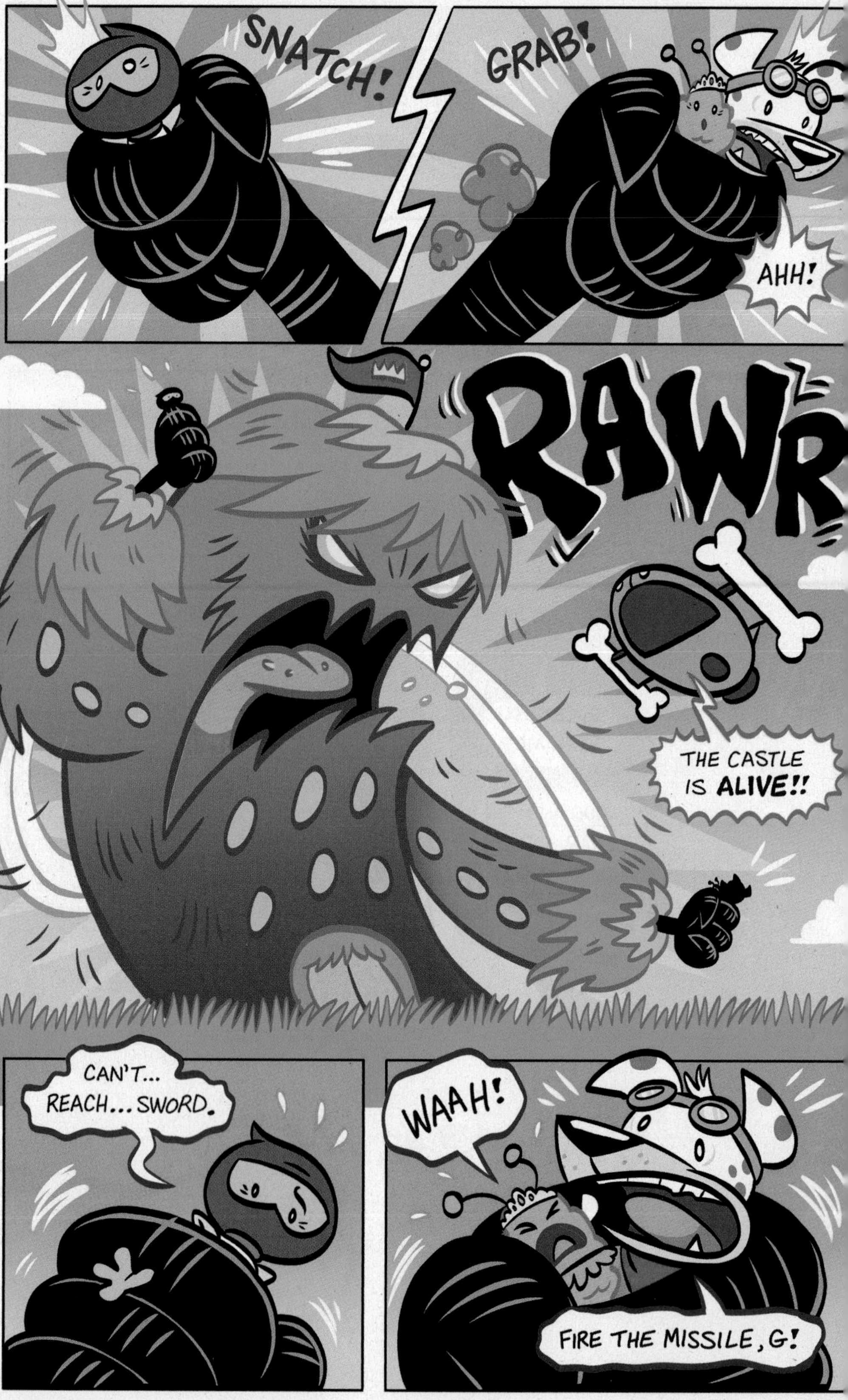
SNATCH!
GRAB!
AHH!
RAWR
THE CASTLE IS **ALIVE!!**
CAN'T... REACH... SWORD.
WAAH!
FIRE THE MISSILE, G!

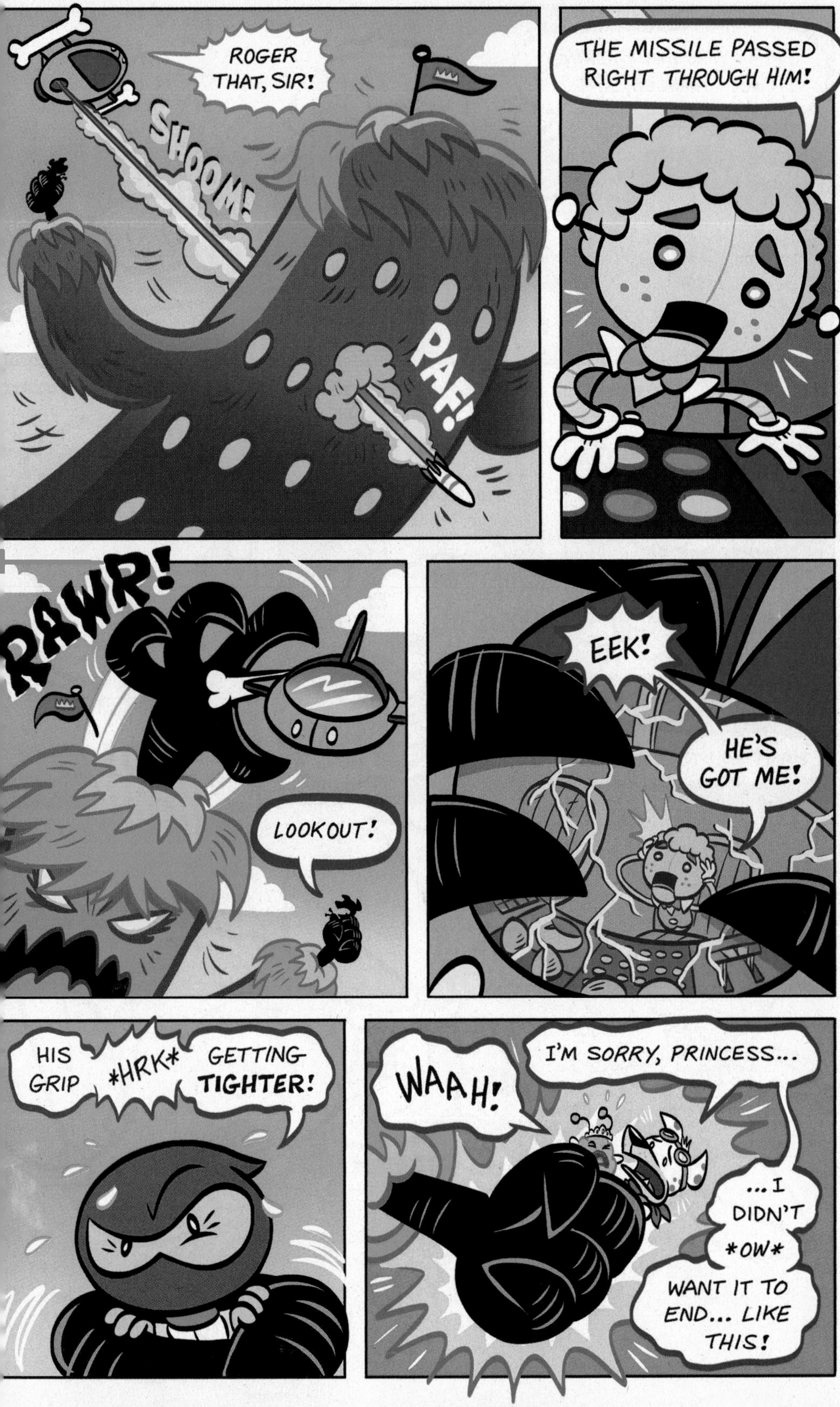
ROGER THAT, SIR!
SHOOOM!
PAF!
THE MISSILE PASSED RIGHT THROUGH HIM!
RAWR!
LOOKOUT!
EEK!
HE'S GOT ME!
HIS GRIP
HRK
GETTING TIGHTER!
WAAH!
I'M SORRY, PRINCESS...
...I DIDN'T
OW
WANT IT TO END... LIKE THIS!

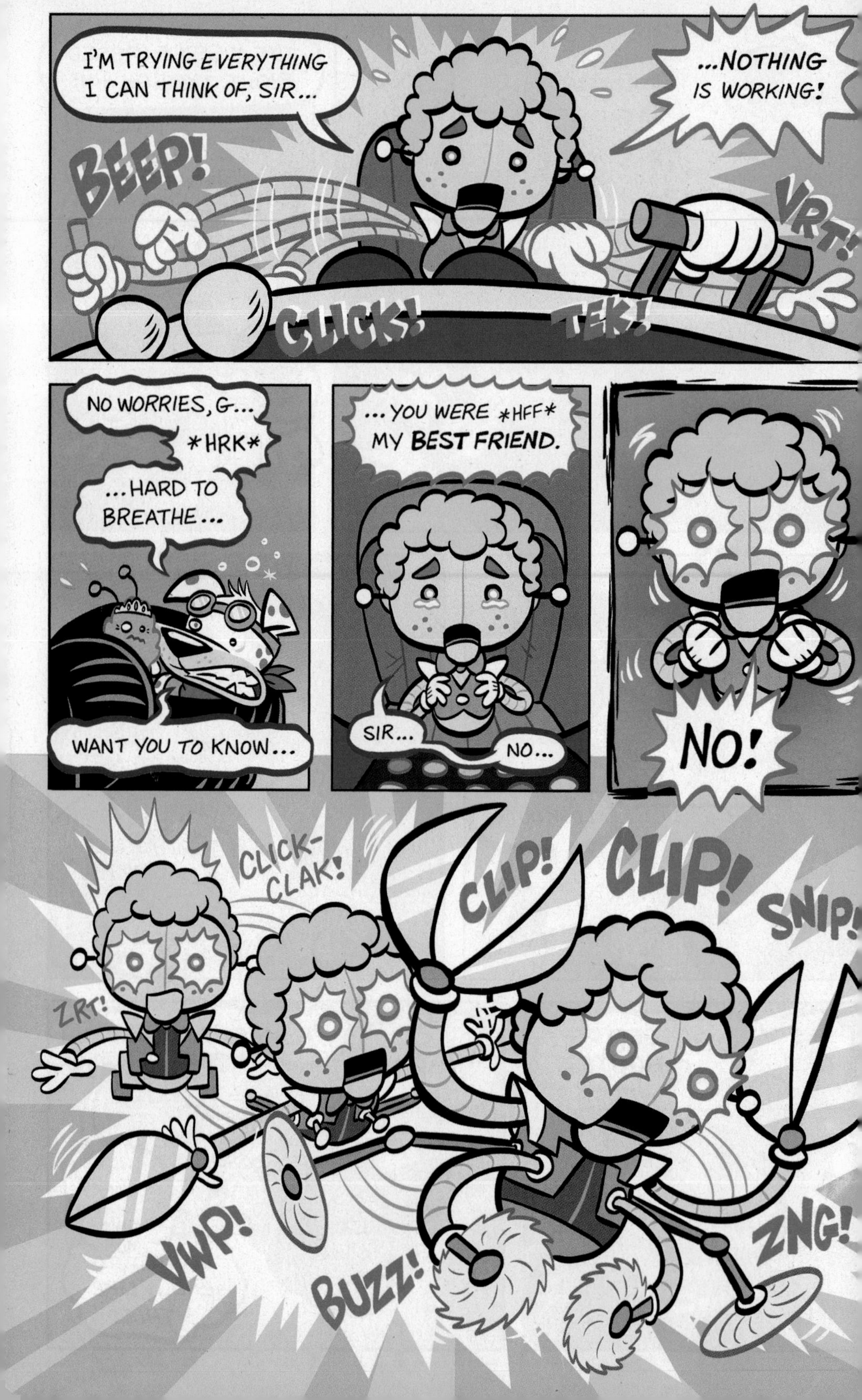
I'M TRYING EVERYTHING I CAN THINK OF, SIR...
...NOTHING IS WORKING!
BEEP!
VRT!
CLICK!
TEK!
NO WORRIES, G...
HRK
...HARD TO BREATHE...
WANT YOU TO KNOW...
...YOU WERE *HFF* MY BEST FRIEND.
SIR...
NO...
NO!
CLICK-CLAK!
CLIP!
CLIP!
SNIP!
ZRT!
VWP!
BUZZ!
ZNG!

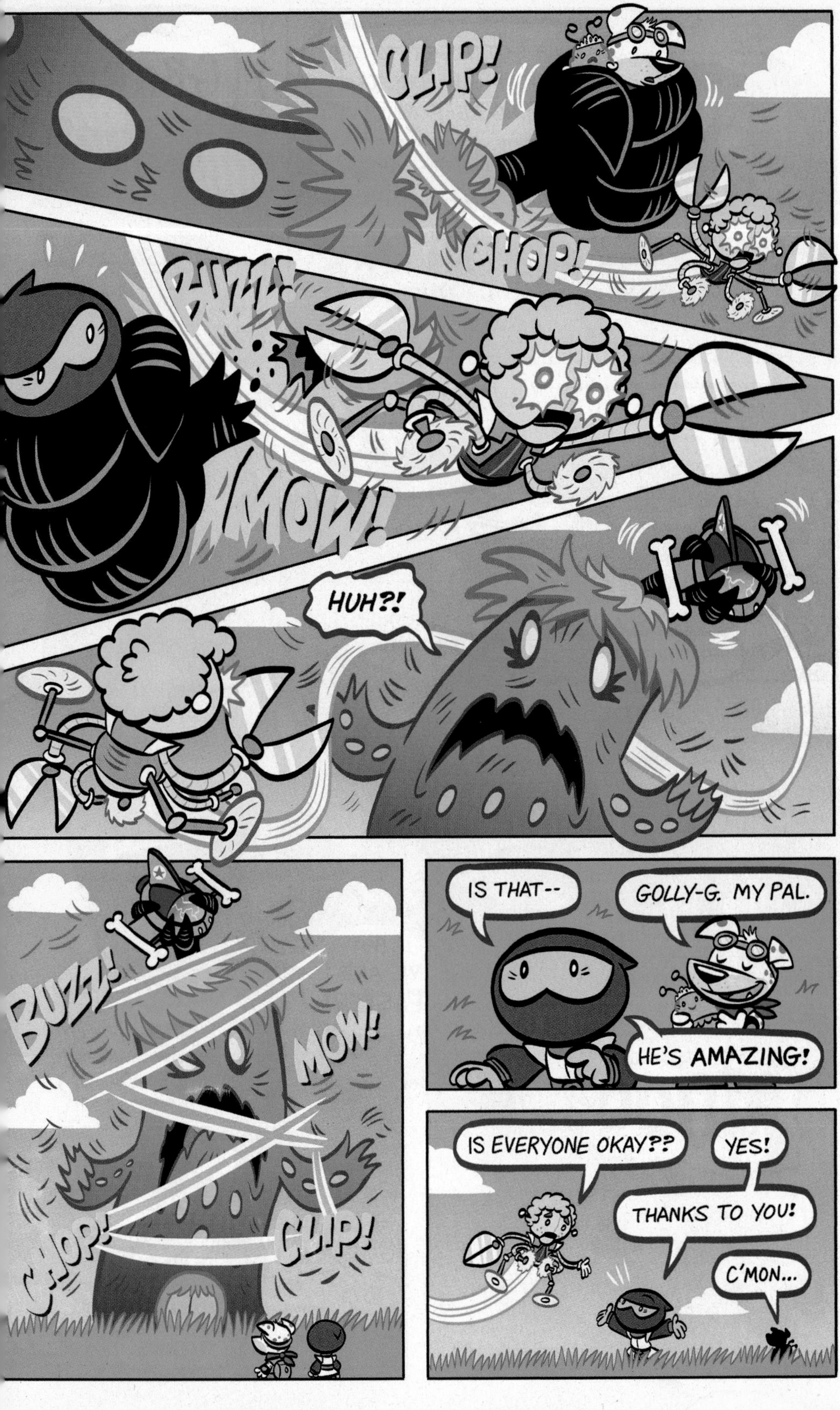
CLIP!
CHOP!
BUZZ!
MOW!
HUH?!
BUZZ!
MOW!
CHOP!
CLIP!
IS THAT--
GOLLY-G. MY PAL.
HE'S AMAZING!
IS EVERYONE OKAY??
YES!
THANKS TO YOU!
C'MON...

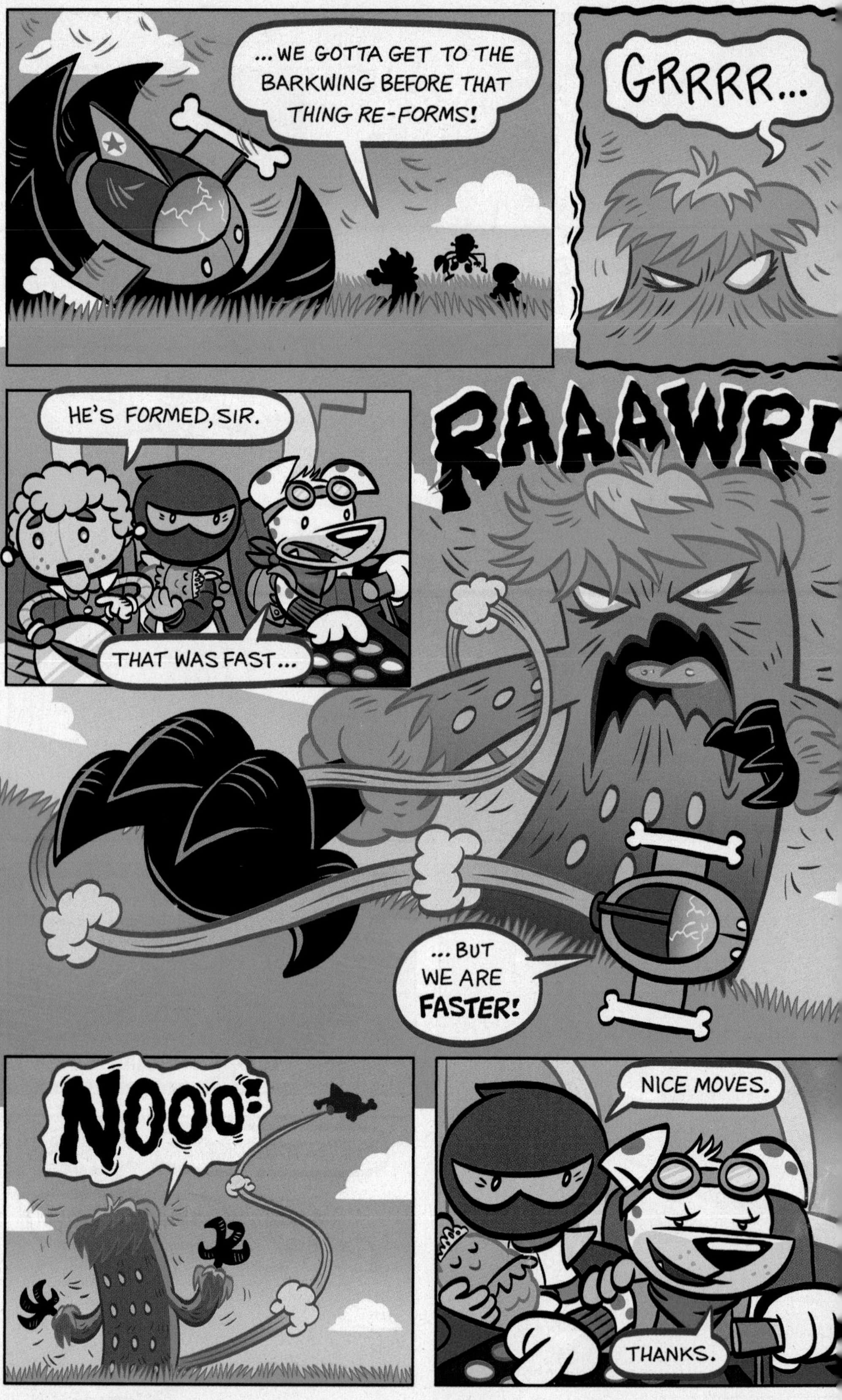
...WE GOTTA GET TO THE BARKWING BEFORE THAT THING RE-FORMS!
GRRRR...
HE'S FORMED, SIR.
THAT WAS FAST...
RAAAWR!
...BUT WE ARE FASTER!
NOOO!
NICE MOVES.
THANKS.

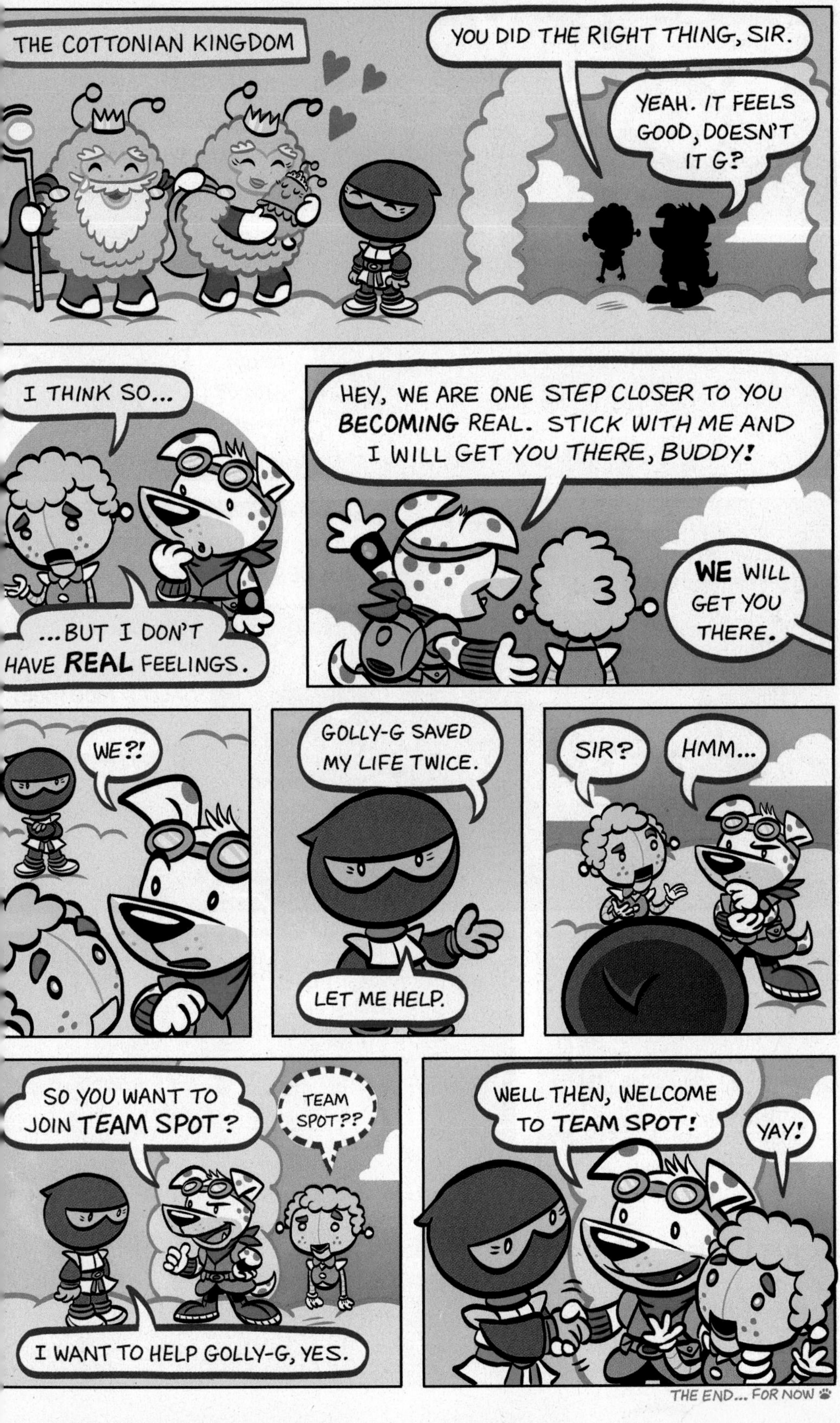
THE COTTONIAN KINGDOM
YOU DID THE RIGHT THING, SIR.
YEAH. IT FEELS GOOD, DOESN'T IT G?
I THINK SO...
...BUT I DON'T HAVE REAL FEELINGS.
HEY, WE ARE ONE STEP CLOSER TO YOU BECOMING REAL. STICK WITH ME AND I WILL GET YOU THERE, BUDDY!
WE WILL GET YOU THERE.
WE?!
GOLLY-G SAVED MY LIFE TWICE.
LET ME HELP.
SIR?
HMM...
SO YOU WANT TO JOIN TEAM SPOT?
TEAM SPOT??
I WANT TO HELP GOLLY-G, YES.
WELL THEN, WELCOME TO TEAM SPOT!
YAY!
THE END... FOR NOW

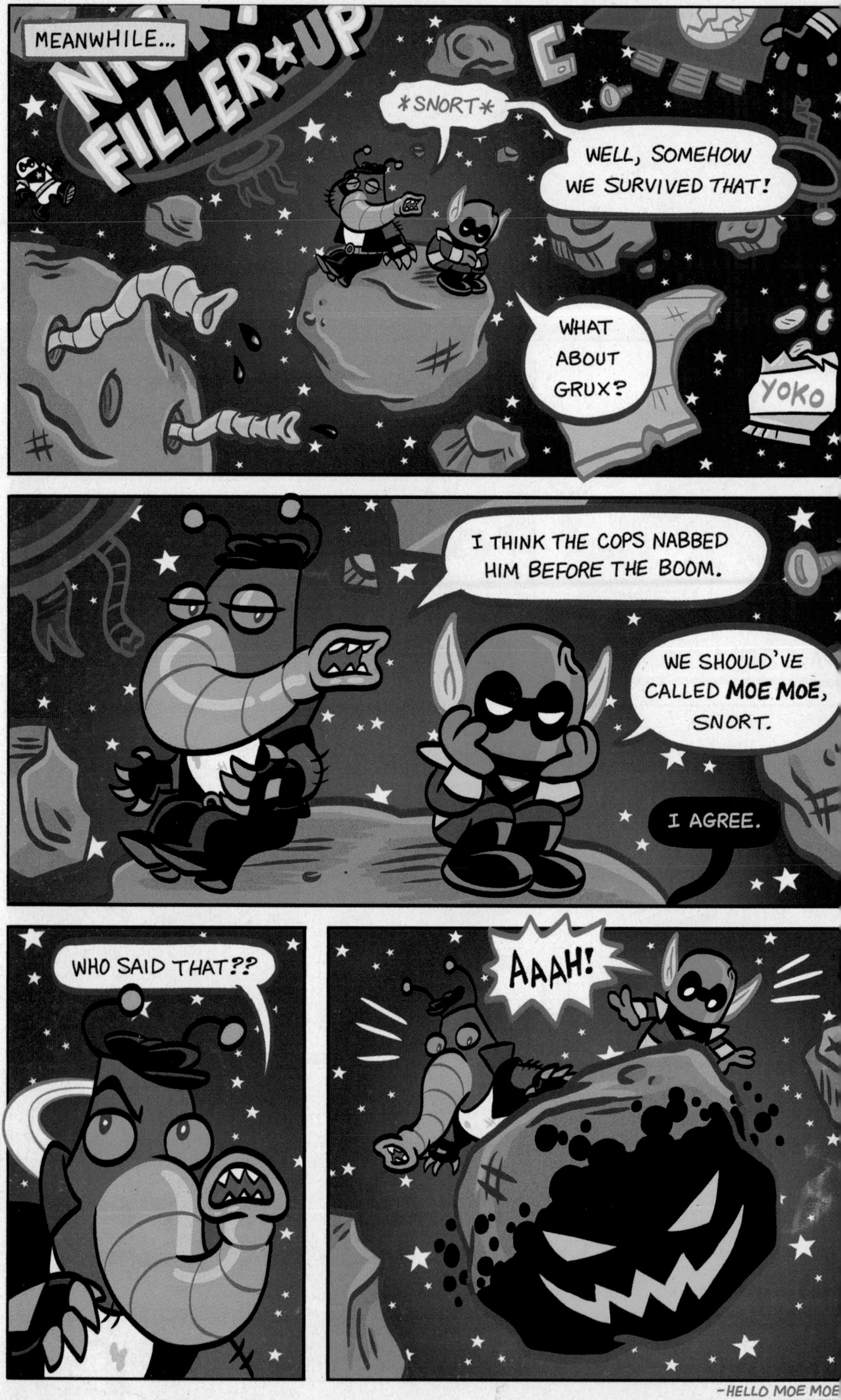
MEANWHILE...
FILLER*UP
SNORT
WELL, SOMEHOW WE SURVIVED THAT!
WHAT ABOUT GRUX?
YOKO
I THINK THE COPS NABBED HIM BEFORE THE BOOM.
WE SHOULD'VE CALLED **MOE MOE**, SNORT.
I AGREE.
WHO SAID THAT??
AAAH!

-HELLO MOE MOE